Mademoiselle

Alice

A Novel

⊂R℘⊃

Also by Janelle Dietrick

Alice & Eiffel, A New History of Early Cinema and the Love Story Kept Secret for a Century

Illuminating Moments, The Films of Alice Guy Blaché

Mademoiselle *Alice*

A Novel

ଓଃ୭

Janelle Dietrick

BOOKBABY
2017

This is a work of fiction. All of the characters, organizations, and events portrayed in this novel are either products of the author's imagination or are used fictitiously.

Copyright © 2017 by Janelle Dietrick

All rights reserved including the right to reproduce this book or portions thereof in any form whatsoever. For information address inquiries to janelledietrick@comcast.net.

Printed in the United States of America

Library of Congress Cataloging-in-Publication Data
Dietrick, Janelle, 1952-
Mademoiselle Alice, A Novel

Issued in print and electronic formats:
ISBN: 978-1-54390-999-9

Blaché, Alice Guy, 1873-1968—Cinema—France—United States.
Eiffel, Gustave, 1832-1923—Cinema—France—United States

BookBaby, 13909 N.E. Airport Way, Portland, OR 97230

Cover: Wikimedia Commons, Rogelio de Egusquiza,
  The End of the Ball
Back cover: LOC, *Panorama of Paris*

*Love looks not with the eyes,
but with the mind,
And therefore is winged Cupid
painted blind.*

William Shakespeare
Midsummer Night's Dream

*The vocation of the artist is to send light
into the human heart.*

George Sand

TIMELINE

1865
July 17: Emile Guy marries Marie Aubert in Paris.
She goes to Chile with him and has four children:
Louis born 1866; Julia born 1867; Fanny born 1869;
and Rose born 1871.

1869
Suez Canal is completed by a French company.

1872
Gustave Eiffel visits Chile in preparation
for several engineering projects.
U.S. surveys four potential routes for Panama Canal.
December: Emile Guy is in Paris on business.
Severe smallpox epidemic in Chile.

1873
July 1: Alice is born in Paris;
Fall: Alice and her siblings are taken to Geneva.

1874
Jules Janssen invents the photographic revolver
to capture eclipses in sequential photographs.

1877
Alice is brought to Chile.

1879
Alice is brought to convent in Veyrier, France.

1880
April: Ancient skeletons are discovered near convent.
May: Alice's brother, Louis, dies.

1881
Emile Guy loses his two print works
in Chile to another merchant.

1882
Étienne-Jules Marey develops a motion picture
camera, improving on Jules Janssen's revolver.

1883
Alice goes to Ferney convent.

1887
February: Work begins on the Eiffel Tower.
December: Eiffel begins working on Panama Canal.

1888
September: Eiffel's workers go on strike.

1889
February: Felix-Max Richard installs
barometers on top of Eiffel Tower.
May 6: Centennial Exposition opens.
May 15: Eiffel Tower opens.
May: Work is suspended on Panama Canal.

1891
January 5: Emile Guy dies.
April 25: Eiffel hosts banquet for Grand Circle.
May 20: Mutualité Maternelle founded.
July 1: Alice is 18.

September: Eiffel is involved in plans to build a refuge on Mont Blanc with Jules Janssen and Joseph Vallot.

1892
November: Eiffel is charged with misuse of funds regarding Panama Canal.

1893
January 10: Trial of Eiffel and four officers of the Panama Canal Company begins.
February: Verdict finds Eiffel guilty.
March: Eiffel removes himself from his company.
June 8-15: Eiffel spends eight days in prison.
June 15: Court overturns verdict; Eiffel is released.
October: Felix-Max Richard, owner of *Comptoir General de Photographi*, loses noncompetition case filed against him by his brother, Jules, and files appeal.

1894
March 1: Leon Gaumont starts work at Comptoir.
March 1-18: Alice starts working at Comptoir.
March 19: New ad for Comptoir appears in *Le Figaro*.
March 22: New ad for Comptoir appears in *Le Matin*.

1895
January: Georges Demenÿ approaches Felix-Max Richard regarding his moving picture camera.
March 22: Lumières project a moving picture.
May 28: Felix-Max Richard loses appeal.
August 10: Eiffel buys Comptoir with Joseph Vallot, Alfred Besnier, and Leon Gaumont.
November: Prof. Roentgen discovers X-rays.
December 26: Alice's grandmother dies.
December 28: Exhibit of Lumière films to public.

1896
Winter: Gaumont company develops company's first motion picture camera with projection.
February: Baby incubator exposition opens in Paris.
April: Alice makes first version of *La Fée aux choux*.
April 29: Alice's sister, Rose, gives birth to a baby boy.
July 30: *Gil Blas* describes a "chaste fiction of children born under the cabbages."

1897
Automobile race from Paris to Trouville.

1900
April-November: *Exposition Universelle*, Paris.

1901
Alberto Santos-Dumont flies around the Eiffel Tower three times.

1902
January-February: Alberto Santos-Dumont flies his dirigible over Monaco Bay.
February 27: Alice's sister, Rose, dies.

1906
Spring: Alice travels to Provence with Herbert Blaché.
Late spring-early summer: Alice travels to Berlin.

1907
January 18: Gaumont et Cie is renamed Société des Établissements Gaumont.
March 6: Alice marries Herbert Blaché.
March 9: Alice and Herbert sail for U.S.
March 19: Alice and Herbert arrive in U.S.

December 28: Leon Gaumont asks London office to ask Herbert to find an office in New York.

1908
September 8: Alice gives birth to baby girl.

1909
Late fall: Gaumont studio and factory completed in Flushing, Long Island.

1910
September: Alice founds Solax Company.

1911
July 31: Herbert and Alice arrive in Europe.
September 12: Herbert returns to New York.
September 16: Alice returns to New York.
November 4: Alice reports in Moving Picture World that she is going to improve the Gaumont property in Flushing, Long Island.
November 21: Alice buys property for building a film studio in Fort Lee, New Jersey.

1912
June 27: Alice gives birth to baby boy.
September: Solax Company moves into a new studio in Fort Lee, New Jersey.

1913
May: Herbert loses his job with Gaumont.

1914
August: war starts in Europe.

1917
April: U.S. enters World War.

1918
February: Spanish flu pandemic starts in Spain.
October: Alice contracts Spanish flu.
November: War ends.

1919
Alice and her two children travel to Hollywood.

1920
Summer: Alice is in France.
December 1: Alice returns to U.S.

1921
Alice sells her property in Fort Lee, divorces Herbert, and moves back to France.

1953
Alice writes in her memoirs that at seventeen she was "literally in love" with a much older man.

1963
Alice says in an interview that she "would gladly have married" her first love, she "adored the man." In another interview, in talking about her work at Gaumont, she refers to "my faithful Gustave."

Part One

PARIS

Chapter 1

WHEN A STORY IS A GOOD ONE, there is nothing to do but tell it. This tale, the incidents of which really happened, is one of the improbable kind, a combination of events not likely to happen ever again. It may be considered that my story is one of coincidence, but it is more than that. It is how I found the love of my life and my vocation—my vocation in the art of cinema when there was no such art.

Memories of the great cities where I have lived—Paris, Geneva, Valparaiso, New York, and Hollywood—crowd my mind, but my story is not one of adventure, although I had my fair share of it, but a journey of the heart, for there is nothing so strong in nature as the chains that draw two people together.

There are many ups and downs in life. I was a sufferer of one of the downs when I was barely seventeen years old. A life of ease was then, by my father's dying insolvent, turned to poverty. My mother also was left without a cent. But as usual, I am starting my story in the middle and telling first those things which happened later.

I have always had a fancy for looking into the past at

Mademoiselle Alice

items concerning those from whom I have descended. The doings of these persons who lived and moved, loved and quarreled, just as we do today, have always been of interest to me.

I have come back to Paris where I was born, but my story starts before that. In front of me are some belongings of my mother's as well as some of my girlish trinkets and keepsakes. A decorative compact opens to reveal a daguerreotype of my mother when she was but sixteen years old. Since photographs were not common in those days, this is the only picture from her girlhood.

My father, who had never met my mother, fell in love with this picture. In those days, marriages in France were arranged and love had nothing at all to do with it.

My mother's uncle, Louis Pujo, rather than be a poor man in France, had chosen to become a rich commoner in Chile where the government of that country was giving away land to Europeans who could train the uneducated peasantry in useful work. My great Uncle Louis went to Chile to make a fortune. He succeeded in acquiring a large ranch, and built a soap and candle factory. In the middle of the nineteenth century, he was the only rich one in the family.

For some years before my parents were married, my father, who was also French, worked in Chile for this uncle of my mother's. There were few steamers in those days and my father was employed to take sailing ships from the west coast of South America to Bordeaux to bring back hides from Uncle Louis's ranch.

My father was a very pleasant fellow, popular with both men and women. Light-haired, blue-eyed, a boyish face on a massive figure, good-natured, careless of everything except the feelings of others, he drew about him many friends. Uncle

Louis was impressed with my father's energy, humor, and intelligence.

One summer, when Uncle Louis came back to Paris to visit his sister, my Grandmère, whom he had not seen in many years, he also saw for the first time his lovely niece, my mother, who was still a convent schoolgirl. Though my mother was born and raised in France, the Spanish enchantment of her ancestors, who once dwelt atop the Pyrenees, was still evident in her dusky eyes and voice.

Since Uncle Louis had no children, there was no one to look after his wife who was frequently infirm and needed the attention of a younger woman. Uncle Louis and his wife spent the summer at my mother's parents' home when my mother was sixteen, and they both took a fancy to her.

Uncle Louis convinced my mother's parents of the advantages of a marriage between my father and mother. This daguerreotype I reverently hold in my hands was provided to Uncle Louis so he could bring it back with him to Chile to show to my father.

"All I had of your mother was that daguerreotype," my father told me. "There was something very attractive in her young and innocent face. She looked out at me with a pair of tender eyes, but there was also in her expression kindness and character. I was delighted with that picture. I found myself looking at it a dozen times a day. Before turning in at night, I opened the case and feasted my eyes on the likeness within. I went to sleep with it under my pillow and dreamed of your mother all night."

It is not hard to imagine a man falling in love with a woman on the screen, and then fail to remember that the players in motion pictures are mere photographs. Is it any more incredible that my father fell in love with a single daguerreotype of my mother?

The following summer, my father came to Paris to claim her as his bride. As part of her dowry, her uncle purchased for my father an interest in a book publishing company in Valparaiso. No one asked my mother if she liked this plan—the deal was made on the day of her wedding, and my mother was handed off like a package.

My father married my girl-mother and took her to faraway Chile where their life was very interesting. Valparaiso was then just a village, but growing there was a European community of French, German, and British expatriates, all in commercial endeavors that quickly flourished after the California gold rush.

While my father worked in the print works, my mother gave birth to four children: Louis, Julia, Fanny, and Rose. And then when she was pregnant with her fifth child, me, she traveled with my father, my brother and three sisters back to Paris where I was born.

But, as I've said, my story starts before I was born when fate stepped in to play one of those tricks so common in human affairs.

While my parents were living in Chile, my father met Gustave Eiffel, and though utterly unalike in almost every particular, they became fast friends.

Monsieur Eiffel had had a secure and predictable childhood. He was one of those child prodigies who astonish everybody. At twelve years of age he had found errors in his textbooks that he pointed out to his teachers. His parents sent him to college where he amused himself asking the professors questions they were unable to answer, then he answered them himself.

Monsieur Eiffel thrived on system. "All action," he liked

Mademoiselle Alice

to say, "should proceed along well thought-out lines; nothing should be done from impulse. Circumstances must be made to conform to rules rather than rules modified to circumstances."

My father, on the other hand, thrived on impulse and adventure. He joined the merchant marine when he was twelve and sailed the world. Those were the days when there was a romance of the sea, when vessels were propelled by the wind in their sails and there was no chugging of machinery below decks. Youngsters were continually running away from home to go to sea. This was my father's bent.

He learned to play cards on ship, using his cleverness, good looks, and wit to make friends and prosper.

A pamphlet fell into his hands along the way directing his attention to gold in California, and he went out there to seek his fortune.

For years, he sought adventure in the wilder parts of America. He was in California for a time, Colorado for a time, and also Mexico. He ended up in Chile with many other Frenchmen who were drawn there by the pull of commerce after the gold rush.

In the year before I was born, Monsieur Eiffel was engaged in building railroad bridges and other structures all over the world. The railroads had come into vogue as a mode of travel, and it was in his youthful engineering capacity that he visited Valparaiso, nestled beneath its encircling hills.

An earthquake had destroyed a customs house and a church, and Monsieur Eiffel was there to design their replacements specifically so that they would stand up to the constant earthquakes. Also, a gasworks was needed.

On this particular day in Valparaiso, Monsieur Eiffel had one of those surveying instruments and he was manipulating it as if he were laying out a new state road.

Mademoiselle Alice

My father, who was lazily curious about Monsieur Eiffel's work, made friends with the not-yet-famous engineer right there on the highway. My father was kind to the stranger and made it pleasant for him in the lonely village, offering him the hospitality of his own small home.

Monsieur Eiffel had been glad to accept. There were valuable books on the shelves of my parents' habitation and interesting curios from all over the world. Monsieur Eiffel also met my mother there in the quaint old flower garden set back behind a cedar hedge.

By this time, my parents had four children under seven years of age. Monsieur Eiffel would gossip delightfully, crack jokes, and suddenly turn around and ask my mother:

"Isn't that a brand new dress you are wearing?"

He fed candies to my sisters and brother and let them climb on his lap while he talked. He made his visit a pleasant affair and everyone in the house enjoyed it.

My father formed a deep liking for the systematic and sensible engineer, and Monsieur Eiffel had never met anyone like my colorful father. My father, precious beyond all fathers, could never be persuaded that the outer needs of the body were half so important as a decently clothed mind. He wasn't the worrying kind and thought the world was a good place to live in. He had a head too full of fun and mischief to ponder darkly on trouble.

Monsieur Eiffel recognized that my father with his amiable personality, and facility for Spanish, English, and French, could be quite adept at sussing out information useful to an engineer who was reliant on making connections in foreign countries to build the large public works he later became famous for.

Because my father continued to travel frequently be-

Mademoiselle Alice

tween South America and France on business, he committed to doing a mission of some consequence on behalf of Monsieur Eiffel. This event proved to be portentous and would shape my destiny.

That year, the year before I was born, the future site of the Panama Canal was being debated and there was any amount of subterfuge used to determine its potential location by Britain, France, and the United States.

Monsieur Eiffel hoped one day to have a hand in designing the Panama Canal, and he asked my father to explore what the Americans and British were favoring as a route through the Isthmus of Panama. Truth be known, Monsieur Eiffel did not much like to travel away from Paris, much less France.

By the time Monsieur Eiffel went back to Paris, my father had agreed to visit Panama on his next business trip, and the resulting events I did not find out until much later.

༄༅༄

A few months before I was born, a smallpox epidemic, especially fatal for children, devastated the population of Chile. The horrors of this epidemic induced my parents to take all four of their children back to France.

My mother was pregnant with me when they sailed, and this is why I was born in Paris on July 1, 1873. Mother often voiced her suspicions that the reason I was smaller than all of my siblings was that she spent two months on that boat, seasick, unable to eat even the minimum that was provided.

Then, after I was born, we were all taken to Geneva. My brother, who was then seven, was placed in a first-class boarding school for boys in Geneva, and my older sister, Julia, then age six, was enrolled in a boarding school for girls, similar to the select school for *jeunes filles* that my mother had attended when she was a child. My father went back to Chile and my mother followed him some months later when I was still a baby.

Thus it happened that, in a delightful suburb of Geneva on the Rhone called Eaux Vives, Fanny, Rose, and I were left with our energetic French grandmother.

Grandmère beamed upon the world in general, enjoying everything from the vantage point of her little Swiss cottage. Hardly more than one room it was, with a white ruffled curtain in the kitchen window, and potted flowers nodding there, too.

My life as a small child was happy in that house of mirth, merry with children's laughter, and comfortable with Grandmère's protecting presence. We adored her because she sought only child-like pleasures, gathering us around her for tea parties in her beautiful old garden, or picnics in a leafy grotto down by the pond. She let us drink from her blue-rimmed teacups, and she dressed for a picnic as if she were going on stage, wearing her lavender dress for anything she called a party.

She managed to keep the cottage heated and comfortable, to tend and sing over the vegetables in her garden, and to keep there also a plot of flowers with which to cheer her home.

Grandmère, as the seasons went by, worked from morning till night to earn an honest living. She chopped and churned and scrubbed. She gathered greens and picked berries. She hitched her cart to a dog and took her vegetables to town. She stitched miles of seams and knitted shawls and mittens and socks. She poured candles and boiled soap in a great iron kettle out of doors. In the same kettle, she fried doughnuts, deliciously light and brown, with the scent of hidden nutmeg. And when her flowers bloomed, she thanked

God for all that her eyes had seen and her hands had touched.

Grandmère was always planning some new pleasure like taking us little ones for a jaunt to the shore of Lake Annecy. We listened eagerly as she told us instructive stories, among other things to be kind to the poor dumb animals who are so dependent upon man for kindness.

We were captivated by a castle with its turrets of varying heights and crenellated walls, looming over the lake. We speculated about who lived there—princesses probably—and what went on inside.

"That was Saint Bernard's castle," Grandmère told us. "He is known as the Saint of the Alps because he trained wonderful dogs to rescue travelers lost in the snow."

There was an indefinable air of joyousness about Grandmère which curved the corners of her lips and twinkled in her eyes. I remember the joy I felt when she bought *pains aux raisins* for us to eat.

At bedtime, she told us all about the wonders of fairyland, to say nothing of real fairies. Grandmère insisted that there was a fairy godmother who was showering on us all manner of blessings.

She read to us from an illustrated book of fairy tales, among them, *Cinderella*, *Bluebeard*, and *Patty and her Pitcher*.

"A voyage into the pleasant unrealities," she always said, "will not hurt you."

I loved the story of the fairy godmother who brings to the poor maiden all that her heart desires. And how I pictured my fairy godmother in the flesh! She had blue eyes and golden hair. I imagined her to be like the fairies I saw in our storybook, dressed in golden spangles and holding a wand topped with a star.

When Julia and Louis came to Grandmère's on school

vacations, they took turns reading me stories. But if they weren't there, Grandmère rocked me to sleep in her arms, telling me the tale of a princess in a golden castle. Always the story had to have a happy ending or I was not satisfied.

We slept three little girls in one little bed in a loft facing the morning sun, where the pink glow of sunrise over the Alps enticed us to the window, where we watched the departure of Holstein cows directed along their paths to the meadows.

It was the tradition in Switzerland to carve into the beams the names of the babies born in that house. I ran my hand over the carvings in the beam next to our little bed. These were the names of Grandmère's children, eight in all, five of whom Grandmère had given life to and then wept as they were taken to Heaven.

You would never know from Grandmère's whimsical outlook that she had suffered such losses. The hand-painted motto that hung in her kitchen said, *Après la pluie, le beau temps*—after the rain, the nice weather—in other words, every cloud has a silver lining.

One morning of family legend, I sat down to breakfast and, on being instructed to give thanks, I folded my hands and said, "My fairy godmother, I thank thee."

After breakfast, the table over which Grandmère presided was covered with a profusion of colored fabrics. She made artificial flowers for the hats she sold in a nearby shop, and the delightful detritus from this occupation made pretty playthings for me from bits of leftover satin and velvet. These colorful scraps were like the fairies' garden, a gay troupe of gauzy winged folk.

After this fairyland was cleared away, Grandmère schooled us in the homely arts and pleasures. While Fanny and Rose podded peas into a shiny tin pan, or churned butter for thick slices of bread, my wee hands were employed rubbing bits of soil off radishes in a bowl of water.

While we were thus occupied, Grandmère sang old ballads from her youth. She was born in the mountain village of Pau on the border with Spain where, on a clear day, the whole range of the Pyrenees is visible.

"*Beautiful sky of Pau,*" she sang, "*when will I see you again?*"

Of course, I never wondered when I would see my mother again because I had no recollection of her whatever.

Then fate instructed its little imp to undo everything that had been done, and to turn it all upside down.

Chapter 2

WHEN I WAS ABOUT FOUR years old, a lady I did not recognize, my own mother, came to see us. She took me in her arms and wept. She told Grandmère that it was time for Fanny and Rose to go to the convent, and she wanted to take me back to Chile with her.

When I saw Grandmère cry, I cried and stamped my feet. Nevertheless, a child's tears were not then an item of any importance to be considered. Despite my tears and Grandmère's saying, "Please don't, she is my little sunbeam," my mother took me away from the only home I had ever known.

I suppose I was young enough to make this painful adjustment, but I have never forgotten that trauma.

We traveled part way by rail and the rest by ship. Some of my readers may have seen the clipper ships of that period, with their tall masts and skyscraping sails. Lost in the bustle, novelty, and excitement of my first journey, I fell asleep, and my memory of Grandmère seemed to fade so far away that I could scarcely remember her face. It grew dim like a dream one has almost forgotten.

The travelers on board spoke many languages and I

therefore resorted to that which all persons who speak different languages resort—pantomime. It was seven weeks later when we arrived in Chile where I was to spend two years.

The little port of Valparaiso was lively all out of proportion to its size, with its cranes removing passengers and cargo to little row boats. Above and behind the town towered the majestic Andes, snow-crowned against a brilliant blue sky.

My first memory of my father is him there on the dock, lifting my mother from the little boat that transported us from the ship. He drove us in a cabriolet up to our home in the rise over Valparaiso.

The mountains loomed black against the evening sky. From the gardens we passed, came the scents of rose geraniums, carnations, heliotrope, mignonette, and a dozen other enchanting fragrances. On the veranda in front of our house were great tubs of pink oleander.

"She looks like you," my father told my mother as he lifted me down from the cabriolet.

Everyone said I looked like my mother, except for my mother who said I looked like my father. Mother told me that as a baby my resemblance to my father had been very pronounced and a source of great anxiety to her. She had sighed as she gazed at my small, determined chin, and my already discernible eyebrows, so like my father's. I became the apple of his eye. I was the baby girl of the family, the small imperatrice who invariably came off the victor with my secretly admiring father.

I was only four years old when my father presented me with a writing set. The only thing that interested me then was the ink with which I made permanent stains on the rug.

My father used to hold me in his lap and there, from a beautiful book, taught me the alphabet. Eagerly I sought out my favorite colored illustrations and then, stumbling over the words at first, I learned to read.

My father also held me sitting before him on the saddle as we cantered wildly about the fields. These rides were wonderful for me but a source of torture to my mother. My father would laugh at her fears as she stood, tense and white, waiting to have me safe in her arms again.

My father had a dog, a great St. Bernard he had procured from the Swiss Alps where this noble breed is celebrated.

When my father came home, this wonderful dog leaped and barked joyously. He stretched up his long length and stood with his two paws resting on my father's shoulders, his devoted eyes on my father's face. My father patted the dog's head and the dog followed him into the house, always watching my father with dignified approval. When my father read aloud to me, the dog flapped his tail understandingly.

When my father was at work, Quatrocentimos, that was the dog's name, stretched out in the quaint, stone dooryard, and I lay down with him murmuring in child language to his accepting and protective body.

I loved that dog better than all the world. If anyone, even my father or mother, punished the dog for a misdemeanor, I would rebel. When the dog was finally allowed to go in peace, I would beg my parents' pardon, but there would be no evidence of repentance in my words or demeanor.

Having a dog did not prevent me from rescuing stray animals. I found them in hedges, gutters, and trash cans, wherever stray animals may be found. I took them in, cleaned them, fed them, played with them, and taught them to do tricks. My mother objected to feeding them all, but she was just as soft-hearted as I was when it came to animals.

I nurtured and loved hungry, ear-chewed cats who, with

Mademoiselle Alice

tender care, blossomed forth as purring pets.

One day, I arrived home with a muddy little lamb tucked tenderly under my arms. A week or two later, I came home with a baby goat. My mother tried to put her foot down, but what could she say? The little goat's big eyes were already gazing at her in adoration.

There were times when my father took me and his dog with him to work. The fire house near my father's business was a place of fascination for me. The moment I heard the repeated ringing of the gong announcing a fire, I would run to the engine house to watch the horses hurried to their places in front of the wagon. They pranced impatiently until they were hooked up, then they dashed out of the firehouse followed by the idle boys and dogs of the town.

I was five years old when this admiration for fire engines first developed itself, and very soon I was allowed to climb up on the hook and ladder truck. I was the pet of the fire company, along with my father's noble dog who would hold the great firehose in his mouth. Quatrocentimos and I were considered a part of the engine house of which the men were very proud.

One evening, my father was coming home while a fire alarm was being sounded. The hook and ladder truck was coming full-speed down the street, the horses galloping, the gongs clanging, the dogs barking, and what was my father's surprise to see his little daughter running along the side of the fire truck? A fireman standing on the footboard reached down, swung me up beside him, and the whole outfit passed out of my father's sight.

The scolding I received that evening was more stern than any before delivered. Nevertheless, the next time the alarm sounded, I was there, and it soon became a regular thing to see me standing on the hook and ladder truck, held in place by a fireman, whenever they were hurrying to a fire.

We lived near the ocean in Valparaiso, and I spent as much time as I could in looking out upon it or in running along the beach inhaling the pleasant tang of salt air mingled with sea smells. The setting sun made a golden track leading to enchanted islands where it was said Robinson Crusoe had his many adventures.

Seeing a ship far out on the horizon was to me an agreeable sight. Once every couple of weeks, a steamer from Europe would put in to the bay, and everyone hurried down to the pier to be present for happy reunions with expected travelers returning.

Still, in my bed at night I dreamed of Grandmère and her white-curtained home, which now seemed like heaven to me. I could still picture the cows grazing in the meadows and the fruit-laden apple trees around the one-roomed cottage. Always there was the thought of going back. If I could only go back. Tears of longing filled my eyes, and the pain of that yearning grew and deepened around my heart.

Little did I know that there was a plan afoot to take me back to Grandmère's, but only for a brief visit, and then to a convent school, the dire fate of well-bred little girls.

Chapter 3

*W*HEN I WAS SIX YEARS OLD, it was determined that I should be sent to boarding school. My father was extremely anxious to give all his children every advantage that he had not had himself; therefore, to the select school for *demoiselles* I went.

There have been many years in my life of which I have not spoken, of which it pains me still to think—weary years of loneliness and severity. As it would take a deep plummet to reach the bottom of my years in the secluded life of the convent, I skim but lightly over the surface of those years.

After the long ocean journey, my father and I bumped along in a carriage on an unpaved road that led from Geneva to Veyrier, to the convent run by the Faithful Companions of Jesus, presided over by the brisk and capable mother superior, Emilie Guers, whose cold blue eyes and tall commanding figure remain vividly impressed on my memory.

During the carriage ride, my gaze swept over a wide range of green valleys threaded with rivers. The great peaks of the Alps rose in the distance, blue-green and wonderful. But the

Mademoiselle Alice

clouds resting on those peaks and the cool winds drifting down brought no message of comfort that day.

Although my father assured me that life henceforth would be a delight of fresh air and freedom, my heart was heavy as we crossed the plain and approached the prison of masonry built at the head of the valley, surrounded by a high wall behind which stood the massive rock of the Grand Saleve.

"This is a school," my father said, "of domestic economy. You must learn all the fine things that young ladies are taught."

Our carriage stopped at the gate, and we were admitted by a lay sister who silently conducted us through a large hall. The walls were gray and the pillars marble. The tall windows showed glimpses of the surrounding gardens. It was spacious but spare, plainly furnished, everything chaste and refined, calculated to relieve the misgivings of visiting parents.

It was here that my girlhood would be spent, stolen, really; here, that my unhappiest recollections would form and they linger painfully to this day.

We were left alone in a reception room for a few minutes to say goodbye. I can never forget that dreadful day Papa and I parted. My father gave me a hearty clasp, a clasp that had something in it so tender and reverent that I was to dream of it longingly in the years to come. Then he left with tears in his eyes. It was difficult at that age to see the unselfishness of my father's desertion. I still remember with desolation the moment the heavy door of the convent closed behind him.

As my father left, Mère Emilie rustled in with the amplitude of her habit, austere and grotesque. Though she was dressed as a nun, she spoke with the audacity of a duchess. She became my jailer, an exacting, irascible jailer, demanding querulously the toils of my undivided service. I would soon learn that she possessed managing abilities which she cultivated by constant exercise. Everyone obeyed her, and everything in her establishment was neat and clean, the perfection of cold sterility.

"Follow me," she commanded. I was led as in a dream beneath the solemn arches, through echoing corridors, up stone steps, beyond grilled gates, far away, it seemed, from the colorful and noisy world of love, song, and jest that I had always known.

I was taken to a dormitory room filled with girls, all of them older than me. I stood stolidly where I was left in the middle of the room, my hair flying in every direction from the long carriage ride, looking hither and thither. The children clustered around me, gaping at me as an object of wonder. I needed no attention until the shadows of night cast a gloom about me, when my stoicism broke down and I began to cry.

Several children endeavored to quiet me without effect. One of the older girls possessed a doll with a soft body and china head, all pink and white, with soft blue eyes, and hair the color of corn silk. The doll wore a pale blue dress with a pink rose under her chin. Taking up this doll, the older girl placed it in my arms.

"There you are little one," she said, "if you'll stop crying, you may have it to keep."

I do not remember this girl's name, but I have never forgotten her kindness. I clutched the doll close to my chest all night.

ଛଠଓ

The memory of a tangled home garden where I had walked with my gentle grandmother faded quickly into the

Mademoiselle Alice

picture of a little girl seated stiffly before a desk within the gray walls of a French convent.

Life became for the most part a mechanical routine, and there were few entertainments to lighten my days or relieve their dullness. It was a vision of years to come passed in lonely service and sameness.

It is seldom that anything unusual occurs in a convent. The rules are so rigid that one need only peruse them to know what everyone is doing. And so, true to the book, every girl rose from her bed at six a.m., was in the chapel by seven, and in the refectory at eight for breakfast.

I felt a little less abandoned when I saw my three older sisters at breakfast, but I was dismayed that we were all separated from each other by half the length of a long table. More dismaying was the fact that everyone was hushed and solemn—no one dared say a word.

The monastic rule of reading aloud during meals was observed. The rules of the convent were read and read repeatedly. None of us dared to forget or ignore them.

The nuns superintended the meal, and enforced the rule of stern silence—everything had to be asked for by signs. The crust of bread and *café au lait* was very different too from the pleasant meals I had been accustomed to having with my mother and father. A feeling of desolation began to again creep over me, and I longed to indulge in another good cry.

After breakfast, we went silently to our classrooms. When the bell rang, I followed Rose into the schoolroom, lighted on one side by three large windows. At one end was a large fireplace. In a niche above stood a statuette of the Virgin Mother, with her hands folded over her breast, beneath which were painted the words: "Behold the handmaid of the Lord, be it unto me according to thy word."

Over each window and painted all around the room were texts of Scripture. Behind the tall reading desk, the teacher's podium, hung a picture of Jesus working in the carpenter's shop at Nazareth, with the text: "He was subject unto them."

We took our places in order and silence, a hymn was sung, and then the business of the morning, which was sewing, began.

In the first class, through which every girl had to pass, we learned basic stitches from hemming to buttonholing. My place was of course in the first class. The hemmers sat in the front, the stitchers next, and so on, while at the top of the class were the buttonholers.

No talking was allowed, as all our attention must be concentrated on our work. It behooved us to work in earnest, for part of the funds for our room and board came from our work.

Midmorning, we were given lessons in geography by the use of globes, history, arithmetic, mythology, or Latin grammar. Lessons proceeded until a quarter to twelve, when we recited the Lord's Prayer and sang a hymn.

Then it was lunch and a half hour of recreation in the yard behind the convent. There was less freedom here than might be supposed. The monitors, older girls whose behavior was judged to be impeccable, kept watch over the little playground where it was their duty to check and restrain evil in the form of attachments between the girls. Such attachments were regarded as incubators for insurrection. Even my sisters and I were kept apart as much as possible.

The afternoon was much the same as the morning, interrupted briefly by a lesson in the lives of the saints or the stations of the cross.

From time to time, Mère Emilie would patrol our classroom. She ruled solely by terror giving rapid orders to her *daughters* regarding their attitude and deportment. If she caught anyone looking out the window for a moment, Mère Emilie would say sharply: "Go to the busy ant thou sluggard; consider her ways and be wise."

Mère Emilie was a stern woman, permitting no gaiety or frivolity in her domain. She imposed the weariness of her own life's routine on her young charges.

Sister Martha was more gently encouraging. From Sister Martha we would learn that in forgetting self and helping others, we would find the secret of happiness.

"The art of sewing is a useful and feminine art," she said, "the foundation of order and economy in every home."

We wore gray dresses of severe simplicity. In part, I attribute my love of pretty clothes to the reverse influence of the convent.

I worked each afternoon until my eyes were burning and my poor little fingers were raw and aching. After sewing, I remember sweeping steps, carrying ashes out of the kitchen, and bringing in wood for the fires. I wore a ragged frock to do chores, and shivered all the time I was washing dishes.

"You must be very grateful to Mère Emilie," my eldest sister, Julia, told me, but later the question was, to whom was gratitude due, for the school mistress was quite old, frequently indisposed, and the hands of the students never failed to supply her every need.

Letters from the remote part of the world where our parents lived used to arrive in batches which had collected at some postal station to be forwarded only as opportunity infrequently allowed.

Mademoiselle Alice

Once, and once only, during my years at this comfortless convent, did I see my father. My sisters and I received him in the dreary drawing room. On that occasion, I had a peculiar medley of emotions. I was strangely at a loss for words, and he seemed to hurry away, perhaps in self-defense, or in a desire to hurry.

It is hard to hold on to one's belief in fairies when one is left alone in the world and everyone goes away. I asked Fanny why our parents left us there at that convent.

"There were," she said, "so many other things in the world to keep them busy."

※

The convent had promised our parents that we would be taught every kind of needlework, and it was in satisfaction of this expectation that a real lace-maker was engaged to teach us how to make lace.

This was the fun part. We held boards in our laps on which we worked multiple bobbins and threads. Day by day we worked with our needles forming little white knots and tiny stars, uniting them by delicate overcast threads that were called *brides*.

While we worked we were treated to the tale of how lace was invented by mermaids who made intricate patterns in coral caverns under the sea.

"Your delicate fingers," we were told, "are well adapted to such fine work."

Before the machines took it over, lace-making was considered an advanced skill, developing in us the lady-like accomplishment of working exquisitely.

"Careful needlework," said Sister Martha, "imparts a certain refinement of manner and a neatness of person."

In addition to these practical arts, I was given as many accomplishments as I had a fitness for, such as drawing and piano lessons.

But if I had a facility for anything, it was for writing. My compositions always received the highest marks.

When winter descended, snow storms of increasing violence whirled around our marble-hearted prison in impassable drifts. All winter the mountains moaned in travail. The muffled vibrations of avalanches and ice cracking boomed across the silence like the smothered roar of a hungry beast. A mournful wail in the wind made this deadly vault of a house even worse.

When Christmas came, our parents were still abroad, and we spent the holidays at Grandmère's little home on the Rhone. She made a merry Christmas of it, and I have since remembered those holidays as the pleasantest of my life.

There was one delight Grandmère provided which never failed to charm me—a browned, spiced gingerbread doll with currant eyes and a colored frosting dress. This recollection still makes me smile—Grandmère in her apron, her loving fingers fashioning the whimsical shapes while I watched nearby, eagerly waiting.

Chapter 4

TWO AFTERNOONS OUT OF FIVE, I was sure to be kept after class for not knowing my lessons. My teachers were all the more severe with me because they knew that if I would seriously apply myself, I might be one of the best scholars in the class.

If my teachers had examined my copybooks instead of examining me at the end of the day, they would have learned the secret of my failures. The blank pages and margins of my copybooks were covered with little sketches. If I fancied a particular subject, there were no sketches in the book; if I disliked it, there were many. I detested Latin grammar, and the book from which I studied this subject was covered with my drawings of faces and figures. The verbs twisted themselves perplexedly about in my mind, so I found escape in drawing and fantasy.

Mère Emilie was an austere person with a will of her own, a very unreasonable person. One could not tell how to please her. Never in my life have I met someone so downright disagreeable. It was impossible to be naturally pleasant before her brusque sarcasms. Mère Emilie knew that the eager attention bestowed upon her by her charges was not bestowed because of affection, but in the hope only of staying in her favor.

Even now I shudder at the recollection of Mère Emilie's seemingly uncontrollable anger.

One day, having committed I know not what misdemeanor, I was taken to a lonely basement room.

"Have I kept and cared for a child," she shouted, "to have her show herself to be so selfish and uncaring?"

There was something in those cold blue eyes of hers as she ordered me to take off my clothes and hand them to her. I took off my jumper and my frock and gave her those and such other articles of clothing as she demanded. Lastly she called for my tights.

I was left alone to shiver in that little room with nothing but a crust of bread and some water for supper. I have never felt so contemptible. I had submitted to Mère Emilie's will without resistance, and wondered how I would ever be able to assert myself under her domineering spirit.

Worse, when the misty half-light disappeared and night fell, I suffered from that which all children most dread—The Dark.

I shuddered helplessly in that black void all alone, my heart pounding away at every nocturnal sound, for there in the silent house, my heart sounded to my ears louder than the ticking of the great clock at the foot of the stairs.

Ever after I scurried past the dark corners of the halls and the shadows on the stairways. The convent afforded many dark holes and eerie corners, and I never outgrew my little-girl terrors, much to the amusement of the rest of my family.

Many years later my misery was vividly brought back to me while reading of poor Esmeralda's pleading for deliverance from the dungeon in *The Hunchback of Notre Dame*. "Let me out!" she cried. "I am cold! I am scared! And little beasts crawl all over my body!"

I thought the humiliation of being locked in that basement was the worst thing that could ever happen to me when one day, when I was eight or nine years old, I was helping to pass the refreshments. I was nervously serving beverages and accidentally spilled red punch, or maybe it was wine, on the coat and shirt front of an honored guest. The man who received this unwelcome baptism was none other than the bishop. When he turned away to blot his clothing with a cloth napkin, Mère Emilie struck me across the cheek with a small cane she carried in her hand, laying open the flesh.

I ran from the room and Sister Martha, who saw the accidental spill and the blow that had followed it, joined me, and when, with wounded feelings and a bloody cheek, I burst into tears, she put her arms around me and soothed me as if she were my mother.

The hatred I felt for the woman who had struck me was only equaled by my affection for the woman who sympathized with me. She tried to comfort me by saying:

"Alice, you are too spirited. You must be something better. But you can do nothing without education."

"I hate her!" I sputtered fiercely. Sister Martha's eyes looked ineffably sad.

"That is very wrong," she said reprovingly. "You must not hate her, dear. You must love everybody."

Oh, that was a lonely time for me. There was much to endure in my ruled, monotonous life. Many hours of unhappiness I spent, my face pressed against a wet pillow.

I lived through those years and grew up like some poor frightened thing under the lash. I often sought comfort from my sister Rose, my pal from cradle days, crawling into bed with her while our jailers slept.

Rose told me that she would have run away long before, but that when I came, a helpless baby, she determined to stand between me and the cruel things that had happened to her. She made this reckless boast in a tense little whisper of fear, however.

The only agreeable impression I retain from my days at Veyrier is that of the long walks we were allowed to take on Thursday afternoons.

Sometimes we walked to the village accompanied by two nuns. We were anxiously urged to blush and lower our eyes for anyone in trousers. If we crossed paths with a boy or a man, the nuns would scurry ahead of us, whispering in terrified tones, *Baissez les yeux! Baissez les yeux! Lower your eyes, Mesdemoiselles*!

Other times we were allowed the unfettered freedom of an afternoon spent in picking wild flowers along the great blocks of stone behind the convent which formed steps up to a high, grassy cliff.

Clambering up the steps, we counted them: one hundred and one. Along the way was a diminutive statue of the Virgin Mary. I loved that dainty statue, standing like a mother doll in her little niche, a mother whose touch alone was tender enough to heal all wounds.

Then we ran further, to the top of the hill where there was a meadow and thirteen trees, glorying in the pure air, and the panorama of mountain and valley, forest and glacier. We played hide and seek, and then, when we were tired, we sat down to listen to superstitions and stories, courtesy of the older girls.

"That cave is for the fairies," Fanny said.

"They don't care to be seen by humans," said Rose, "that's why you sometimes glimpse them flying away."

But this land of fairies, water sprites, and enchanted forests in the light of day was also the land of ogres, ghosts, and vampires at night.

Commonly seen in the Swiss Alps are lights that sometimes appear in the night over marshy ground. These ghostly forms were the subject of many stories told to us by the older girls. Sister Martha explained that these forms were not ghosts, but illustrative phenomena called *ignis fatuus*, dangerous and misleading lights representing deceptive goals or hopes.

"Each one is like an empty fire," she explained, "the pleasurable glow that illumines no path."

The path of the railroad had not yet reached our convent, but the laying of train track was begun the spring after I arrived. And during the excavation for this purpose, discovered in the ground on the property of the convent, were human skeletons.

"Yes, skeletons," one of the older girls said to a number of us wide-eyed listeners, "large and small, both children and grownups."

"They were ancient," she added knowingly.

Many were the nights I lay in bed thinking of those long-dead children and parents. Ghosts of said skeletons were purported to prowl the corridors of the east wing of the convent. I was not at all sure which wing was east, so in the silent darkness of whichever wing I was sleeping in, images of terror haunted my mind.

It was perhaps because of those skeletons and my life's dreariness, that stories of adventure appealed to me with an overwhelming force. The more bloody and hair-raising they were, the better.

From my father, I inherited an absorbing passion for books. He had given me a beautifully illustrated book called *Whittington et son Chat*. I fell in love with this story, familiar to many school children, about a boy named Dick Whittington who went to London on foot. He bought a cat for a penny and worked in a wealthy merchant's kitchen. He was mistreated by the cook, but became friends with the little girl of the house, who was named Alice. Eventually, because of Alice and his cat, Dick became enormously rich. When my father read me this story, he always gave me a little squeeze when he got to the part about "little Alice."

I was so weary of my self-effacing life, that my dissatisfaction may have been partly due to the charm pictured in the books of adventure I read.

I was usually bored by the children's books provided for me at the convent, and would surreptitiously procure volumes of yellow literature from the older girls, novels of pirates, shipwrecks, and train robbers, which were, of course, taken away from me whenever I was caught reading them, this deprivation being followed by a lecture on depravity and, as often as not, some sharp raps over my knuckles.

Nonetheless, I concluded that not all men of adventure were criminals. There were respectable men, such as my father, who were in the adventure business.

The only literature approved for my consumption was older, much older, like Greek mythology and Scripture. We learned Bible verses by heart and recited them before breakfast every morning. Also, certain portions were read aloud to us before bedtime every evening. This bestowed upon me a fondness for noble words and an early acquaintance with the higher themes of life.

෨෬

Meanwhile, fate was doing things without my knowledge. My father had been successful in Chile. He had two print works, one in Santiago and one in Valparaiso on *Calle de Esmeralda*. On that street he had three German competitors who also sold books, musical instruments, and sheet music and, on the surface at least, they seemed to be his friends.

My father being in financial difficulties had, in order to keep his print works out of the hands of his creditors, placed them in the hands of one of these merchants, Carlos Niemeyer, who owned a shop just two doors down from my father's. On the face of it, my father sold him his print works for a small sum. My father straightened out his affairs, and then wanted his print works back. But Carlos Niemeyer said no, no, no, the print works were legally his and he meant to keep them.

My father was astonished and enraged. He had had absolute faith in Niemeyer's fidelity. But there he was. Either he had sold the print works to Carlos Niemeyer, in which case they were his, or he had placed them in Niemeyer's hands with a view to concealing his assets from his creditors. Despite the evidence in my father's favor, Carlos Niemeyer kept the print works and became wealthy.

One day, my father was bound and gagged by several men and taken to an abandoned dwelling outside of town. He somehow managed to escape, but then discovered that both of his shops had been taken over by his competitors. It is an illustration of the very different conditions that may occur in the life of a single person.

Mademoiselle Alice

From my father I learned that, without realizing it, we live on the brink of ruin all the time. I have heard of famous persons dying of starvation, persons upon whom money had flowed like water. Prominent actors and actresses furnish some examples. Once a person finds himself without money and without friends, he quickly realizes the condition he is in. Few there are who can keep their heads on straight at such times.

My father had to leave Chile, also leaving behind my mother, until he could find his feet again. He made his way back to France. To my great relief, he could no longer afford the expensive boarding school in which we had been prisoners. My father took me and Rose to a slightly shabby, but less regimented, boarding school in Ferney, France, situated in the chateau that had belonged to Voltaire a century before.

Voltaire was still a very popular figure, and the house was open to tourists. His bedroom was kept as it was in his time, but it was much defaced by visitors who tore the bed linens to shreds, collecting relics as souvenirs.

I had a bed in a garret which was not a bad sort of place. Our tiny attic room could be accessed only by a ladder stair and we were able from its window to obtain a view of the town of Ferney and the surrounding country.

It was with a renewed sense of adventure that I ascended the ladder stair and transformed our tiny loft into a study. The wooden box I used as a desk was always littered with scribbled pages, and next to it a pile of books lay heaped upon the floor. I knelt before the wooden box writing stories while the last rays of daylight filtered in from the window.

The rambling rooms of the chateau were a marvelous place for games. We pretended to be damsels in distress, also kings and queens and knights errant.

Mademoiselle Alice

Ferney was still imbued with the spirit of Voltaire, renowned for his wisecracks and indifference to authority. The nuns spoke of him with shocked admiration. The best part was that playwriting and playacting seemed like the most natural thing in the world there. In Voltaire's time he had used the barn as a theater. He also had a portable stage, painted green and gold, inside his house which held only eight or nine players. It was the perfect size for a children's play and we were given the opportunity at Easter to put on a morality tale.

Rose and I both played angels, and when I stood on that green and gold stage, wrapped in white draperies, I was transformed. I watched the audience as the audience watched me go through each scene. All about me were eager faces upraised and joyous hands applauding. In all my professional triumphs, I have never since known the thrill of that first appearance, the friendly faces everywhere.

I was judged to have a very good voice and also permitted to sing on stage. I heard sympathetic townspeople in the audience say, "Isn't she wonderful?" even though my acting was probably atrocious.

I always looked forward to Easter because I loved the flowers waking from their wintry sleep, the new clothing of the earth. I prayed fervently that my parents might be restored to me. When the sun shone warm and opened the leaves, I believed again that they would return.

"Isn't it remarkable," Sister Martha said, "that out of a bulb no prettier than an onion should spring fragrant white lilies, proof of awakening to new life?" All of these things bore significance for me.

Also, on Good Friday we had hot cross buns for breakfast.

After two years at Ferney, I looked forward to my confirmation in June. I chose Lily as my confirmation name because

Mademoiselle Alice

it is associated with Saint Anthony who is the patron saint of animals. Guests were assembled to witness the distribution of prizes. Some of us received ribbons, and others received edifying books about church or French history.

Finally, our father came to fetch us. He took us to Paris where we were reunited with Mother, Fanny, and Julia. I was then almost thirteen, the age when a girl throws away her doll and begins to aspire to things less childlike.

Chapter 5

MY OLDER BROTHER LOUIS, at thirteen, had contracted a serious infection and died. There is nothing more disturbing to a parent than the death of a child, and this great sorrow darkened my father's visage. I saw through my father's pain; moreover, he took naturally to me, and after Louis died, in a measure I dropped into his place with my father.

My father was a sportsman from his head to his toes, and since he had made a companion of me, he taught me what a sportsman should know. I became an incorrigible tomboy. I pulled on trousers under my skirts to climb trees and ride horses. I stood in rubber boots in streams of rapidly running water casting for trout. Those days in which my father escaped from work and took me on excursions were pleasant days for him and golden ones for me.

My father allowed me to draw out from him some of the particulars of the most romantic and exciting adventures in which he had taken part. When he talked of his adventures, I listened to him with rapt attention, now and then giving up little exclamations of interest and delight.

For a long while after this great change in my life, I could do nothing but think about my new-found happiness. It bubbled up in me like a spring of limpid water. We had a nice house in a suburb of Paris with an attic and wide porches. It seemed that my father and mother were bent on making up for the many years they had been deprived of their children by the affection they lavished upon us. I don't know whether they or I were more delighted at our reunion.

My three sisters and I were all two years apart. When we stood in a row, my father liked to say, we looked like a flight of stairs.

I was always the youngest, the smallest, and the pet. Father would sometimes call us characters out of books. He called me Beatrix, shortened frequently to Trixie, after a character in a story by Balzac. My mother and sisters called me Baby Betty.

My sisters were all quite grown up by then, when we were all finally reunited in Paris. My sisters no longer needed our mother, whereas I was still young enough to drink in her praise and attention.

"You have a Madonna-like face," she told me, "yet your smile can transform it into dancing merriment."

And my mother proved a good wife, faithful to the details of home-keeping, sweet-natured always, and lenient to my father's whims.

"Your mother," he told me, "is the pride of my heart."

She was an adoring and pleasing wife from the time she entered her husband's home. His will was her law, and this was evident in the most trivial matters. Sometimes it seemed he was hurrying away from her. Her dainty perfection seemed to weary him. But after several days of freedom, tramping in the country or fishing in the wild, my father was sure to come back to my mother's welcoming arms. Her smile would be as sweet when he returned as when he left.

༄༅

It is hard to find a person with a superior intellect who is not handicapped by some glaring defect. My father's besetting sin was the gaming table. My mother pleaded with him to keep away, but all her pleadings were in vain. Just as soon as my father made a deal by which he pocketed a handsome profit, he would go to a gambling den and, as often as not, lose it all to men who were his intellectual inferiors.

"Papa, is it wicked to play cards?" I asked him. "You play cards sometimes, don't you?" He made no response to this.

It is interesting how certain callings might be considered criminal in one age and respectable in another. In the middle of the nineteenth century, the professional gambler in the west was quite a respected and prominent personage in the community.

An anecdote I have heard my mother tell about my father's long-term relationship with the festive tiger dated from the first year of their marriage. There was a saloon in Santiago, Chile, that had a roulette wheel. It had a cover and the men would spin the wheel, continuing to bet until the wheel stopped spinning. When the cover was lifted, they would find out how lucky or unlucky they were.

My father betted and lost, betted and lost, while my mother looked on. She was holding in her arms my older brother who was a baby at the time. My father noticed that one of the other players was quietly winning, and winning repeatedly, betting on the red five. My father got to thinking.

"There was a worm in South America," he told me, "that

gets into the furniture and eats holes in it. On that roulette wheel the worm had eaten the wood beneath the red five so that you could hear the hollow sound the ball made when it fell into that spot."

After making this assessment, my father was able to win back more than he had lost.

My father told tales of gamblers and gold miners outwitting the desperadoes of the plains. He used to hide his gold in a pickle jar and bury it under a bush, sometimes losing track of its location. The desperado was to me a fascinating person, and the wickeder he was, the more I admired him. It is a curious psychological fact that wickedness is attractive because it is wicked.

One day, when my father and I were on one of our outdoor excursions, he related the following story:

"Poker is all about bluffing," he said. "I was on the road, a stranger in town, so I put on a simple clergyman's collar and entered a saloon. As the card players were arranged around a table, I stepped up in my white collar and remonstrated against the sin of gambling. 'Oh, come on,' said one of the men, 'we'll show you how it's done and you'll get used to it in no time.' The players begged me to join them. They pulled me down into a chair and put the playing cards in my hand."

"That was the first part of my bluff. For a while I asked numerous questions about the value of the cards and the rules of the game. It seemed that nothing but an occasional case of blind luck prevented my being frozen out. Several times when my pile of chips was severely reduced, I held the winning hand in a large pot and saved myself while one by one the other players dropped out of the game. At last there was only me and one other player. I purposely made blunders, but I held hands that enabled me to keep even."

Mademoiselle Alice

"My opponent saw that I was having a run of luck and ceased to bet until that run had ended. Then he made several bluffs with a view to winning the pot. Every time he tried this, I laid my hand over his. I bluffed and bet and pretty soon I was holding most of the sum invested. When my opponent searched my face, he saw nothing but piety and benevolence. Finally my opponent went too far and he lost. He cursed his luck while I scooped up all the money there was on the table."

My father's face grew dark all of a sudden, and he would not tell me what happened after that. He cut off my questions.

"What happened after that?" I wanted to know. "What happened after you won all the money?"

"That's the end of that story," he said gruffly, but I knew it wasn't the end of the story. Something happened after my father won the game, but his dark countenance discouraged me from pressing him.

He told me that the game of life is similar to a game of cards. Having good cards is the same as having good luck. Few there are with such aptitude for the game that they can win with poor cards. A poor hand usually means losing the game. In other words, success usually comes with opportunity, but not always.

Chapter 6

I WAS NOT QUITE SIXTEEN shortly before the opening of the Exposition Centennial of 1889. Monsieur Eiffel's tower was almost completed, and it was receiving accolades from all over the world. I knew that Monsieur Eiffel lived near us, and that my father worked for him in a position of trust.

My father had become the foreman of Monsieur Eiffel's iron works, working steadily until he was as necessary to the works as the engine that supplied the motive power.

"I can get on without anyone under you," Monsieur Eiffel told my father, "but not you."

His gratitude dated back many years, but more recently to my father's assistance during a strike of the iron workers.

Construction of the tower had started in the middle of winter. Through the first year, the men were working on the ground to build the tower up to the first level. In the late fall of the second year of construction, working conditions presented new challenges. The wind was biting, the frost and snow debilitating. The men were required to climb up to pound in rivets at increasing distances from the ground.

Freezing temperatures made this work difficult and dangerous. A strike was called, and my father, anxious to get it resolved, brought the demands of the workers to Monsieur Eiffel. Within a short time, Monsieur Eiffel supplied the workers with waterproof garments, sheepskin clothing, and a four-cent raise. Everyone went back to work.

Monsieur Eiffel used to come to our place and talk with Father about things I didn't understand—tariffs and free trade, raising money to build railroads, and all that.

Mother said that he was a widower and had, since his wife died some years before, not been in the slightest degree affected by any woman. Nonetheless, she said, he was sporty and charming in his attentions to the ladies, and there was something about him that drew the fair sex to him.

"He is so distinguished," Fanny said, "with that touch of gray at the temples."

"Such fine eyes," said Rose, "are they gray too?"

"He's such a good and honest fellow," my father said, "kind, gentlemanly, and successful in business—yet he's kind of a woman-hater."

"Oh, I wouldn't call him that," my mother objected, "it's just that he has so many fussy females in his own family."

"You mean his daughters?" my father asked.

"Yes, they are so spoiled! Then too, he is absorbed in his profession, so he no doubt feels it wise to steer clear of any complications."

"He probably has a horror," my father replied, "of the matrimonial guardhouse." My mother sniffed at this.

When Monsieur Eiffel visited us, he and my father would go into the study and talk about business. I used to listen from the top of the stairs and wonder what they meant by bonds,

Mademoiselle Alice

guarantees, and dividends, for at that time I didn't understand a word of it.

The study had been tastefully furnished by my mother and a cheerful fire was always burning on the hearth. Indeed, there was an air of comfort about it which you find in some rooms and not in others. On the wall over the fireplace was a large photographic portrait of me.

At the time my portrait was taken, my hair was short, because I had had a fever and it had all come out. When my father left the room for a few minutes, I could see Monsieur Eiffel arise from the easy chair where he had been sitting and, with his back to the door, gaze up at my portrait for several moments.

As Monsieur Eiffel was taking his departure, he received at the same time an invitation to dinner that same evening. When he came back later, he wore a gray flannel suit and a colorful cravat. As always, he was fastidiously correct in his dress, winningly courteous in his ways. There was something altogether very attractive in his appearance.

I took pains that evening to make myself look older. The fashion then for girls under seventeen was that the skirt should not reach much below the knees. But I was petite and put on one of my sister's skirts that went to the floor.

I took rather longer than usual making myself ready. I brushed and swept up my hair three times. The longer skirt, the hair piled on my head, were the signals that a girl was no longer a child, but a young lady.

When Monsieur Eiffel was formally presented to "our little Alice," he looked at me appreciatively and said:

"Mademoiselle Alice, having heard no end of chatter from your father about his interesting little daughter, I have long desired to make your acquaintance."

Mademoiselle Alice

For one fleeting moment, the world seemed to stand still, and a tremendous silence told of a great happening. There was something in that pair of gray eyes through which he looked at me that seemed to penetrate my very soul. But I responded demurely as was my upbringing.

"*Et moi aussi,*" I said, "and me also," and dropped my gaze.

We were soon enjoying ourselves at table. Monsieur Eiffel was very entertaining and charmed us all with his conversation.

Within half an hour he had me completely infatuated and set my mind waltzing through paradise.

I was at an age when a girl's heart goes out naturally, and mine went out to Monsieur Eiffel. Even though he was close to my father's age, he seemed rather boyish to me. He talked a great deal about the experiences he and my father had shared over the years.

My mother, remembering her guest was a learned man, introduced a historical riddle game by way of entertainment. Monsieur Eiffel was very good at questions about ancient Greece and Rome, but not China and Japan. After a number of brain teasers, Monsieur Eiffel looked at me with a thoughtful frown in answer to my mischievous gaze.

"Got the answer?" I asked.

"I may be better able to answer," he said with mock condescension, "when I shall have given it sufficient thought."

"Well," I said archly, "let us know when you are ready."

He laughed. I noticed that when I talked, Monsieur Eiffel often laughed with a mingling of amusement and admiration.

Later that evening, I learned what Monsieur Eiffel and my father had been discussing. My father was to accompany a large shipment of prefabricated iron pieces from Monsieur

Eiffel's workshop in Paris to Colón, Panama, the city where supplies were being collected to be used in the construction of the locks Monsieur Eiffel had designed for the Panama Canal.

What was my excitement to learn that Monsieur Eiffel was going to be spending a lot of time with us.

"Papa is going away for six weeks on business," Julia told me, "and Monsieur Eiffel, is going to stay at our house to protect us."

Monsieur Eiffel was to take his breakfast at our home and dinner at his club.

"Papa told him he needn't trouble himself to stay with us in the evenings," Fanny said.

"He can come in at any hour he pleases," said Rose, "he has a key."

Monsieur Eiffel was well pleased to oblige my father. No doubt, the thought of long evenings among my father's well-chosen books was inviting.

And so it was that my romantic interest in Monsieur Eiffel flowered in the secret recesses of my heart.

Nothing was further from the mind of my father, who had seen me grow up from a baby. Indeed, the last Christmas he had given me a doll. I had received it with evident gratitude, but as soon as my father's back was turned, I took it up to the garret where I left it.

As for Monsieur Eiffel, he had no use for schoolgirls, as his associates were chiefly men.

Late in the evening after my father left on his business journey, Monsieur Eiffel let himself in, but I did not see him then. On the following morning, after my mother and I breakfasted with Monsieur Eiffel for the first time, I asked him:

"Which way do you go when you leave the house?"

Mademoiselle Alice

"Right down the avenue," he replied. "Can I do anything for you?"

"I go down the avenue to school."

"Oh, you do," he said.

It didn't occur to Monsieur Eiffel to walk to school with me, but when it was time for him to leave the house, I left at the same time. The morning air was delightfully dry and cold, without a cloud in the sky. I wore a saucy little red felt hat and a gray wool skirt with a scarlet sweater to match my hat.

Monsieur Eiffel looked over at me and I looked up at him.

"Perhaps," I said, "you wouldn't mind helping me with my books."

The fact that my hair was piled on my head, exposing the nape of my neck, was an indication that I was "of age"—which I wasn't, but in those days, it meant I was old enough to be married.

I talked to him about my years in Chile, my mother, my sisters, and my brave, strong father, whom I loved with all my heart, who had crossed the ocean in his youth to put his talents to better use.

There were neither miles nor hours in that walk. Monsieur Eiffel had been bored by women—highly educated women, too—and here I was holding up before him pictures, giving each the peculiar coloring of my own individual vision.

Now, there is that in some girls which attracts them to men much older than themselves. An older man is not forward, but he is susceptible to her attentions because he is conscious that he is passing beyond the sphere of young ladies, and he is highly appreciative of any notice whatever that they might pay to him.

As for me, I was very proud of having him for a companion and wondered with a thrill what it might be like to be loved by a superior being such as him. I did not care a bit for boys.

He permitted his eyes to dwell upon me for a moment and I lowered mine with that modesty one expects to find both in young girls and in eminently correct young ladies.

Walking in cold weather was my delight, and on this cold morning I felt as if I would rather run. There was ice in the little ditches beside the road, and they afforded especially good stretches on which to slide. I slid on every one I came to.

"Good gracious," exclaimed Monsieur Eiffel, "don't fall!"

I laughed, and then I astonished him by bursting into song, a ripple of song, merry and lilting.

"You sound like a nightingale," he said.

I had not quite let go of all my childish ways, and yet I saw myself as a young woman.

When we reached a point where our ways parted, I said:

"Mother told me to ask you to dine with us this evening."

This was true, but it was I who had suggested that we invite him. It was a rather bold thing to do, and not the sort of thing that my sisters would have considered even decent.

"Your mother is very kind," he said gallantly, "and you may tell her that I will dine with her with pleasure."

Monsieur Eiffel dined with us that evening and several other evenings while my father was out of town.

After dinner Monsieur Eiffel would sit chatting with my mother. She asked him about his men's clubs, perhaps to determine his daily schedule.

"I most often frequent the Grand Circle on Montmartre where there is always chess, whist, and billiards."

"Do they serve dinner there?"

"They do. Then once a month *La Marmite* has a banquet."

"Where is *La Marmite*?"

"It doesn't have a clubhouse. We meet in the Continental Hotel usually. The membership has expanded so with politicians, literary men, and artists. This year they made me president. And on Monday nights I frequently go to the home of Edouard Pailleron, the playwright."

"Edouard Pailleron?" my mother asked thoughtfully, calling on her keen memory. "Wasn't he one of those men who signed the artists' protest against your tower?"

"Yes!" laughed Monsieur Eiffel. "You know, he probably wrote it!"

My mother laughed in surprise and delight on being let in on this little secret.

"All of the men who signed that protest are friends of mine. One of them was on the committee that approved the tower a few months before."

"Really?" asked my mother.

"Really," Monsieur Eiffel said. "It was a joke. The protest appeared in the newspaper on Valentine's Day, that was my first clue, and it was full of clever *double entendres*, fit only for the men's club."

"Why did they oppose the tower?" my mother asked a trifle confused.

"They didn't oppose it at all. It was like saying, 'you lucky dog,' a congratulatory slap on the back—all in good fun."

Sometimes Monsieur Eiffel would read the evening paper while I pretended to study or read—then he would play checkers or dominoes or some other game with me. I chatted at him like a magpie all the while.

But whenever it came to my addressing him by his name, I avoided doing so by not calling him by any name at all. I was passing a very delightful season and I found myself wishing that my father would not hurry back, because when he came he would doubtless appropriate much of Monsieur Eiffel's company to my loss.

I was hovering between childhood and womanhood. Indeed, I thought I was a woman, but my parents, and certainly their friend, Monsieur Eiffel, regarded me as a child. When occasionally I gave flashes of being a grown woman, Monsieur Eiffel would look genuinely frightened. He had been asked to afford protection to his friend's wife and daughters, and anything like a complication would be terrible. At such times, if he contemplated taking himself out of the equation in our cozy home, he would not see how he could desert his post, and yet if he stayed he may have feared that he might form an attachment with me or I with him.

He may have been conscious of the fact that he was drifting into an untenable position. What had he been doing? Turning the head of his friend's daughter? If Monsieur Eiffel thought this, he was wrong. It was not he who was turning the girl's head, but she who was turning his. In any event, he stayed.

There was something very delightful between us, but there was a dignified aloofness about his manner which forbade familiarity. Maidens who had admired his face and other sterling qualities retired disheartened at his unapproachable demeanor, while he looked at them, one and all, with pitying tolerance. They were certainly pretty and amusing to him, but impossible as interesting companions.

Deep in his heart, I believed, was a hope unconfessed that he would eventually meet a woman whose mind could follow his own down the intricate paths of learning, and I was convinced that I understood something about him, about his sympathetic and artistic nature, that other women of his own age did not.

Mademoiselle Alice

When my father returned from his business trip, he welcomed Monsieur Eiffel with his usual cordiality. My father thanked him profusely for having accommodated him during his absence.

"It has been a pleasure to me," Monsieur Eiffel told him, "to afford Alice some amusement during your absence."

"Didn't you enjoy it, too, Monsieur Eiffel?" I interrupted him with a pronounced reproachful look.

"Very much, very much!" replied Monsieur Eiffel, embarrassed and reddening.

"I dare say you've been very kind, old man," said my father, and there was something in the appellation of "old man" that I could tell grated on Monsieur Eiffel's nerves.

"Would you like to walk over to the club with me," my father asked, "for a game of whist?" They left together and I did not see Monsieur Eiffel again for almost two years.

§)Q3

The next day I walked under the Eiffel Tower, just completed, into the Exposition Centennial. The Centennial was a celebration of new technologies. Visitors were gathered round an exhibit of various typing machines. Men were competing in a contest to see who could type the fastest.

Visitors were also gathered round an exhibit of Thomas Edison's phonograph playing music recorded on wax-covered cylinders, and other of his electrical contrivances.

There was an exhibit of photographs—these were photographs done in an artistic way, a rather new idea then. Photographs were still looked down upon as cheating art because they recorded all the details of a fine painting without employing the skills of a trained painter.

Mademoiselle Alice

There was an exhibit of a painting I was very much taken with: Burne-Jones' *King Cophetua and the Beggar-Maid*. A poem by Tennyson served as the theme for the painting. The little beggar-maid appears in rags, barefoot, at the court of King Cophetua. Her ineffable beauty is expressed in her large, clear eyes, deep and pure. The young king is looking at her ardently, as if in prayer. According to the poem, he loves the little beggar-maid and will make her his queen.

Exploring the exposition grounds, I found villages representing distant lands, and one could imagine oneself on an adventure without the discomfort of traveling on ship. One of these was Rue de Cairo which purported to contain all the mysteries of Egypt. In a distant corner, was a mysterious tent inhabited by a gypsy fortune teller.

Madame Zanubia was rather short, very stout, and had a round, red face with sympathetic dark eyes. Heavily laden with tawdry jewelry and mystically attired in a loose robe painted with the signs of the zodiac, she sallied forth from her tent distributing business cards printed with her stock in trade: "The Egyptian Oracle, Secrets of the Future Revealed. Love Affairs a Specialty."

It was more than curiosity that drew me into her weirdly furnished tent, redolent of sandalwood. She had a stuffed owl, a small pet alligator, beaded curtains, and other fusty furnishings and emblems of her craft.

In the dim light, the prophetess sat down before a table on which stood a crystal globe, about the size of a large grapefruit. While the light burned low and the music from outside played a melancholy air, she gazed into the crystal ball.

My father called these kinds of places spook parlors. I knew it was wrong to consult a fortune teller, but Madame Zanubia reminded me of Grandmère, kindly and sympathetic.

"What is your particular trouble?" she asked.

I sat down at her table and I am sure I told her all she needed to know in order to diagnose my case without my being aware that I had told her anything at all. The golden tide which was flowing into her treasury no doubt came from silly, lovesick girls like me.

Taking a pack of cards, she dealt them face up, examining them closely as she did so.

Madame Zanubia then bent over her crystal ball and made mystic movements with her hands. She paused, peering into the globe as if to discover certain secret formulas, the better to thoughtfully interpret its revelations.

"You are going to marry and live happily ever after," she assured me.

"Oh, how do you know that?" I asked, amazed. "Do you see that in the globe or in the cards?" A girl of sixteen is fairly easy to amaze.

"Every word of it," replied Madame Zanubia, "that's my business. That will be fifty cents."

"Certainly," I said. "But can you show me those cards again and tell me what each one of them means?"

She patiently went over all the cards again and then she grabbed my hand.

"Let me look at your palm," she said. "The lines of your palm are a little confused." Then after a pause: "Yes, here it is. He awaits you with longing heart."

I left cheerful and happy having been assured that the Fates were on my side.

But if Monsieur Eiffel was waiting for me with a longing heart, he would have to wait a rather long time.

Later that night, I heard my father and mother talking about me.

"She is flirtatious," my mother said, "almost immodest."

"I wouldn't call Alice flirtatious," my father said. "It's just a way about the girl that draws admiration without her seeking it."

"Do you think she is unconscious of it, or just taking a mocking delight in her power?"

"I remember when you were credited with the same failing," my father said.

"Monsieur Eiffel is so sure of himself," my mother mused, "I think that is what appeals to her."

"I rather rely on my observations," said my father, "that they fancy each other."

"He takes a paternal interest in Alice," my mother defended. "I am sure he admires her girlish beauty and more so enjoys her intelligent conversation."

"Is he not a man?" my father demanded. "You know as well as I do that any man exposed to a girl in petticoats is perfectly capable of making a fool of himself."

"Honestly," my mother responded doubtfully, "I cannot see Monsieur Eiffel making a fool of himself."

"Nevertheless, I think I should take precautions against any unwise attachment on Alice's part."

On hearing this, I froze. My father decided to send me back to boarding school and that I would go immediately.

Chapter 7

AS A GIRL, I CONFESS I was reckless, but I will not admit that I was bad. Indeed, looking back to that period, I wonder at my own innocence. I was simply uninhibited when it came to the turnings of my heart.

As the old proverb goes, love laughs at locksmiths. My father had locked the proverbial stable door after the horse had escaped. A girl's heart may escape during a flash of lightning. That is why in French the term for falling in love at first sight is *coupe de foudre*, the cut of lightning.

But the course of true love never runs smooth.

I was loath to go back to the prison of the boarding school in Veyrier, where for so long, most of my girlhood, I had been sealed off in that cold palladian, especially when there were so many interesting things to do in Paris.

I wrote to Monsieur Eiffel that I was broken-hearted, and I enclosed a small picture of myself looking very grown up, a duplicate of the picture he had studied over our mantel.

But boarding school failed to solve the problem. The new quiet life was very strange to me after living in Paris for a few years. I had become a city-bred young woman and my natural gaieties spelled my disaster. I spent my afternoons trying, but failing, to fix my mind on routine work.

Why should I, like the busy bee, improve each shining hour over dead languages, mathematics, or philosophy for which I would have little or no use since the probability of my coming to want was rather remote? But I was bright enough to get what I wanted, and in one respect I knew very well what I wanted.

Novel reading was frowned upon for young girls of excitable feelings and wild imaginations, but I loved to read stirring, chivalrous stories, and romantic verses. On long, idle afternoons, I pictured to myself Monsieur Eiffel, a man of noble sympathies, the hero of every book I read. Somehow the very thought of Monsieur Eiffel sent me into a delicious chaos of uncertainty.

I read of love, thrilling through pages of wondrous happenings, and reflected that even modern times must have happily unusual experiences and glorious triumphs. Having gained my knowledge of love and its ways entirely from certain books, I learned that ideal lovers approached their fair ones always in an attitude of reverent homage.

Seated upon my bed in the dormitory room, I dreamed upon many a moonlit night of the home that would be mine—and when that home would come.

I liked to read in the evening by lamp light. This reading was, in the opinion of Mère Emilie, a concession to frivolity. Her constant discipline on this point imbued me with the idea that every desirable thing must be frivolous.

My eldest sister, Julia, had returned to the convent as an instructor and lay sister, teaching the next generation of girls in gray dresses to play the piano.

"I have prayed for wisdom and strength," she said, "to bring up these little souls and make them good citizens."

Julia was my opposite and was never known to do anything that was not eminently proper. She had subsided into a quiet maiden lady and seemed to find happiness in service, while I regarded my return to the convent as a corrective stint in the reformatory.

The nuns had been instructed by a letter from my father to keep my mind occupied with harmless amusements, and they did their best.

I was taught the newest stitches in crocheted lace, I was taught cribbage and chess, and every night at nine I was tucked into bed like a ten-year-old. I was willing to do almost anything to get away from the discouraging narrow-mindedness of my well-meaning jailers.

Among my idiosyncrasies was a love for practical jokes. Indeed, I had a keen eye for the ludicrous and was very mirthful. This was my greatest real fault. Practical jokers are a burden on society, and the only thing that kept me out of trouble in spite of this propensity was that I was small in size and childlike in demeanor, resulting in my being much petted by those adults enlisted to teach me.

I had hardly been settled in before Mère Emilie laid out a course for me to pursue.

"I shall give you a good education," she said, "and an education is a foundation on which a woman may build a career. I don't propose that after giving you an education, some man shall come along, talk a lot of nonsense to you, and render all that I have taught you wasted. You must begin by putting all notions of love and marriage out of your head."

Mademoiselle Alice

It occurred to me that my father may have enlisted her assistance by putting the notion in *her* head that I may have developed an attachment for a man who was too old for me.

It evidently did not occur to her that I was rather young to agree to place myself in opposition to nature's laws. Nevertheless, she said she hoped that I would repay her kindness in educating me by making myself the old maid she was herself and spend my life working, instead of surrounding myself with the prattle of my own children.

She was probably a good woman despite her crankiness. At the same time, there was ever in my childish mind a sneaking admiration for this witch of a mother superior who with her small, wrinkled face had triumphed in her walled-in world. Still, I had a wicked desire to torment the despotic old lady

I was constantly being punished for some petty offense or for breaking the routine and then leading my schoolmates to rebel against the tyranny of the school mistress. The unbroken quiet of long afternoons of sewing had become appalling. I found myself possessed of a hysterical desire to break in some way this insistent monotony.

Although I was a very bright scholar, before the first term of school ended, my course was cut short by my being discovered in a prank which resulted in my expulsion.

Even though the school was of a very good class, Mère Emilie was more interested in making money than in the welfare of the students. She received plenty of money for her pupils' tuition to warrant giving them every comfort, including excellent food, but she skimped on this in all possible ways.

One day, when the food had become so bad I could stand it no longer, I led a group of willing co-conspirators in what is called an old-fashioned barring out. We bought provisions with spending money we had from home, took possession of the schoolroom, and locked the door. This rebellion did not last long, for the door was broken open, Mère Emilie entered, and soon quieted our little feast. She questioned us as to our leader, but no one would tell. When she proposed to punish us all alike, I assumed the whole responsibility and was expelled from the school.

"I was born," I told her, "with the Dickens in me and must work out my career in his service."

"Nonsense!" she replied. "You were born to ease and comfort. Your silly prank was the result of self-will and an exuberance of spirit."

"It was one of my jokes," I said not altogether ruefully. "They always turn out the wrong way. Don't you know what it means to have reckless impulses, doing or saying something you are bound to be sorry for the next day? Well, that's me."

The last thing she said to me was: "Remember, you will surely be tempted into marriage because you are very good looking. Men will try to draw you away from the path of duty, but you must not listen to them. What they will want of you is to make you a slave. Be constantly on your guard."

It occurred to me then that she, Mère Emilie, had made me a slave. This I had not realized when I was a child. Also, it was rumored around the school that she had had an unfortunate love affair in her youth which had determined her to a life of spinsterhood. Because of this, she had resolved to save her young charges from the possibility of like sorrow.

When Grandmère came to fetch me, Mère Emilie described my behavior to her in detail, adding loftily:

"This ordinarily improving school, I must say, has failed in its object."

Mademoiselle Alice

"Alice is young," Grandmere responded gently, "but that is a fault we all get over."

I spent a few days with Grandmère, and then returned to Paris where I wanted to be.

ಬ∞ಃ

"My darling," murmured my mother when she saw me after a few months absence, "you positively shock me. I did not realize you were growing up. I have always thought of you as my little girl."

During the few months I was away, my father had lost contact with Monsieur Eiffel. My mother explained briefly what happened in the embarrassed voice of one who wishes to convey the fewest facts necessary to forestall any other questions.

"Your father lost a lot of money," she said, "and then there was no more work." My mother turned away so as to hide her concern from me.

I knew that my father had been working with Monsieur Eiffel on the Panama Canal, and that that endeavor had recently ended in scandal and bankruptcy. It was in all the papers.

My father had been wealthy, but his fortune had dwindled, and as it dwindled, he and my mother, who had been a famous hostess in earlier days, had gradually withdrawn from society.

It was surprising to me how soon we lost all of our friends in society. For a while, we were invited as before and, having a wardrobe, my sisters accepted some of the invitations they received. But within six months the men who control the sale of women's garments had so changed the fashions that our clothes were no longer in vogue. I had not had a coming-out party yet, or been fitted for the social life that my older sisters had enjoyed, but I cheerfully fell heir to the garments they discarded.

Since Fanny was plumper than I was and Rose a little taller, there was always material enough in their cast-off dresses to allow for remodeling. And I was so clever in the remodeling that my sisters gazed at me in wonder and disapproval. I put together charmingly mismatched reincarnations of their old clothes.

"A lavender waist with a blue skirt?" Fanny said. "Sorry, Baby Betty, they do not match. What is worse, they almost match."

My sisters did not always understand why I cared so little for social life. I was the only member of the family who cared for the artistic in life and who had not been fashioned from a perfectly conventional mold.

I got my ideas about fashion from gazing at the pictures of actresses displayed in theatrical papers. I was fascinated by Adelina Patti, a famous opera singer, who played all the leading female roles—*Esmeralda, Carmen,* Marguerite in *Faust,* and Juliet in *Romeo and Juliet.*

Adelina Patti was beautiful and she fulfilled my romantic fantasies by marrying her co-star, a handsome tenor, when she was playing Marguerite. My magazine said "she looked like a child, a delicate and adorable little creature." I was naturally impressed by the fact that she received $5,000 for each performance she gave in New York and San Francisco.

"I cannot believe you read such rot!" my father scolded.

At Ferney, I had become enamored of the mystery of the foot lights. When my father realized this, he opposed my going to the theater. He feared I might learn to care too much for it.

He did not know that, in the dark hours of the night, I was stage-struck, and fancied that I looked somewhat like Adelina Patti, an undersized young woman with a Madonna-like face. It goes without saying that I dreamed of becoming a great opera singer or actress. All along I craved praise, consequence, flattery. Never did I let my father know of my desires, however, because I was proud, too proud, to accept that my chances of becoming a great opera star were too negligible to be taken seriously.

"Sometimes notions opposed," Rose said wisely, "become strong desires."

I saw Monsieur Eiffel only once during this period, from a distance, at the *Carnaval de Paris*, an annual outdoor masquerade charity event that all Parisians attend. Rose sewed spangles on gossamer elfin wings and went as a fairy godmother. I made my own costume from rags and tatters of rose and gray china silk, a picturesque beggar-maid dress. Fanny was dressed as a shepherdess and objected to my costume, saying it was rather *negligée*.

We made our way to rue Saint-Antoine where musicians played on an outdoor stage. Robin Hood danced with Mother Goose, Napoleon with Dolly Madison, and a Crusader with Miss Muffat. Clowns and Columbines, pirates and fairies, soldiers and milkmaids flew past in a mad whirl, but all were masked and I had no idea who among them might be Monsieur Eiffel. I kept an eye on Henry the Fourth as his form looked familiar. At some point in the dancing his mask fell off, and although he replaced it instantly, Monsieur Eiffel's identity was revealed. My heart gave a fierce little tug when I saw him.

ಸುಂ

For Christmas that year, I was too old to receive gifts such as toys and dolls. The question between my father and mother was what more substantial article should be provided for me? They finally decided that an *escritoire*, one of those diminutive French writing desks with curvy legs and claw feet, would fulfil its purpose and encourage my creative pen.

On Christmas morning when we were assembled to open gifts, what was my excitement when I caught sight of the desk. It stood forth as pretty a piece of furniture as I ever saw.

"Is that for me?" I asked.

"Open it and see," said my father.

I lowered the front and looked in every pigeonhole and pulled out every sandalwood drawer until I came to the one that had a little brass key in its little brass lock and, turning the key, found the card on which it was written: *For Alice from Papa and Mama.* I threw my arms around my father's neck and then my mother's.

During this period, my father was taking various jobs to keep us fed and clothed, but it was hard on him to see us suffer from any want. He determined to marry off my sisters and then, when I became of age, me.

Marriage in Europe has always been brought about in different ways from those prevailing in America. In the United States, the great bulk of the marriages were made for love; in Europe they were largely arranged by the parents. A self-respecting girl was not supposed to fall in love until she was engaged, after the object of her thoughts had openly declared himself. We were raised not to think of a man "that way" until he had proposed.

Also, the bride was expected to have a cash dowry, and the amount had to be settled upon before she married.

Mademoiselle Alice

There were places, notably Geneva, where most of the marriages were brought about by this craft. The prospective groom was expected to deposit sufficient money to pay all expenses before he would be introduced to a prospective bride. He might, after seeing her, withdraw, and she had the same privilege. Everyone availed themselves of this brokerage system, from the highest classes down to those who could not really afford it.

It was through this brokerage house in Geneva that two of my sisters' marriages were arranged. First Fanny and then Rose, both of them over eighteen. I was just seventeen and my father thought he had more time to marry me off.

"I've been thinking what an awful thing it is," I told Rose, "for a girl to trust her whole future to a man, not knowing whether he's going to make a good husband or a horrid one."

"Mmmm," Rose said agreeably. "I often heard Mère Emilie say she wouldn't marry the best man on earth."

"Yes," I said, "Mère Emilie has a very clear idea of men's faults, in spite of her not knowing any."

I heard my parents talking about arranging for me to marry.

"What are we going to do with Alice?" my mother said. "She has no more idea of responsibility than a kitten."

"She is not fitted for any branch of business that I can see," Papa said. "She must learn naught of love until calm reason comes to her. Love is all right, but love alone will not carry her over the rough places in life. You know she could never be satisfied as a poor man's wife."

"Not with her indulgent father," my mother chided, "supplying her every whim."

"She is almost at a marriageable age," my father said, "and should be married as soon as she turns eighteen. We are living up to our income, but if anything should happen to me, she would have to go to work, and that would end her chances for marrying in the set to which she belongs."

"Work does spoil a girls looks," my mother agreed.

Chapter 8

AFTER I CAME BACK from boarding school that last time, I was aware of there being a great trauma in my family. A policeman came to the house and took my father away, my mother weeping and clinging to him. I did not see my father for some time. Then he came home, and the trouble seemed to be over.

And there was another scene I witnessed, my father holding my mother's hands, and they were talking with great earnestness.

My father was never the same man after the misfortune that came to him. He stopped going to his club, and experienced greater difficulty in gaining a livelihood for those dependent upon him.

He got terribly run down and came home one evening sick and discouraged. He had caught a severe cold and had, on this memorable evening, come to his home never to leave it again. The seasoned outdoorsman would die quietly in his bed.

During his last illness, he worried a great deal as to what was to become of me if I was deprived of his care.

"I wish you were a few years older," he said to me one day. "I would pick out a husband for you. I would know the relief of your assured future before I must leave you."

As I could not bear the thought of him leaving me, I felt it best to change the subject.

"Papa," I said reproachfully, "would you expect me to marry a man without love?"

"I would rather rely on his good qualities to win your confidence and respect. It would be better than a romantic attachment. Certainly, it would be more enduring."

While he was slipping away, at the slightest sound he would start. He would enquire if he was hearing a gun from a sinking ship, or a melancholy foghorn. At the last he was sure he heard the thin clang of a distant bell.

A light came into my father's eyes, a tinge of red to his cheeks. I put my arms around him and kissed him as I had done when I was a child. Then his words became indistinct and he closed his eyes.

During the night, my father drew his last breaths. My mother was praying by his bedside, Rose and I were wondering at our first sight of death that would take our father from us and make our mother a widow.

There were a few long breaths, the intervals between them growing greater, a rattle in his throat, and he was dead. His face instantly became white as chalk.

I was unaware of time passing. It seemed that time had ended. I heard voices behind me mingled with the sound of my own sobs. I remember being on my knees beside my father's bed, hysterically clinging to his body, while my mother tried to draw me away.

I became aware that there was someone standing behind me, wringing his hands. I turned, and saw two strange men in our home.

"Don't take him, don't take him!" I cried. My mother held me as long as she could while they picked up my father, and then I followed the men into the street, crying bitterly.

༄༅

That was January 5th. The next day, my black gown bespoke the laying to rest of my beloved father. I stood, hopeless and dry-eyed, in the midst of an empty house echoing with my father's voice, stilled finally and forever. The house suddenly seemed desolate without the one on whom we all depended. It seemed to me that when my father went out, solitude stepped in, and his death had wrung every drop of happiness from my life.

And yet I dreaded the thought of leaving our home.

I wondered: what was the trouble that had preyed on my father's mind to the very end of his days? Whatever it was, I felt sure that it had given him a measure of sorrow that helped to accelerate his decline. He had ended his days a broken down man of business over whose record hung a cloud. What that cloud was I did not yet know.

It was the twelfth night of Christmas, the Epiphany. In other years, we would have had a cake with a hidden almond in it. Tradition had it that the youngest child of the family would be entrusted with the job of distributing the portions of cake to the other family members. Whoever found the almond in the cake would be queen for a day.

I was overwhelmed with the seriousness of my loss. Caprice and indecision, the indulgences of childhood, were no longer available to me. We would have to leave our home, and the first thing to be done in preparation was to clear out family belongings that had accumulated for years.

I gathered together a few of my father's books, looking them over tearfully, before I put them with my things. Some of the worn books, which I had been read from as a child, awakened a host of memories: *Arabian Nights*, *Gulliver's Travels*, and *Pilgrim's Progress*.

I went to the attic and looked about at the confusion of miscellaneous articles. There were pictures, old furniture, empty frames, rugs, fireplace fenders and irons—every conceivable article. There were crates and trunks, some full, some half empty. The sight was discouraging, but I resolutely went to work to separate everything into groups to be disposed of in different ways. Old schoolbooks, packages of letters, my own dolls, were packed away or placed in a pile to be gotten rid of. The work of selecting what should be discarded brought me before a cold, dead past, and a corresponding loneliness.

In one of the trunks I found some old bedding,—blankets and pillows. I removed them and was thinking that I had emptied the trunk when, feeling in the bottom, my hand came across a tin box.

Upon opening it I found there the evidence of my father's existence, his papers and mementoes.

Pitiful indeed were the little treasures contained in the tin box—a sailor's keepsakes. Bits of sea glass, pretty shells and stones, my mother's face smiling from a tarnished frame, a baby's photograph, my mother's loving inscription penned on the back. There were also a few letters, intimately tender, from wife to husband and husband to wife.

The first letter I opened contained a pressed flower that had been there for many years. It was from my father to my mother promising that if she would forgive him for past sins, he would mend his ways.

A letter from my mother's uncle to my father warned him that if he ever entered a gambling house again it would be all over between him and my mother.

Truly, a tombstone is not the only reminder of one who has lived and moved, talked and laughed, worked and loved, on the face of this earth.

On unfolding the next document, I assumed that I had come upon something of importance. It was my father's will, executed years before, making a few small bequests and leaving the rest of his estate to his wife and his daughters who remained unmarried at his death.

I felt like an interloper reading my father's will. The baby of the family is not normally expected to take care of such things. But I was not the baby any more. Just as I had instinctively taken my brother's place when he died, I knew I needed to find a way to take my father's place as breadwinner now that my mother was alone.

Trembling slightly, I read further that Papa had appointed Monsieur Eiffel to be my guardian, and directed that if my father died before I reached the age of majority, my share of my father's property would be left to Monsieur Eiffel in trust for me until I should reach the age of twenty-one when it was to be paid either to me or to my husband should I marry.

Monsieur Eiffel was to provide a home for me, if necessary, and to direct my education.

Among the provisions of the will was a list of assets that described my father's property as consisting of a bank account and a large amount of stock in the Panama Canal Company.

Mademoiselle Alice

I had to stop reading and consider for a moment—the question in my mind was whether the stock in the Panama Canal Company was worth anything at all as I knew that the company had been put in receivership two years before. As I understood it, my father's investments in the Panama Canal Company were what brought about the family misfortune. Some rich men with money to fool away might in about twenty years be able to complete the canal, but at present the stock was worthless.

I wondered wistfully how my father had allowed his affairs to drift so hopelessly.

I folded up the will, taking little comfort from the promise of worthless stock and an empty bequest when I reached the age of twenty-one.

It was indeed fortunate that Julia had already been educated as a teacher, and entered the novitiate, her needs circumscribed and met by the religious order. Fanny had married in Geneva the previous spring, and Rose's marriage had already been arranged to be carried through in March.

"I think I prefer," Fanny had said when she was preparing to leave, "to marry someone I know nothing about, rather than, say, the boy next door, someone I have known forever. Mystery is a prerequisite of romance. Look at our parents—they did not know each other."

Rose was a beautiful girl with light hair and languid brown eyes. While she was packing to go to Geneva, I asked her how she felt about her upcoming marriage.

"It was in accordance with our father's wishes," she said. "I owe him that."

"I don't see why," I said.

"We were sent abroad to school," she said, "and we must

repay that kindness by a gratifying marriage."

"But you have had other suitors," I said. "We all have our love affairs," she said, "and they are easily put in abeyance."

After she left to get married, it would just be me and my mother.

൙ൠ

Here is one of the bitterest of many bitter tales.

My father's untimely death had found him deep in debt. His lawyer told my mother that his estate was heavily entailed and that the sale of his effects would surely be insufficient to cancel that indebtedness. Everything had to be sold, including my little escritoire.

I knew the family finances were low and wondered how my mother managed to keep our heads above the surface. Care and worry lined her brow. As the days before we had to leave our home counted down, even hunger visited us. It took money just to buy bread and butter. I found it remarkable how small an amount of food is necessary for the existence of the human body.

In the words of Edgar Alan Poe, unmerciful disaster "followed fast and followed faster."

One drizzling winter night, Mother sent me out to buy my supper with only fifteen cents. When I reached the crossing, I looked timidly at the heavy teams and the slush in the street, then scanned the faces of those about me. Paris suddenly seemed like a menacing place. But when one is hungry, one can think of nothing else.

As I walked, I considered what I could buy with fifteen cents. One roll and a cup of coffee, I decided, would be all that I could expect, so I made my way into an inviting cafeteria. I

Mademoiselle Alice

followed the others with my tray, keeping my face resolutely turned away from the tempting array of food before me.

Perhaps, I thought hopefully, as I sat down at a long table with other diners, the scant meal would at least take the edge off my appetite. The Parisian's breakfast generally consists of a cup of coffee and a roll, but such scant provisions would by no means be considered sufficient for supper.

It was not until I had finished my roll that I saw the doughnut on a plate opposite me. It was a light and brown doughnut, tempting and taunting me with its delicious hint of hidden nutmeg, like Grandmère's own. That the doughnut might be part of a satisfying meal belonging to an absent table companion, I did not stop to think. I only knew that I was penniless and hungry, and that my table companion had departed, leaving a half-finished meal behind.

I hesitated no longer. The voice of hunger was insistent— why waste food that had been discarded? I helped myself, rapidly eating the remaining ham and potatoes on the plate opposite me, when suddenly my table companion came back, and my departed senses returned with a jump. I was mortified at what I had done, but my mouth was so full, I was unable to make an apology. My first thought was to run away from those who knew of my disgrace. I picked up my tray and left the table and the cafeteria without a word. Also, I regretted that I had no time to eat the doughnut.

Here then is a startling example of how a person without sufficient funds might struggle against the sordid things of life, yet drift helplessly with the murky current.

ଚ୍ଚାର

Mademoiselle Alice

I had not intended to bother my mother with my father's will, but on our last night in our home, after all the preparations for removal had been made, I showed her the will which, under the circumstances, seemed completely irrelevant to the situation we found ourselves in.

"Oh, dear!" she said. "He signed this will when you were only ten years old, after Louis died!"

"I didn't want to show it to you," I said. "I didn't think it made any difference under the circumstances."

She read it carefully with a pained expression on her face. Then, she formed a plan. She would live with her Uncle Louis, who had come back from Chile and had a very small place, until she could find a job, and I would go to live with Monsieur Eiffel as directed by the will.

Because of these late unfortunate circumstances, I had no other home to go to.

My mother sent him a telegram regarding my father's wishes and, without any further explanation, told him that she was sending her "little girl" to him.

Chapter 9

I HAVE LEARNED THAT the unexpected usually happens where I am concerned. Even under sad circumstances, the unexpected can provide a bit of comedy. The story I relate to you here happened as follows.

Telegrams are usually associated with death or disaster, so when Monsieur Eiffel received a yellow envelope, his two married daughters, Claire Salles and Valentine Piccione, who were with him at the time, waited in suspense as he read the brief message.

"What is it?" one of them asked impatiently, while his puzzled expression changed to one of amusement.

"My deceased friend's little daughter is coming here tonight!" Monsieur Eiffel told them.

"A little girl, coming here?" said Claire. "How delightful!"

"Is she coming to stay?" asked Valentine.

"Apparently so," said Monsieur Eiffel, perplexed at this unexpected disruption of his comfortable bachelor routine.

"We will have to put a room together for her," said Claire.

Mother told me that Monsieur Eiffel had acquired a beautiful mansion on rue Rabelais across from the Jockey

Club, but that he seemed to prefer the solitude of his bachelor apartment on rue Prony since most women seemed to disappoint and bore him. It was to his rue Prony apartment that my mother directed the carriage driver to take me.

It was dusk but not yet suppertime when I betook myself bag and baggage, to Monsieur Eiffel's front door on rue Prony. Rain came pelting at my back and the wind screeched down the street behind me.

My knocking threw wide the door. I stood there in the doorway wearing a thin little suit never intended for cold or wintry weather, while my gloves—well, my gloves had been sewed up so often for holes in the fingers that I carried them now in pretense.

Standing before me were Claire and Valentine, whom I did not yet know, and they were gaping at me, speechless.

"Did you not hear me knock?" I asked. "I am Mademoiselle Alice, Emile Guy's youngest daughter."

I suddenly felt awkward about my imposition and their seemingly shocked lack of warm welcome.

"May I come in?" I asked.

"Of course, dear," said Claire, "come in, come in."

Claire was clearly the beauty in charge. She had a glorious crown of golden hair and, I would soon learn, everyone took orders from her.

"I'll fetch Father," said Valentine, the meek and mouselike younger sister. She ran upstairs and I heard her telling Monsieur Eiffel: "She's here. Change your cravat."

"Why should I change my cravat for a little girl?" I heard him ask.

"She's not a little girl," I heard her say. "She's beautiful."

I suppose I was much changed, but I had retained the same characteristics. I was conscious of meeting again the man with whom I had flirted shamelessly when I was emerging from childhood.

It seemed that since Papa's directions having been laid down in his will when I was much younger, and since he and Monsieur Eiffel had not seen each other for some time, and my mother's telegram had said she was sending her "little girl," it was supposed by Monsieur Eiffel and his daughters that I was a child.

While we waited for Monsieur Eiffel to come downstairs, Claire told me that I must wait until she made different arrangements regarding my room. I followed her with my bags and was behind her when she threw open the door to my temporary home. I was never more amused in my life. The room was strewn with playthings, including dolls.

Claire and Valentine, laughing, explained that they had taken great pleasure in planning for a little girl visitor as soon as they became accustomed to the idea of her coming. The guest room had become a regular playhouse as they drew on their own stock of toys saved from their younger days.

Claire and Valentine had made an excursion downtown as well, and wandered among the toys to their hearts' content, coming home tired but radiant.

"We saw so many things we enjoyed," Valentine said.

"Valentine played with everything she saw," Claire explained, "she was absurdly fascinated by a cow that mooed when you turn it over, and I could not tear myself away from the dear little dolls' accessories."

Monsieur Eiffel seemed much surprised when he saw me, though really the surprise was with me.

Papa was over fifty when he died and I remembered Monsieur Eiffel to be about the same age as my father. But Monsieur Eiffel did not look much over forty and was as young in his actions as in appearance. It seemed to me all at once that he had been growing younger as I had been growing older.

He had the same fine face I remembered, so seriously kind. There were patient wrinkles now about his mouth and eyes, his temples were touched with gray. He was older of course, but with a certain grave distinction.

"Mademoiselle Alice!" he exclaimed. "Your mother said she was sending her little girl!"

"Yes, I apologize for the misunderstanding."

"Not at all. Claire and Valentine have set up a playroom for you. See? You like it?"

"It's charming," I said. "I don't mind a bit."

Later, I overheard him talking with his daughters about me and asking their opinions as to whether it would be proper for him to keep me with him. I could not hear their whispered responses, but they all seemed to agree on some conspiracy regarding what to do with me.

Finally, Claire and Valentine left, and I was left alone with Monsieur Eiffel.

We dined together and he was very good and sympathetic and said so many nice things about Papa, regretting that he had lost contact with him in recent years.

"Papa often told me," I said, "that if he were taken from me, I could count on you for anything." Monsieur Eiffel winced at this.

"He was like a brother to me," he said, "and I have missed him greatly. Your father so cared for you—he had known so well your worth, that he begged me to be a party for a time to his cherished plans. To humor him, I agreed to watch over you during his absence."

"He had a hard time since you last saw him," I said. There was again an awkward silence.

"I remember now," he said, "he told me to take care of his little girl."

Then he imitated my father's way of talking, making me laugh for the first time: "'She is an irresponsible and thoughtless creature, but sound and good at heart. Watch over her and use your influence, if possible, in persuading her to stay off the stage.'"

I started laughing so hard there were tears rolling down my cheeks.

"He was afraid I would become an actress," I said.

I saw by his expression that I had touched a sympathetic chord. And sympathy is an effective weapon with which to attack a woman's heart. He responded instinctively to my every mood. He seemed to take such a kindly interest in me and was so sympathetic with me in my bereaved condition that I felt greatly comforted.

I constantly found him looking at me with a singular expression. It was as though I was connected with something beyond myself. There was tenderness in his gaze.

His honest gray eyes looked straight into my soul, and as I looked back, I dropped my gaze, for I knew what would be revealed there if I looked back at him too long.

Could it be that he felt that he was placed toward me in the position of an uncle? I certainly did not have for him a corresponding feeling. I thought him a very attractive and interesting man.

After the dinner dishes were cleared away, Monsieur Eiffel put on his coat and told me to get my bags.

"Come, come, little one," he said. "I will take you over to Claire's house."

"Does she have room for me?"

"She has lots of rooms."

It is awkward to rely on the kindness of a friend of your father's. It is more awkward to be quickly shunted off to another residence. A bit nonplussed, I retrieved my bags from the playroom that had been prepared for me.

"I am sorry to have imposed," I said.

"Not at all, Mademoiselle Alice. We are happy to have you." Then on the way out of the door, he quipped:

"If you proposed to make this house your home, you would have to marry the old man who lives in it."

"Well," I said, "the unexpected usually happens where I am concerned."

"Indeed," he said, "it is one of the most delightful things about you."

On the way to Claire's in his carriage, he explained that his daughter's house was really his own house which he had acquired only a year before.

He kept a library and office there while Claire lived in the house with her husband and children. When Monsieur Eiffel felt the urge to entertain his many friends and business associates, Claire would play hostess and handle the arrangements. He actually preferred, he said, his bachelor quarters.

I had passed completely from childhood into womanhood. Nevertheless I had not recovered from my girlish fancy, and though I endeavored to conceal this fact from Monsieur Eiffel, I probably failed. Unfortunately, my relations with Monsieur Eiffel had changed. His treatment of me was more reserved than ever.

౸౦ଔ

Mademoiselle Alice

Monsieur Eiffel took me to a beautiful part of Paris where his stone-front mansion at 1, rue Rabelais overlooked rue Matignon, a street abounding in gardens. From many small-paned windows glowed lights within. Through the glass I could discern an inviting fire of logs upon the hearth. I was cheered by the prospect of comfort and help.

It was very grand, that house. In the entryway, big red roses in the carpet seemed to jump up at me. The living room had a great stone fireplace, green plush sofas, shaded candelabras, and lovely antique tapestries hanging from its lofty ceilings.

I was received by Claire who was very cordial to me. I was installed in a spare room and became a member of the Salles family. Although Claire was very gracious to me, she regarded me with amused curiosity.

But I was still in an awkward position. While Monsieur Eiffel was my father's friend, and had known me for years, Claire and her family were strangers to me, and I was conscious, in spite of their kindness, that I was imposing.

On awakening in the morning, I detected the aroma of coffee. I made my way down a long hall where rooms branched out in a perplexing way. A balcony promised a view of the manicured garden beneath, but I hurried downstairs, and entered the kitchen where Claire was almost purring over a bowl of oatmeal and cream. There was a toast rack on the range, to say nothing of a dish of radishes and some tempting butter on the breakfast table.

"Help yourself," said Claire. I helped myself to a slice of toast and sat down.

"I should not have to impose on you for too long," I said, wiping the crumbs from my mouth. "My stay must be short because of my needed attendance upon my mother."

These were the years before it became customary for young ladies to earn their own living. I was more self-reliant than most society girls of that day whose intellectual and practical faculties were generally under-developed because their slightest requirements were attended to by servants.

Claire had apparently been thinking about what to do with me. She had her hands full with her social life and her two boys.

"You may act as my social secretary," Claire said. "If there is not enough work in that line to occupy you, you may tutor my two boys."

"How old are they?" I asked.

"Two and five. They are of the rambunctious variety."

To Claire's surprise, I gladly accepted the charge.

The hours I would be required to teach the boys each day would not be many, and I would have time to acquire other skills as I desired to eventually be able to support myself and my mother.

The boys had grown beyond the need of a baby nurse and I could not quite be called a governess. The boys called me their friend which was perhaps the best name of all.

I had been well-educated, and settled down to the work of instructing the Salles children. Within a short time, it became evident that Claire was pregnant with her third child. She was in her confinement, as we called it.

Although I dearly loved the Salles boys, teaching them was tiresome for me because I was so young. I had only had a wee taste of the world's pleasures, and it was terribly unstimulating for me to be confined to the company of two little children.

The day would invariably end in a dull nursery tea and a long lonely evening in my own room, or sitting on an upper balcony where I could listen to the distant strains of music from the rooms below if Claire and Monsieur Salles were giving a dinner or dance that evening.

If there was no dinner or dance in the evening, I would light a lamp in Monsieur Eiffel's library and look over the books. It was evident that the man who had filled these shelves was a well-educated and intelligent person. I have never before come upon a library, other than my father's small collection, in which every book was so beautifully bound.

Monsieur Eiffel had many atlases, for he was much interested in geography, and a revolving globe four feet in diameter. I was surprised that some of the books were modern. I found *Saint Elmo* to read, and other tales of standard fiction, where heroes were older and wiser than a new generation.

A fine, broad fireplace warmed the huge, high-backed armchair nearby. I liked nothing better than to throw myself into that armchair and bury myself in a book. Those wonderful old books were interesting enough to make me forget everything.

My taste for literature extended to almost every branch, but fiction was always my favorite. I mostly read the best fiction of the nineteenth century.

On the occasions when Monsieur Eiffel visited Claire and her family, he would find me there in the library, humming some tune or other. We sat over stacks of books in pleasant discussion, sometimes several hours at a time. Long we chatted under the yellow light of a floor lamp, sharing sympathetic and understanding stories of lonely years past.

I was charmed with his knowledge of any subject he touched upon. The result was that the afternoon would pass without his reading a word, devoting it all to conversation with me, though I confess he took the first opportunity to set me to talking. He was not only a good talker, but a good listener and, as we know, a good listener is even more entertaining than a good talker.

He was surprised when I told him I was born in Paris.

"I thought you were born in Chile," he said.

"No. My parents came back to Paris and installed me in Geneva with my grandmother."

"So you are a country girl?"

"A country girl in the city."

There is an unwritten, unspoken language between the sexes, and Monsieur Eiffel, unbeknownst to himself, was talking it all the while with his eyes. His gaze followed me as I dawdled over the shelves, now and again reaching for a book, turning the pages for a while, then passing on to another. I would pose standing on one foot, the other encased in a slender boot showing beneath my skirt, a feathered boa drooping from my shoulders adding to the picture.

I knew perfectly well that, at that moment, he cared less about the books than he did about talking to me. Had I not felt toward him something like what he felt toward me, there would not have been any such understanding between us.

෴

While I lived at 1, rue Rabelais, I acquired the habit of taking early morning walks, because you have to get up very early to catch the sleeping beauty of the Seine. Any other time of day it is wind-ruffled and restless, but there is an hour at dawn when nary a ripple disrupts its mirrored surface. A walk along the ever-lovely quay was refreshment for my eyes.

I often saw wagons lumbering along, loaded with camp equipment and human beings—gypsies with no home other than what they had with them.

I circled back along the Champs-Elysées. The chestnut trees had blossomed and stood in all their wealth of white. The fashionable windows fascinated me and made me forget that I was poor.

Deprived of home, fortune, and loved ones all in one year, I enjoyed one undisturbed morning hour each day, a golden hour in which to walk about, tripping on loose cobblestones, dreaming of the good things the future might bring, for surely of late, fate had dealt harshly with me in the justice of things, and my future must be bright to compensate for the loss of all that had gone before.

Chapter 10

SHORTLY AFTER I MOVED in with the Salles family, my mother and I were invited to a banquet for three hundred guests to be given by the Grand Circle of Paris, an important club composed chiefly of commercial men and civil servants. Monsieur Eiffel was among those hosting the event along with other engineers, ambassadors, and consuls to and from South America.

The name of the club, Grand Circle, signified a vision of the future when it was foreseen that both the successfully finished Suez Canal, and the unfinished and abandoned Panama Canal, would make it possible to sail from Gibraltar, the western limit of Europe, around the world over that circle of the globe closest to the equator.

My mother rejoiced very much to go, and further that she would be able to introduce her youngest daughter into society, the unfinished business left by my father's untimely death, and which she could not have otherwise done because she had no fortune.

Claire was made aware of the upcoming banquet, and she became part of the plans that were being laid for me to be presented to society. She asked me to come into her little sitting room and close the door.

"Please give me your attention," she said.

I was a demure little miss of seventeen, and seated myself gingerly, as though I feared I might break the chair with the hundred pounds I placed on it. But I was embarrassed, mortified really, that I had nothing to recommend me, and cast my eyes to the floor, barely listening to the lecture I was receiving.

Claire proposed to do everything in her power to enable me to make a match during the limited time that had been set aside for this purpose.

"It isn't necessary," Claire explained, "for me to go over the circumstances of your being here. The power of wealth and the difference between it and poverty are growing greater every day. There is much that I can do for you, but there is a great deal that I cannot do. I can put you forward for a limited time, enabling you to mingle with those with whom we associate, thus giving you an opportunity to make an advantageous match. But you must remember that it will not do me any good to sponsor a girl for any length of time who hasn't a cent in the world."

"Yes, I understand," was my demure reply.

But as my face flamed, I also felt a slow burn in my heart. Of course, I knew exactly what she meant. With nothing to live on, there was no escape from the impending doom of poverty except a good marriage.

To my mind, families of pretentious standing and fortunate circumstances were matters of indifference, but it was obvious to Claire that I had nothing to wear to the ball.

"My father," Claire continued, "has asked me to outfit you for your coming out. This Grand Circle ball is rather exclusive, and my sister and I cannot attend. Both of us are in our confinement. This will be a grand opportunity for you to meet young men of good standing."

She further advised me to "brush up a bit," but her recommendation failed to impress me.

"Love is a matter of the soul," I said knowingly. "It has nothing to do with clothes." Whereupon she admonished me to make myself pretty all the same.

The next morning I was driven in the family carriage to Claire's dressmaker who was a natural artist, endowed with a fairy wand for her highness's adornment. In a posh little studio lavishly draped with chiffons, silks, and laces, she made up a simple costume for me that accorded well with my figure.

It was pink overlaid with thin white stuff embroidered with a delicate tracery of green leaves. It was rather plain in the front, cut low about the throat, but in the back the flounces on the skirt were gathered into a trail of roses in pink, mauve, and yellow. I arranged my hair in a modish fashion and consented to borrowing a necklace of Claire's.

I had white stockings and little, pink slippers. They were the sort of slippers a princess of past dreaming might have chosen to slip on in the firelight.

When Claire saw me so festively arrayed, she remarked that I looked pretty enough, but she fretted that the men would not pay any attention to a girl with no chic.

But the men of that set had been deluged with chic, and as soon as I appeared in the ballroom, I was besieged with introductions. My dance card was soon filled with names and, as I sailed over the shiny parquet floor, the simple manner in which my hair was done along with the unstudied arrangement of my costume, so unlike the elaborate gowns of the other women there, attracted many eyes. I saw more than one young man looking at me with a glance that was unmistakably admiring.

The ball was held in a grand hotel famous for its lavish furnishings. French doors linked the opulent dining and reception rooms. Ornate crown moldings layered with gold leaf framed the sparkling glass ceiling, and the walls were hung with wine red silk.

The heavy scent of countless roses, crimson draperies, and little scarlet shaded lights on the tables gave the dining room a gala air. The faces of those gathered about the numerous small tables glowed above the rosy lights and were reflected in the many mirrors.

Many curious glances were cast in Monsieur Eiffel's direction, for his distinguished figure had become well-known. His skill in his profession garnered him much praise. Elevated on a dais he sat, looking very different in evening dress, very correct with a gardenia in his lapel.

Prompted by the president of the club, he made a little speech welcoming the guests to the banquet and stating the reasons for the sumptuous feast.

"I would like to propose a toast," he said, "to our many friends and compatriots who have joined the community of those with more adventurous spirits who have established businesses in South America."

To Monsieur Eiffel's right sat Jules Simon, one of our most respected statesmen, who also gave a speech and received much applause.

These were men of business, fortune, and government, who dispensed a good deal of money in connection with philanthropic capitalists. If millions of francs were needed to found a hospital, Monsieur Eiffel would be one of several wealthy persons to make up the amount.

My mother's Uncle Louis was with us, back in Paris after forty years in Chile. Also at our table was Dr. August Coignard, who had founded the French hospital in Valparaiso where my mother had donated her time.

My mother and I were possibly the only single women at the banquet, and thus we attracted the attention of those of the party who were unattached. The sparkling wine was flowing and, when the banquet was at its height, Jules Simon joined our table. He was then founding a new company called *Mutualité Maternelle* with other important men, the purpose of which was postnatal care, a new science in those days for the prevention of infant mortality. France was then suffering from a high rate of infant mortality among those women who worked in the needle trades especially.

Dr. Coignard pointed to my mother's many years of working with him in Chile. Suffice it to say, connections were made, and my mother was soon after hired as a director of the *Mutualité Maternelle*.

ಸಂಬಂ

There is some question as to how far a man is responsible for a girl's falling in love with him. In this case, Monsieur Eiffel would not have prevented it even by refraining from the little compliments that he considered due any woman. I was confronted by that which dazzled me and was dazzled.

I thought he was the most agreeable and most amiable man in the world, and therefore I would have been aggrieved if he thought ill of me. We are most ambitious for the esteem of those who most merit our own. No one can tell what a girl of seventeen is going to do, and when she does it no one can stop her.

When I saw him marshaling the dancers, I admired him immensely, and when he stood in the middle of the ballroom, giving his orders by clapping his hands, I thought him the embodiment of manly strength and beauty.

Women had made open advances to him. They had attacked him through his vanity and through his senses. They had all failed.

I was sitting at my table, looking at him, yearning for him. Presently he looked aside and straight back into my eyes, as though answering my silent call, and miraculously he crossed the room to my side. I am sure the color came and went from my cheeks as he advanced toward me, but he was ready with a reassuring greeting.

"Mademoiselle Alice! My little nightingale!"

Monsieur Eiffel seemed touched by the worship of a beautiful girl young enough to be his daughter. He returned my gaze and asked me to dance. I looked up at him with a frightened glance, as if to say: "This honor cannot be for such as me."

Nevertheless, we danced, and with such grace that others ceased to dance to watch us. Every movement was perfect, yet it seemed natural, not calculated.

"What a beautiful little girl you are," he teased.

"I'm not a little girl," I protested. "I'm a woman—almost eighteen!"

"You don't mean it. I thought you were younger."

"How old would you take me for?" I asked him.

"Fourteen—perhaps a year older."

"Oh my word, you are way off. I'll be eighteen in two months."

"You don't mean it!"

"Oh, yes. I know you consider me a child. You forget—eighteen is legal age for a woman."

He danced with me several times during that evening. The memory of those dances has remained with me ever since. We floated in voluptuous circles to entrancing music.

"Let's go and sit down," he suggested. "We ought to be talking instead of dancing."

After the orchestra stopped playing, many guests stayed late, sitting around talking and drinking coffee. We spent the remainder of the evening together in one of the little nooks intended for romantic *tête-a-têtes*, absorbed in each other's conversation.

"You are too good for society," he said, "too fragile and unspoiled. You're like a wildflower. I have seen haughty women in wonderful clothes, but there are not many like you, as natural and unaffected."

He introduced me to a close friend of his, Jules Janssen, who was dressed in a black frock coat and a large white cravat. He appeared to be much older than Monsieur Eiffel, looking for all the world like Saint Nicholas with his long white beard and understanding eyes. Both men were members of the *Société Astronomie Française* and *la Marmite*.

"Monsieur Janssen is a scientist and astronomer," Monsieur Eiffel said by way of introduction. "He travels the world taking pictures of eclipses. He invented a camera that takes many pictures per minute. How many per minute, *mon ami*?"

"About forty," Monsieur Janssen said.

"Did you take that camera with you to South America?"

"No, unfortunately my trip to Chile was a few years before I invented it."

Mademoiselle Alice

"Like you," Monsieur Eiffel said to me, "Monsieur Janssen also spent some time to Chile." Then he turned to Monsieur Janssen.

"Mademoiselle Alice was born in Chile."

"No, no," I said, correcting him for the second time. "I was born in Paris, but I went to Chile when I was little."

"Pardon me," Monsieur Eiffel said gravely, then turning to Monsieur Janssen: "My lady is a *Parisienne*."

Both men laughed, but there was kindness in their attentions to me. Moreover, I liked being called "my lady."

Chapter 11

MONSIEUR EIFFEL HAD a great many friends and interested several of them in getting me invitations. I had no acquaintances among young men near my own age, and this seemed to trouble him. He hunted up several youngsters and brought them to the house for my companionship. They seemed very boyish to me. They were all very nice, but I didn't care for them much except to socialize in a superficial way.

I played a merry game of hearts with them all, leaving my own heart untouched.

Young men of those days were accustomed to frolicsome company in the young women they honored with their attention, but I was a serious girl having seen a great deal to indicate to me that life was not a bed of roses. I quickly became bored with the whirl of dinners, dances, and small talk.

After a few months had gone by and I didn't make a match with one of these boys, Monsieur Eiffel said to me:

"Mademoiselle Alice, you must remember that you can't very well make a home without marrying."

"You seem to have done so," I said.

"But I am not you. You are young and pretty, and at the marrying age."

In this way, Monsieur Eiffel treated me with a certain reserve which I did not relish. I wished that he would not keep a barrier constantly between him and me.

I met so many attractive men that my interest in them was neutralized. I had already met the one man who was capable of inspiring me with a grand passion.

Still, I did not really think about marriage. There seemed to be plenty of time for that later. All I desired was to live on just as I was in the company of this delightful man.

I wanted Monsieur Eiffel to escort me to functions, but he would not. He didn't tell me why, but I knew that he feared people might accuse him of appropriating me to himself.

He even introduced me to his two sons, entirely likeable lads, who were close to my age. His youngest son, Albert, in fact, was exactly my age and held no appeal for me whatever. Years later, Monsieur Eiffel told me that Albert, after a date with me, had told him: "She's all right, but I think she likes you, Dad."

One day, a young man invited me to go to a play with him. Monsieur Eiffel stopped by tired and despondent about something that had gone wrong during the day. Claire suggested that he go to some place of amusement. He demurred on the ground that it would not benefit him to go alone.

"Why not take me?" I suggested.

"I thought that you already had an engagement?" was his reply.

"I'll break it," I said eagerly.

He looked at me surprised, and said he would not have me do that in any case.

Mademoiselle Alice

I assured him I preferred to go with him, but could not make him understand that I would rather to spend an evening in company with an older fellow like himself instead of a young man nearer my own age. Monsieur Eiffel, with his many interests, had made a strong impression on me. He seemed to find me particularly congenial as well, and I preferred him to any of the young men of my acquaintance.

Half an hour afterward, I received two tickets to the play, *L'Ami Fritz*, with a note from my young escort stating that he was unavoidably prevented from taking me to the theater and hoped I would find someone to take his place. I went merrily to Monsieur Eiffel waving the tickets over my head and asked him to be the substitute.

I wore my ball dress and put on all my finery including a number of gold and silver bangles. I knew I looked very pretty and, more than that, I wore on my face the unjaded and youthful expectation that was fast fading from the face of my escort.

I had been to the theater but once or twice in my life, while the drama was an old story with Monsieur Eiffel. But in my enjoyment he discovered renewed interest.

The curtain went up on *L'Ami Fritz* which had been playing in Paris for many years. The play was a romance, an old-fashioned love story about a comfortable, middle-aged bachelor named Fritz and the farmer's daughter, Suzel.

The first scene takes place in a garden set with a rustic dining table under a tree. It was a real tree, too, introducing naturalism to the stage. Several men were sitting around the table, dipping their spoons into real bowls of steaming, cabbage soup. The men drank wine with their dinner and one of the guests, a rabbi, made a wager with Fritz that he would marry in spite of being hardened against it. Fritz bet one of his vineyards that he would not.

Mademoiselle Alice

I thought it was all wonderful, just like a story book. There was continual happy chatter during the performance. Everybody was dressed in high style, delighting my eyes looking from the costumes on the stage to the fashionable women around me.

When at intermission the curtain fell, Monsieur Eiffel took me where we could get an ice cream, which to me was an extraordinary treat.

As the play progressed, Fritz falls in love with Suzel. The couple sings a romantic duet while Suzel climbs up into the cherry tree from where she hands Fritz some ripe fruit.

The players, many of them mouthing their lines and overacting, were to me real people, their joys and sorrows were real emotions, while the hero and heroine seemed to be enacting my own feelings.

In another scene, Suzel gives the rabbi water from a pitcher at the well. He asks her to tell him the story of Rebecca in the Old Testament. I knew the story of Rebecca. She was chosen to be a bride because she was kind enough to give water to a stranger.

In the last act, Fritz and Suzel are betrothed, and the rabbi donates the vineyard he won in the wager as Suzel's dowry. In the end, the two lovers are united in an embrace.

Monsieur Eiffel, blasé himself, and having seen the play a number of times before, regarded me with infinite satisfaction. When I felt my arm against his, a thrill ran through me. When I turned my face toward his, looking for shared appreciation of some noble sentiment expressed by one of the actors, he smiled sympathetically and with wonder at my animated excitement.

That broke the ice between us. Monsieur Eiffel thereafter permitted himself to show me some attention. He never would have allowed himself this indulgence if he had not seen me blithely turning away the handsome young men he provided for me. More than that, he appreciated something in me that young men did not.

That night I went to sleep dreaming that Monsieur Eiffel was the hero and I the heroine in the play that had been enacted. This love that had entered my heart was a serious and perplexing problem, to be constantly considered, and I found it impossible, no matter how hard I might try, to transfer that love to another would-be suitor.

Chapter 12

*M*Y MOTHER HAD A QUIET WAY with her and an abundance of common sense. While I failed to find a husband among my many dance partners at my first ball, my mother succeeded in being hired to assist at a clinic near the Sorbonne, and to direct the education side of *Mutualité Maternelle*.

The business of the company was carried on by volunteers of means and social standing, along with a few paid assistants like my mother. She took me with her to work on her new job.

The first mission of *Mutualité Maternelle* was to collect a fee from working women, and then to pay working mothers to stay home for one month after giving birth so they could breastfeed their babies. It was said that this one change in employment practices would cut the rate of infant mortality in half.

The second mission of the company was to educate the new mothers as to hygiene and the danger of giving their babies unsterilized cow's milk. This educational purpose involved visiting new mothers in their homes, bringing them a layette, and also encouraging them to bring their babies to a clinic where the health of the newborn could be monitored.

I watched wide-eyed as the babies were washed and powdered and wrapped in blankets. Then they were carried into the doctor's room where their weights were recorded and the physician inspected them and asked their mothers about the care they were able to provide for the baby.

Meanwhile, Monsieur Eiffel and I continued our *tête-à-têtes* in his library. From the stars in the heavens above to the creatures of the seas below, there appeared to be nothing which this brilliant man had not searched out in study.

He was interested in French history and his own place in it. I gladly helped him with one of his pet projects—researching his ancestors. Together we pored over ponderous volumes of genealogy from the library.

There were no frills about Monsieur Eiffel even though he was very well-dressed. Indeed, it would have been impossible for him to pretend to be anything but a plain man. His plainness consisted in not putting on airs, and in a solidity for which he was respected. This solidity would suddenly drop like a mask and reveal a remarkable tender-heartedness.

He had been a widower for so many years that he was more like a bachelor. His own comfort and his independence were his guides.

One day, I felt sure he had a story to tell me. He told me about his wife who had died more than a decade before when their children were still small.

"She was in delicate health," he said, "and we are prone to become more attached to one who is depending on us for comfort than to one who has no need of our care. I had bought a vacation house in Sevres and we planned the place together, and while it was being readied for our use, we went out there to watch our conceptions materialize."

"Before it was finished I knew that my wife would not live to enjoy it. She was not conscious of the seriousness of her malady and continued to look forward with happy expectation to our vacations. On no account would I break her anticipation. Instead, I consulted constantly with her on how we would have this and how we would arrange that, keeping her interested in what could never be realized in order to shield her from the truth."

"While the house was being remodeled, I continued to make changes to prolong the construction. When the house was finished, I laid new plans for the grounds. One spring—the last of her life—we drove out there frequently and I worked with and directed the men in planting the garden while my wife sat on the porch, making such suggestions as occurred to her. "

"Meanwhile, she was growing more and more feeble. But not until the day she left me did she realize that she would never share with me that on which we had lavished so much thought and care."

"All was finished at last. The place was ready, and my wife's stay on earth came to an end. Perhaps, had I not lost the motive power for what had so long occupied me, I would have borne my bereavement more stoically. As it was, I became one of those who nourish a grief."

He stopped talking for a moment, remembering, taking deep breaths. I listened to this recital with sympathy, and my hand crept into his while his own closed over mine. Gravity lay in his gray eyes—gravity and sincerity.

"And, oh, I am so glad," he said, with evident happiness, "that I have been able to give you a home."

Mademoiselle Alice

Needing to lighten the mood, he then told me a humorous story.

"The ladies of Paris soon learned that I was a widower. After I had been a widower for a while, I became ill for a week. A lady who lived opposite me first became aware of my illness and hastened to send over delicacies. The news spread down the street on both sides and everybody, all the widows and unmarried women in Paris, it seemed, sent broth or fruit or jelly. Had I consumed it all, I would have died of gluttony."

"When I recovered, I found a basket in my entryway filled with visiting cards bearing the names of the ladies who had sent delicacies to me."

"As soon as I was able," he explained, "I began calling on the ladies who had favored me with a gift, and I did not cease until I had thanked every one of them in person."

"When I finished, I had an acquaintance with many ladies. Some were very old and some very young, but I had five children, and I could not see bringing another woman into my home. My sister and brother-in-law moved into my house and took care of the children while I attended to business. I had to travel quite a bit. More than I wanted to."

He told, too of his busy years of civil engineering which carried him to the far parts of the earth, bridge-building in the mountains and over rivers.

"I must be boring you," he said.

"I could never be bored," I said, "by the stories of your life."

※

The one fear that haunted Monsieur Eiffel's daughters was that he would one day get married. He always disavowed any intention of committing this crime, and declared his firm resolve to live and die in single blessedness under the care and dominion of his daughters.

Still, his daughters took turns in standing guard over him lest he should present them with an undesirable stepmother.

If Claire had to be out of town, it was Valentine's turn for duty. If Claire and Valentine were otherwise engaged, their sister, Laure, kept Monsieur Eiffel company.

One day, after a long session in the library with Monsieur Eiffel, it appeared to Claire that her forebodings were in danger of being realized. She saw Monsieur Eiffel and I, sitting each of us on either side of a reading table, talking together in whispers and laughing softly. But it was, no doubt, the way we looked into each other's eyes that revealed to Claire that her father had discovered a kindred spirit.

Monsieur Eiffel sensed her recognition of this development and, to throw her off his trail, he declared loudly that he would always take the tenderest "paternal" interest in me. Nevertheless, Claire whisked him away on some pretext or other.

Later that day, I was curled up in the hidden refuge of the armchair by the grate, and I overheard her say to Valentine:

"Serves her right. These social climbers need a lesson now and then."

That was all I needed to hear. It was enough. For two days, I was so cross there was hardly any living in the house with me.

The next time Monsieur Eiffel came by, he found me unusually quiet in his library.

"My little nightingale," he said, "why do you not sing?"

"I cannot sing," I said.

Mademoiselle Alice

I told him I felt I needed to move out, and he apologized for the careless indifference to my welfare that marked the attitude of his society-loving daughters.

"My mother needs me," I said.

"Perhaps you can come over to my rue Prony apartment to help me continue with my research."

I had a lump in my throat and couldn't say anything.

"Perhaps both you and your mother can come over here on Thursday nights." He took my hands in his. "We will have wine and music and a bite to eat. Will you come?"

"Of course I will."

His kindness touched my heart.

Chapter 13

*M*Y MOTHER WAS ABLE to find an attic apartment for us at 5, rue de Tournon, one of those ancient streets bearing the stamp of ancient times, and I moved in with her. The topmost apartments were quite looked-down-upon in those days because everyone knew they used to be the servants' quarters.

My imagination was captured by one of the apartments below, the former home of Mademoiselle Lenormand, the famous fortune teller who correctly advised Josephine that she would marry Emperor Napoleon. The residence of the prophetess for forty years had been at the extremity of a dark courtyard, and over the door there remained a sign that read: *Mademoiselle Lenormand, Libraire.* Because fortune telling was illegal, she was officially a bookseller. It was rumored that a stuffed owl peered down from the bookcase.

My mother had only worked for *Mutualité Maternelle* for a few months when they decided to stop paying her. Since many women of the comfortable class were volunteering to take her place, she had to resign in order to find a paying job.

My mother's most important possession was her sewing machine, and she found work making buttonholes in coats and

Mademoiselle Alice

waistcoats for a ready-made clothing company. She made every effort to support herself and me, but the pay was always miserable. Every job always had to be supplemented by piecework she did at home. Evenings we often spent fabricating artificial flowers, an art we both learned from Grandmère.

It was fall and the dressmaking season was at its height. Parisians are passionately interested in matters of dress. Half the women of Paris worked in the needle trades. My mother, my sisters, and I were among the lucky ones because our convent educations enabled us to obtain better paying jobs with Paris dressmakers rather than the lower paying jobs in factories.

We went to 1, rue Rabelais on Thursday evenings where Monsieur Eiffel's daughters played the piano for us. I played too, the few pieces I could remember by heart. My mother did the best she could to keep me well-dressed, making over the clothing that my sisters had worn. I made a very good appearance, especially on Thursday nights.

Monsieur Eiffel had one of the first-ever phonographs, given to him by Thomas Edison at the Exposition Centennial. He explained how it worked and I listened with interest. I showed that I understood the contrivance because I always said "Yes" or "Indeed" and "How clever" at exactly at the right time. When he asked: "Do you follow me?" I always said, "Perfectly."

"How did you come to have a daughter," he asked my mother, "who understands these things so well?"

My mother was much pleased that her daughter had a mind capable of understanding the explanations of Monsieur Eiffel. With her patient smile, she said proudly:

"Alice has always attended the best schools. Besides, she has pronounced scientific tastes. You see," she explained, "it is

Mademoiselle Alice

so like what I had hoped for myself—life here in Paris among people who really live and use their talents. While we were in Chile, my musical ability and other accomplishments were buried under the cares of a village household. We lost many advantages. But now," she said, her face shining with satisfaction, "Alice is living my dream. Her music will be appreciated and, of course, all her clever ways."

While she conversed, my mother occupied herself with embroidery. A modiste for whom Mother had sewed agreed to give her small parts to embroider at home. She was sewing day and night to earn our bread and butter.

It was at one of these musical evenings when the subject of my future employability was discussed by Monsieur Eiffel and my mother.

"She sews beautifully, but she finds it tedious," my mother said.

"I did enough sewing at school, Mother."

My mother continued talking to Monsieur Eiffel.

"She is like her father—passionately fond of poetry and literature, the pleasures of the mind."

"Perhaps Alice would like to pursue a course of stenography," Monsieur Eiffel suggested. "The stenographers in the Chamber of Deputies draw a fine salary."

"Are women allowed to secure such positions?" I asked.

"I think they are required to pass the baccalaureate," he answered me, but turned again to my mother.

"Alice could get a job with a company. In the future, businesses will likely employ stenographers instead of paying men to hand-copy every blasted piece of correspondence. But first they will have to purchase typewriters and they are expensive."

Mademoiselle Alice

The typewriter had not yet proliferated, and men who had good handwriting, both legible and beautiful, was desirable in business for important letters and contracts.

Finally, Monsieur Eiffel turned to me.

"Mademoiselle Alice, a good friend of mine, a professor at the Sorbonne, was a stenographer for the Chamber of Deputies. If he would be amenable, would you like to take lessons in stenography?"

"I would," I said. "I would be most grateful for an introduction, if you would be so kind."

Monsieur Eiffel was always true to his word. He said, cryptically, he knew of a way that a certain sum of money by which I might receive some education as a stenographer might be awarded to me.

I wondered about this later. I was of an independent mind and wanted to know how I qualified for this award of funds.

I went to the address of one Professor Charles LeFebvre that Monsieur Eiffel gave to me.

"I am Mademoiselle Alice," I announced directly, "and would like to take stenography lessons. Will you kindly tell me your price?"

I was fully aware of the anxious note in my own voice as he drew forth a chair.

"Do not worry," he said reassuringly, "Monsieur Eiffel has acquainted me with your situation."

"There is a fund," he told me, "placed in my care, for instructing pupils of promise. That money may be expended on your education."

"I am so glad," I said with a sigh of relief, "for I feared the lessons might be more than I could afford."

So my lessons began, and the three afternoons each week when I appeared for instruction came to be bright spots in my life. Professor LeFebvre gloried in my advancement, then troubled himself continually because of hardships he feared I might be secretly enduring, while I calmly accepted his devoted friendship, installing him as my confidant and adviser.

He provided me with practice cards and copybooks to help me learn the language of stenography. Some of the practice cards were quite artistic, using the stenographic symbols to compose a picture in penmanship.

He took me to the Chamber of Deputies and to the Senate where stenographers are at the top of their field and have the highest status.

He also took me to the Sorbonne where I was the only female in the class, to practice my skills by taking down in shorthand the lectures of Professor François Aulard, a scholar of the French Revolution. The competency test for a stenographer was to take down one of Professor Aulard's lectures for an hour, and then to transcribe it on a typewriter under the tyranny of the stop-watch.

Professor Aulard was a great story-teller and had a most interesting story to tell.

"After the Revolution of 1789," he said, "the National Assembly was jammed with French citizens, no longer willing to accept the *fait accomplis* of lawmakers. Citizens wanted to hear the discussion. A method had to be devised to write down what the lawmakers said."

"Ten men sat around a table, each with a stack of numbered strips of paper. The first man would write in longhand the first three or four words on a strip numbered one, and then nudge the man sitting next to him who would take down the following three or four words on a strip numbered two, and so on, until the debate was over. Then the numbered strips were assembled in order and printed for everyone to read."

"Two men, they were all men," he said, looking pointedly at me, "stood by and listened to the entire debate so they could review the strips of paper for sense and accuracy."

"In the decades since then, we have seen many systems of stenography invented. France, Britain, Germany and America have all created their own systems which are very popular."

While I was taking private lessons from Professor LeFebvre, he observed how thin I was, and instituted the fashion of serving afternoon tea in his study.

"It's quite the custom," he assured me, watching with satisfaction my hungry enjoyment of a sugared roll while he poured the tea and instructed me.

I proved to be an apt scholar and absorbed in a short while what some might be years in learning. Monsieur LeFebvre, my teacher and my friend, was delighted with the success of his efforts on my behalf, assuring me when I expressed my gratitude that it was his pleasure to teach me.

With much practice, I learned to write at the same rate that most people talk, and to read pages of inscrutable curlicues.

"It's like a secret language," I said to Professor Lefebvre.

"It is a secret language. It has been used by spies."

"Spies?" I said. "How intriguing! Should I write my diary in shorthand?"

"You should if you have secrets and don't want anyone to know what you are writing."

ಐಡಿ

Typewriters were uncommon even in offices during those days, and were never to be found in households, but Monsieur

Mademoiselle Alice

Eiffel was interested in the latest technology, and he procured a typewriter for himself. He suggested I make myself useful to him by typing the various lectures and manuscripts of his coming books on the sciences, etc.

This was to his advantage but also to mine as he knew that after I acquired the skills necessary to obtain a job, I would also need a letter of recommendation, and such a letter from a great man of affairs such as himself could be invaluable to me.

I begged him to tell me where the money for my private lessons came from. As I suspected, the money donated for my education came not from an established fund, but was a personal gift from Monsieur Eiffel. When I asked him about it, he averred at first, saying, "Your father's will provided for your education." He tried to conceal the fact that this money did not come from my father's estate but from his own pocket. After I pinned him down on the subject, he finally admitted it.

"It was my pleasure to donate that money," he said. "I ask but one reward—that you type my scholarly papers."

This was one of those times when Monsieur Eiffel invented ways to make my mother and I think that what he provided for us was our own, and that we were not indebted to him for it. He saw that someone would have to take care of us since we had very little to live on and no one to tie to.

༄༅

In those years, my three sisters lived near Geneva, so my mother and I traveled by train to see Grandmère for Christmas. Fanny was expecting her first baby, so we had the additional joy of awaiting the birth of my mother's first grandchild and my first little niece or nephew.

Mademoiselle Alice

Grandmere's kitchen was cheery with its glowing fire and snowy cloth on the table. There was again the delicious odor of ginger spice cake baking and, best of all, Grandmère herself smiling a welcome to us.

Even in winter with all the snow about, there were birds that came to be fed, and to sit in rows on the red berry tree.

A few days after Christmas, Fanny had a baby girl she named Yvonne Emilienne, after our father.

It was the sight of my little niece, nestling under her lace covers, that gave me the idea—though it was more than an idea for it became my constant longing. I had so long felt that I was robbed of my childhood, and I felt this loss even more keenly since the loss of my father. My baby niece in her lacy nest awakened a heretofore repressed need of my own. I wanted a baby with my whole heart, someone to love and someone to love me. The thought grew to fill my dreams, day and night.

But I could not have a baby unless I was married. I had matured rapidly, and my mother began to form plans for me, but I was not inclined to follow them. The matter of bringing about a match between me and a young man miscarried, and no further attempt was made by my mother to find a husband for me. I had little to do with young men and maidens my own age, and when with them I felt as if I was not part of the same age group.

Of course, there was another reason why I did not marry. I had given my heart to Monsieur Eiffel, and it was not mine to give to anyone else.

Women, even those who were educated, were expected to marry and remain at home. Widows and old maids had few choices. There was domestic service and factory work for the uneducated. There was nursing and teaching for those fortunate few who had training enough to gain such employment.

Mademoiselle Alice

One day, when I was wondering how I would make my own way, I received a note from Professor LeFebvre saying that the firm of Lageze et Cazes, at 18, rue des Quatre-Fils, a factory specializing in the production of varnish used in inks, was looking for a stenographer-typist.

I was interviewed by the head of the concern, Monsieur Lageze. He immediately made me aware that he was of the opinion that the motive that drew young women into the business office was the hope that they might thereby secure a husband.

"I don't think I'd ever have a girl in the office," he told me the day he considered me as a possible stenographer, "except I can get a girl cheaper. I want you to understand before you start that I don't want any flirting around here. There have never been any matches made here, and I don't want any man here courting any girl I might hire."

I flushed with something near to rage. I would have liked to tell him to keep his job and his advice. But I really needed the work, so I tightened my lips, told Monsieur Lageze I understood, and was hired.

He had agreed to try out one of the new typewriters and gave me a very small salary to begin with. Indeed, I felt that I was not worth much to him at first, but I was attentive to my work and soon I was producing documents on the typewriter twice as fast as the men did with their elegant handwriting—much to their chagrin.

I felt much out of place in that varnish factory. As I took my place at the only typewriter in the outer office, a painful hush fell over the room.

The chief clerk, a revolting man with black teeth, whose duty it was to initiate new clerks, made a wry face behind his hand, and I heard him say something about soured cream.

Mademoiselle Alice

I was the only woman in a large room crowded with men. They looked at me with suspicion and discomfort. I was taking a coveted job. Men had always been the recipients of the higher education that was required to read, calculate numbers, and spell correctly in the business world.

But I went to work with a will, rejoicing in the change from the tyrannies of the school. However, I soon learned that a place of work has its own tyrannies.

The chief clerk concluded he might talk as much nonsense to me as he pleased. However, I was unused to being spoken to in so mortifying a manner.

"Why are those lovely eyes perpetually averted?" he asked. "Surely, *madame*, we should be better friends."

Calling me *madame* instead of *mademoiselle* was an insult to my virtue and he surely knew it. I felt my cheeks grow hot and made an effort to recover.

"My friends do not call me *madame*," I said coldly.

"Oh, they don't! You will hereafter find me charming, eh?"

"No sir, it is the sunshine of your absence that I most desire."

This retort did not please him, and he felt a show of force was called for.

"I am the manager here," he said, "and I will be watching you."

Thereafter, I dressed as plainly as possible and wore my hair in a most unbecoming manner. Still, he liked to stand in a threatening attitude beside my desk and make tantalizing remarks. I could do nothing but pointedly ignore him.

One day, when he was walking around, supervising the work of others, he inflicted on all of us his singing:

Mademoiselle Alice

"*If a body meet a lady coming through the rye, and if a body kiss a lady, need a lady cry?*"

And then, suddenly and unbelievingly, he turned my head and kissed me on the mouth, a sloppy, disgusting kiss. I wiped my mouth on my sleeve while he walked away, laughing. The other men laughed as well, and he hummed as he went on his way: "Need a lady cry."

I did not cry. I glowered with indignation. Like a cat, I would show my claws. I rose from my desk and started at him with a clenched fist.

"You will swallow your garbage or I will tell someone who will make you!"

He turned on me as though I were the one who was both bold and presuming.

"Look at this kid," he said, "trying to strike me!"

A general murmur of alarm riffled the men. They could neither defend me nor feel comfortable siding with my tormentor. I had to return shaking with anger to my desk.

I should say that this was my first kiss, and in those days, it was considered quite improper for a man to kiss a woman before they were engaged. At the convent we were warned that if we kissed a boy, we might well grow an unsightly mustache.

Later, I was required to explain this entire sorry episode to Monsieur Lageze while trying to hold back my tears. Monsieur Lageze's politeness greatly relieved me. He called the chief clerk into the office and gruffly told him to stop his disrespectful behavior or lose his job.

After that, I tried to put the chief clerk away with looks so reproachful that he would leave me alone. I told him that if he wished me to respect him, he must not speak to me again in any personal manner. But a leopard cannot change his spots.

Mademoiselle Alice

At the end of that long week, I paid a visit to Professor Lefebvre and told him my story. He was aghast. To him and to Monsieur Eiffel, a more chivalrous generation of men, women were something to be revered, protected, a thing of beauty not to be profaned.

"Patience, my child," said the professor, "We will get you out of there."

Chapter 14

I WAS EKING OUT a miserable existence by hammering a type-writing machine from morning until night. Although I worked twelve hours a day, I still could barely earn enough to pay rent, buy food and the necessary clothing. My mother had found work in the Paris needle trades at little more than half of what I was making as a stenographer-typist. Worst of all, life at this job was very dull. I yearned for something livelier.

I looked for jobs on the "Men Wanted" page, and scanned the newspaper from day to day looking for items about Monsieur Eiffel. He hosted numerous banquets and was the recipient of many honors. Then one day, a great calamity fell upon his reputation and fortune.

One night in November, on my way home from work, the newsboys were calling "Extra, Extra," along the streets, and I stopped to buy a paper with its headline screaming: "EIFFEL CHARGED WITH MISUSE OF FUNDS."

I snatched the paper from the boy's hand. In the past, the newspapers had covered Monsieur Eiffel's extravagant entertainments, his generous gifts to charity. Now I read that he had been accused of a crime, and the newspaper painted an incriminating picture of widows and orphans left destitute, of families destroyed because of his alleged misuse of funds.

The charges against him were related to the Panama Canal scandal which had become public during the Exposition Centennial three years before.

I read every word of that newspaper. It was apparent that the public had turned on Monsieur Eiffel. The outcry was over the fact that he had made money on the project while the investors had lost their savings, and in large amounts. I took the newspaper home and asked Mother what she thought about it.

"I never blamed Monsieur Eiffel," she said, "for the failure of the company, although your father was very bitter about it. Monsieur Eiffel had been hired to redesign the canal after the Panama Canal Company had wasted many years trying to cut through a mountain."

"Why did Father invest so much in the company?"

"Monsieur Eiffel encouraged him to invest. The Suez Canal had been finished a few years before, and its investors all made money. Your father knew from his own experience what completion of the canal would mean to business with the Americas."

"I don't remember exactly—why did Papa go to Panama that time?"

"He accompanied building materials to Panama. There were going to be ten locks designed by Monsieur Eiffel, but only three were finished. Before your father got back to Paris, the company was in receivership and all those building materials had to be left on the banks of the Chagres River. Monsieur Eiffel had to turn the assets of the company over to the receiver and stop working on the project. That's when your father became unemployed."

"Is that why Father lost contact with Monsieur Eiffel?"

"Your father was angry and, I think, sort of broken hearted. Monsieur Eiffel grew richer while he grew poorer. But also your father had to find other work, and that took all his time."

Even though my father had lost his own small fortune, I did not doubt for a moment Monsieur Eiffel's innocence.

The worst attacks on his character were printed on the editorial pages.

"*Vous avez toupet formidable!*" wrote one angry reader. "You have incredible nerve!"

"His conscience is more easily satisfied than his cash requirements!" wrote another.

"The antics of Bonickhausen!" someone scoffed. "Good to be hanged!"

I knew that Monsieur Eiffel had, years before, changed his name from Bonickhausen, the name of his grandfather, to Eiffel, the region his ancestors had come from early in the eighteenth century. Although this region was presently part of Germany, at the time Monsieur Eiffel's ancestors had left it, it was part of France. Unfortunately, for a Frenchman to be born with a German name accrued to his disadvantage.

While Monsieur Eiffel's loyalty to France was not questioned by those who knew him personally, the name he was born with at once excited suspicion in strangers.

It was immediately clear from the newspaper that all the great achievements of his life, as well as his financial success, would go down the drain of scandal. His reputation up to this point had been impeccable. The public's adverse reaction to the case, I knew, would send him fuming helplessly into seclusion.

Mademoiselle Alice

ഌᘉ

Two months later, there started a month-long trial. The Palace of Justice was surrounded by crowds of angry onlookers—the public was not interested in material facts or exculpatory details.

Little by little, the testimony was printed in the newspaper. Most of the investors' money had been spent before Monsieur Eiffel became involved. The plan before he had joined the company as a contractor was to dig a canal through fifty miles of mountain and jungle. Eiffel's plan, which he had developed over many years, involved a lock system that enabled ships to float up one side of the incline and down the other. The Panama Canal Company had run out of money while Eiffel's company was in the midst of building the locks.

On the day of the verdict, I begged off work using the excuse of a family emergency, and managed to slip into the courtroom. There on the bench sat the judge in all his solemn dignity, and below sat the accursed defendant.

The sensational climax came like a thunderbolt down upon the silence of the courtroom.

As everyone waited, a man walked up the center aisle carrying an envelope. The envelope was thrust into the hands of the judge. Even as the judge read the missive, he rose to his feet and his voice rang out imperiously:

"Gustave Eiffel—guilty!"

There was some cheering in the courtroom followed by the judge pounding his gavel.

Monsieur Eiffel, who had borne all in silence, turned his face away from the vindictive gaze of many eyes. He was sentenced to two years in prison and a fine of 20,000 francs.

Mademoiselle Alice

A few weeks after the verdict, I took up a newspaper to see under large headlines a notice of a change in Eiffel's engineering company of which he was president and owner.

He announced to the press that he was withdrawing his name and himself from his own company which was failing to receive new business because that which had been its most compelling asset, the Eiffel name and reputation, was now a liability.

There were several months before his prison sentence was to start while an appeal was made to the higher court. Unfortunately, the appeals court was slow to hear the case and render a decision. It was June when Monsieur Eiffel's prison sentence began. He sat in prison while the appeals court judge heard Monsieur Eiffel's lawyer present the case for overturning the judgment against him.

Eight days after Monsieur Eiffel began his prison sentence, the court found that the charges against him were brought more than three years after the offenses were claimed to have been committed, and the charges against him were therefore barred by the statute of limitations.

Of course, it was gratifying to have the prison sentence overturned, but the public regarded the decision as unfair because they saw the rationale for it to be a mere technicality. When Monsieur Eiffel was to be released, the newspapers did another extra edition.

In plain sight of a spitting and shouting crowd, he walked out of prison a free and honest man, but stripped of his former luster.

Everyone who was Monsieur Eiffel's friend went directly to 1, rue Rabelais to congratulate him. I went with my mother.

He was very emotional. He hugged me, he hugged my mother, he hugged everyone who had come to see him like they were long-lost friends who he was very grateful to see again. Everyone told jokes and tried to make him feel better.

He needed to talk about his incarceration and told everyone gathered around him a story.

"I was in the Conciergerie!" he said, still in disbelief and shock over his reversal of circumstances. "The same prison cell as Marie Antoinette! I spent most of my time working out chess problems."

"When one of the jailers saw me playing chess by myself he asked me if I often played."

"'There are no chess players in this town,' I told him. 'I have tried all who pretend to play the game and have derived no pleasure from it. You see, I am reduced to working out problems.'"

"'I too sometimes amuse myself in that way,' said the jailer, drawing a chair to the table on which the board rested. 'Let us see who is the better player.'"

"In the first game between us, the jailer checkmated me in eight moves. I was so intrigued by my opponent's plan of attack, I asked him to go over the moves again so that I might learn from them."

"'Perhaps I would play better for a stake,'" Monsieur Eiffel told his opponent, and taking a gold Louis from his pocket, he laid it on the table.

"I must have lost twenty gold Louis," he told his assembled friends who laughed at the story, "and I did not play any better. I played worse. Then I became almost as good a player as my opponent and started to win again."

"I did not know you ever played for money," said one of Monsieur Eiffel's male friends.

"I never did before and I never will again," he answered.

Mademoiselle Alice

After many of the guests had left and I had a moment alone with Monsieur Eiffel, I took a rose from a vase and placed it in the buttonhole of his lapel.

Now when a lady puts a flower in the lapel of a man's coat she must, of necessity, stand very near to him. He looks down into her face. Her hair smells good and her breath is sweet. Monsieur Eiffel encircled me with his arms. I was not sure if I should take his embrace as romantic because he had already embraced everyone at his spontaneous welcome-home party several times. But it was romantic for me.

He looked at me with his puppy-dog eyes, and he knew then that which he was very glad to know: that I did not seek his love for the benefit of his money and social position—but for him alone.

Chapter 15

ONE SUNDAY soon after Monsieur Eiffel's release from the Conciergerie, we took a promenade together along Quai Malaquais, where we rummaged for books among the metal boxes that line the banks of the Seine. I liked to read a certain amount of poetry every night before bed, and I was always on the lookout for small, gilt-edged books of poetry while Monsieur Eiffel searched for sets of leather-bound volumes, the complete works of famous authors.

For those of us who delight in old texts, Quai Malaquais is a fairyland. A few steps away is the *École des Beaux-Arts*, its students painting in the open air while crowds of Parisians enjoy the sunshine. Over our heads were the tremulous leaves of aspens, and in the courtyard opposite the bookstalls, a statue of Voltaire laughing at everyone from his pedestal.

A flock of white pigeons swirled over the statue and settled at its base, pecking at the oats blown over from the horses being fed where the carriages were parked along the quay.

The little courtyard surrounding the statue also served as a stage for street musicians who played so merrily as to cheer even the most grumpy visitor.

Mademoiselle Alice

Behind the statue of Voltaire were a few stately mansions of past grandeur, oh, very far past, still holding their dignified place. Bookstores had taken over the ground floor of each mansion, and the upper stories were turned into apartments. Outside each window was a small iron balcony adorned with green things the tenants had put there to catch the warm rays of the sun.

"My father came here to sell books," I said, "those he could part with."

"I am sure he did," Monsieur Eiffel said. "I come here frequently, as well. That is the Bureau of Civil Engineering right over there." He pointed to the building next to the École des Beaux-Arts. "My friend, Edouard Pailleron, lives just down the street."

"I would love to live on this street," I told him, "with its booksellers and all these people milling about."

"The artistic temperament," he said, "craves a beautiful setting."

The mansard roof of one of the old stone mansions caught my eye. A casement window belonging to one of the attic apartments was opened wide, its white curtains blowing softly in the breeze, while two potted geraniums nodded on the iron balcony.

"We had a window like that," I said, "at my grandmother's house."

"Did it have this many pigeons everywhere?" Monsieur Eiffel asked.

"No," I laughed, "but we could look out and see birds hopping about on the trees and in the winter their little tracks all over the snow."

One day not too long after this, Monsieur Eiffel was hurrying by the statue of Voltaire when he glanced up at the

Mademoiselle Alice

old stone mansion and saw the window I had pointed out to him. He noticed someone removing a piano from the building and, thinking that someone might be moving out of one of the apartments, he decided to enquire.

Though he had not passed down Quai Malaquais with the intention of finding a lodging place for me and my mother, that is exactly what he did, and for this, the little attic window was responsible.

"I asked the woman who opened the door," he told me, "if the room on the top floor was vacant."

"The one," I asked excitedly, "with the red geraniums in the window?"

"That's the one," he said, "and she let me see it."

While ascending the gloomy staircase, he was told that the little two-room apartment was to be vacated the following morning. The concierge inserted a key in the lock and left him there to inspect the apartment.

The tiny rooms were as inviting as their window promised. Realizing that an apartment with a view of the Seine might disappear as soon as it became available, Monsieur Eiffel paid the advance price asked, and brought the keys to me and my mother. This was one of many thoughtful things he did for us.

I loved that apartment, a tiny place with a low-ceilinged bedroom under the stairs and a kitchenette. From the small casement window, I looked out on the merriest street in Paris. Along the quay, street merchants offered everything from balloons to haircuts. Up and down the Seine steamed the crowded *bateaux-mouches* and *hirondelles*. There were glimpses here and there between the trees of Notre Dame's trim spires and the blue roofs of the Louvre.

And across the tall chimney tops, romance called to me.

Mademoiselle Alice

ುಂಡ

Most of our furniture had been disposed of at auction, but there were a few nice pieces my mother had saved from the wreck of our fallen fortunes. Now she put what she had left in our little flat, just enough to make it dainty and comfortable.

When I came home after work, I would take off my hat and cloak and sink into a cushioned chair with a grateful sigh. My mother would get out a little wicker tea wagon and we would have tea. She prepared all our meals on a primitive gas ring in the miniature kitchen

I fondly remember evenings spent beneath the shaded lamp, engaged in writing or drawing. The small table beneath the window became quite naturally a place for the exchange of simple confidences, for comforting recollections of home, and beloved scenes of happy times.

Then too, we had the companionship of a little gray cat.

When we moved in, I heard faintly from without a muffled cry, and as I stopped to listen, the cry was repeated, louder and more persistent. Following the direction of the sound, I drew aside the curtains. There upon the tiny iron balcony huddled a small furry creature whose golden eyes begged piteously for shelter.

"Poor thing!" I said as I opened the window. With a meow of gratitude, the little gray cat sprang into our apartment. I looked down along the smooth side of the building, down five stories to the courtyard below, wondering how she got up to the mansard roof and to the window of our apartment. The little cat was already calmly grooming her wet fur before the warmth of the fire.

After a few minutes, she was transformed from a wet alley cat into a gorgeous blue Persian. At first she kept her distance,

Mademoiselle Alice

but after she was fed she rubbed affectionately against my legs and gazed up at me with her great, topaz eyes. She climbed into the most comfortable chair and made her home with us. Maggie, I called her.

A few days later, Monsieur Eiffel called again, making as an excuse tickets to the opera.

At the appointed time, I was gowned and ready to go. This was my first opera in the magnificent *Palais Garnier*.

Outside it was adorned with golden statues of the muses, Harmony and Poetry. Entering the lobby, ablaze with gaslights, my astonished eyes took in everything from the extravagant marble staircase, to the gilded busts of the great composers, and the domed ceiling where there was a painting of Apollo and Orpheus.

We ascended the broad marble steps to a balcony overlooking the lobby, and gazed down the cascading staircases at our fellow opera-goers. It was like another visit to fairyland. The gowns, furs, evening clothes, and hats were so exquisite as to make me gasp in admiration.

"People like to see and be seen," Monsieur Eiffel said. "That's why the lobby was built this way."

Then we went to the Grand Tier, through draperies of red velvet to Monsieur Eiffel's reserved box. The floor and the ledge overlooking the gallery were also covered with red velvet. The auditorium was ornate with gilt carving on every surface. From the domed ceiling hung a gorgeous chandelier with thousands of prisms descending.

In this palace of crystal, gold, and marble, every performance was a gala.

The one whimsical note was the painting of a curtain hanging from the proscenium arch. This huge canvas was

Mademoiselle Alice

painted with rich, red and gold drapery, complete with gold braid and tassels.

"Look at that curtain!" I said.

"It was painted by Marcel Jambon," Monsieur Eiffel said, "a fabulous scenic artist. He paints much of the scenery as well."

Strains of music took possession of me and I leaned forward as far as I dared to watch the dancers. And then my thoughts floated out with the music and I danced with them. If only I had that blue satin gown, I thought, seizing it enviously in my imagination

"What are you thinking?" Monsieur Eiffel asked.

"I was just making believe," I said, "waltzing off in that blue satin dress. The music gets hold of me like that."

The story was Charles Gounod's Faust. Doctor Faust is an old alchemist, disillusioned with life, and about to end it all by drinking a goblet of poison. He curses happiness, faith, and science, calling on the Devil to assist him.

In response to Faust's invocation, Mephistopheles appears offering the old doctor first Fortune, which he refuses, then Glory for which he cares not, and finally Youth. While Faust hesitates, Mephistopheles shows him a vision of the young and beautiful Marguerite who is spinning fine thread on her spinning wheel. Faust is sorely tempted and he signs the pact with the Devil. Immediately, he metamorphoses into a handsome young man.

After some courting scenes, Marguerite is in a garden and she picks a daisy—Marguerite is the French word for daisy. She plucks off the petals one by one.

Faust asks her: "What is that for? A bouquet?"

"No," Marguerite says, "it's a game."

"What kind of game?"

Mademoiselle Alice

"You will laugh at me! Go away!"

She pulls the petals off, one by one, murmuring to herself.

"What is that you are murmuring?" Faust asks.

"He loves me, he loves me not. Loves me, loves me not."

She pulls off the last petal with pure delight.

"He loves me!"

"Yes, he loves you," Faust says. "Let the words of this flower be God's affirmation."

The whole house cheered and clapped ecstatically.

At intermission, we went to the *Salon du Glacier* where refreshments were served. The ceiling and walls were decorated with Bacchanal paintings: little gods behaving badly. The menu was displayed in Gobelin tapestries: fruit, coffee, tea, wine, and ice cream. The extravagantly dressed patrons walked about laughing gaily until the music started again and everyone went back to their seats.

After the performance, Monsieur Eiffel led me backstage where, in addition to ateliers for making costumes and props, he pointed out a complicated rigging of pulleys and counterweights for curtains and scenery.

Behind the stage, there was a beautiful reception hall decorated like the Hall of Mirrors at Versailles. Monsieur Eiffel, as one of the Paris Opera's most famous patrons, was allowed to go backstage where he developed special relationships with the singers and dancers.

After the opera came a supper in an exquisitely decorated tea room where atmosphere abounded and the music lured my soul far from the mundane things of earth. We had, at Monsieur Eiffel's suggestion, a dainty plate of chilled melon, then a delicately blended salad, followed by a luscious stew in a covered white ramekin. We finished off our supper with coffee and tuilles.

Mademoiselle Alice

While we were sitting there, a well-dressed couple, who knew Monsieur Eiffel socially, came to our table to say hello. After they passed by, I heard the woman say: "That's his daughter."

Monsieur Eiffel heard it, too, and caught my eye with shared amusement. This became a feature of our relationship. Society had become accustomed to seeing him with one of his daughters, and rarely if ever felt compelled to question my identity.

Chapter 16

I HAD BEEN WEARILY maintaining my post at the varnish factory when Monsieur Eiffel told me about a position for a stenographer-typist in downtown Paris, and he insisted that I should speak to the owner, one Felix-Max Richard, who was, he said, "a worldly sort of man."

"I know him," he said. "He is interested in everything, and he will find the idea of a young lady in the office most pleasant."

The result was that the next morning, I walked into the *Comptoir Général de Photographie* at 57, rue Saint-Roch to apply for the job. It was on the first floor of an old city building, just three blocks from the magnificent opera house.

Outwardly calm, but with a pounding heart, I held in my hand a note from my stenography professor, lauding me for my natural talent for the art of stenography, and a letter of recommendation from Monsieur Eiffel:

"To whom it may concern: This is to state that Mademoiselle Alice Guy has been in my employ as a stenographer-typist for some time. She is strictly honest, neat, and efficient. She is notable for her understanding of temperament. She is leaving my employ only because she has finished the work for which I retained her. She has my highest recommendation."

He signed the letter and included his address and telephone number.

I wore a plain black suit, old and worn, spectacles I had acquired after measles once upon a time, and a sensible pair of shoes. For luck I donned my little red hat and, assuming a businesslike air, entered the office of the Comptoir.

I gave my name to a young man, some twenty-seven or twenty-eight years old. He bowed to me as deferentially as if I were a belle, and placed a chair for me near a desk at which he seated himself. Then he waited for me to state my business.

"I heard that you were looking for a stenographer."

"And?" he asked.

"And I am one."

"Indeed," replied the young man. He evidently had never heard of a female stenographer.

"Yes. You'll find that I am business-like, quick, and competent."

"Mademoiselle, I do not think I am the person you want to talk to."

"Are you not Monsieur Richard?" I said.

"No, no. He is out. You might speak to Monsieur Gaumont. He is the manager."

"If you please," I said.

My disappointment that Monsieur Richard was not there added to my anxiety. The young man asked me to follow him to an office where another man with a bushy mustache was working at a roll-top desk.

I stopped on the threshold. Monsieur Gaumont was looking at papers full of figures, and did not look up right away. He gave the impression of being in the middle of the busiest morning of the busiest week of the busiest year. I stood watching him for a few moments. Then, just when I was starting to feel even more uncomfortable than I was already, he finally raised his eyes to look at me.

"Come in," he ordered. He frowned as his visitor was revealed to be myself, clearly a person of no importance.

I had to introduce myself again and state my purpose since the other young man had forgotten my name. I had tried to look older by the simplicity of my attire, but I was such a slim little creature, the childish naturalness of my bearing probably seemed inadequate to the importance of the position for which I was applying.

"My dear young woman," he said, "you cannot possibly have the qualifications. You have no idea of the requirements, and besides, you are not a man."

"I understand stenography," I insisted, "and I can operate a typewriter." I was very proud of my commercial education and my experience also was hard won.

He then voiced his opinion in a tired tone that I was too young for the job, but I had been through too much to let that stop me.

"I'll get over that," I said simply.

"Very well, then," he laughed, "let's see what you can do."

To test me and perhaps to give himself time to get used to the idea of a female stenographer, Monsieur Gaumont began dictating at a high speed. I had to ask him to slow down.

"Wait a moment!" I said, "I have to correct something."

Presently, flushed and laughing, I looked back at him.

"Ah," said Monsieur Gaumont wryly, "perhaps I should think more slowly."

Mademoiselle Alice

He frowned continuously, no doubt desiring very much to let this laughing young person know that the purport of his message was no joking matter, and that his own heavily pressed time was not to be squandered.

"Women are not normally reliable enough," he said, "to hold a position of any importance. I'll tell you the straight truth—I am most frightfully irritable and impatient."

He suppressed the slightest of smiles, and I could tell that he admired me for my nerve. I also knew that that which was a strike against me, my gender, could be turned to my advantage. In eyes raised to his, my appealing expression baffled reproof. He realized to his dismay a disinclination to hurt my feelings.

I typed several pages of dictation, checking to see that every word was spelled correctly, and handed my work to Monsieur Gaumont.

"Ah, it's quite competent," he said with a frown and a dismissive nod of his head. He forgot to ask me for my references, so I volunteered my letters of recommendation.

"Excellent," he said as he briefly looked them over.

He told me that he was not really in a position to decide my fate as he had only been working at the Comptoir for a couple of weeks.

"We will have to find out what Monsieur Richard thinks."

Monsieur Gaumont told me to come back later that afternoon when Monsieur Richard would be there. This was all I wanted in the first place.

When I came back later that day, I met Felix-Max Richard for the first time. He was a handsome man, late thirties. He looked strong and healthy, having the tan of an outdoorsman.

"Mademoiselle Alice, it's a pleasure," he said.

Mademoiselle Alice

Making an effort to engage his mind, I asked him about the company motto, printed around the edge of a decorative frame.

"I was taught Latin in school," I said, "but I am not sure what these words mean—*per lucem semper novitas?*"

"Ah, very good," he said. "It means 'the light is always the novelty.'"

Monsieur Richard was impressed. "Where were you educated?" he asked.

"I was educated in convents near the Swiss border. More recently I have had lessons in stenography. I taught myself to type."

"Ah, it's a wonderful thing, stenography. I have been to the Senate and watched the stenographers."

"My professor took me to the Chamber of Deputies to watch. Also to the Sorbonne."

"The Sorbonne? The Sorbonne lets girls in?"

"Not really," I said. "I was the only girl. The pupils in stenography are allowed into Professor Aulard's class."

"The famous historian?"

"It was very interesting," I said.

Messieurs Gaumont and Richard looked at each other and declared themselves astonished at such a sensible young woman.

"Do you think I will be able to fill the position?" I asked.

"The salary is not high," Monsieur Richard said. "One hundred and fifty francs. Is that satisfactory, Mademoiselle Alice?"

"Yes. When shall I commence work?"

"Tomorrow morning, if you will."

Then he turned to Monsieur Gaumont.

"Do you have anything for Mademoiselle Alice?"

Mademoiselle Alice

"Perhaps I could show her around," he said.

Monsieur Gaumont seemed to know everything about the many products the Comptoir stocked and sold. He showed me the company catalogue from which customers could order chemicals, photographic papers, and plates.

He showed me cameras of all sizes, both domestic and foreign, the most popu-lar of which was the Photo-Jumelle—a nifty, hand-held camera that anyone could learn to use.

I do not think I was ever happier in my life. I was sure I would be able to make a place for myself in this downtown office as I had a splendid groundwork of experience from my varnish factory job, and I very much looked forward to learning the work I was about to undertake.

Many, many times I have been thankful to the kind fate that steered my feet straight into that camera manufacturing business.

I returned home elated, and ran up the dark stairway to our apartment two or three steps at a time.

I was too excited to sleep that night, and my mother, with her usual indulgence, allowed me to keep her awake while I drew rosy pictures of my future. Long we talked of my good fortune. Mother finally told me that I must try and get a little sleep and bade me good night. It seemed but a moment later when she woke me up in the morning.

The next day, I took up my duties at the Comptoir and began my new vocation.

೫೦೧೩

I often left my place before the typewriter to welcome the timid customers who waited in the doorway. Then I was back again, telephones and buzzers seeming to call me on every side. Cheerfully and tirelessly I responded to every demand, giving correct prices, dates of shipment, and other details incumbent upon the carrying out of a successful, merchandising business.

The Comptoir was advertised in the newspaper as *Photography for Amateurs*. This was a new idea made possible by smaller cameras. Previously, people generally went to a photographer to have their picture taken.

In order to promote our cameras and photographic supplies, we gave free lessons every morning at 9:00 and 10:00 a.m. I had to learn photography myself so as to be able to teach customers how to operate the cameras, develop the film, enlarge, color, and retouch the photographs. We sold everything for the dark room, from chemicals to cardstock, and special papers lined with silver foil. Silver foil might be used for a seascape, or a red-tinted photographic paper for a fire scene.

With the protection of the counter and the pleasant mask of business, I was able to look frankly in the face of everyone who came in, male or female, and I enjoyed being out front. There was no more: *"Baissez les yeux!"*

I enjoyed the hurry and noise of the business world. For me, the crowded city was a joyous place, filled with friendly hearts and hands. I was deeply interested in those whom we proudly called our customers. In my eager desire to please, I did not distinguish between the great men of science and the working girls who were on their lunch breaks expressing an interest in photography.

Monsieur Gaumont was a man of splendid business dexterity, and made many successes, but his quick temper, impatience, and lack of tolerance made him difficult. On many occasions, I had to use all of my tact to keep him from losing his temper. He was inclined on the spur of the moment to

Mademoiselle Alice

blame someone unrestrainedly without considering the exigencies of the occasion. When he later calmed down and had time to consider the conditions, he would come back to a fairer frame of mind. Nevertheless, I found that if his ire was directed at me, I was less able to persuade him with reason.

If I was so much as five minutes late for work, Monsieur Gaumont was at the door remarking dryly: "Did you miss the train, Mademoiselle?"

One day, everything went wrong. Monsieur Gaumont scolded the foreman of the workshops, scared the office boy, and barked at me. In the mail he found a misdirected letter which had been returned to him, and summarily discharged me before lunch. I came to him after lunch, in tears, begging for another chance, and he grudgingly gave it.

"No more mistakes," he warned me.

He did not brook any carelessness and we all worked in a state of fear.

I sat before a typewriter on a stand by a window looking out at the *avenue de l'Opera,* alive with carriages rolling homeward from the park. The steady clack of horses' sharp-shod feet on the pavement provided a pleasant form of music.

But soon, my desk was moved into Messieurs Richard and Gaumont's office. The stenographer's sanctum was then separated from their office by a heavy curtain.

"Dictation, Mademoiselle Alice," Monsieur Gaumont would call. He didn't seem to have time during business hours to say *please,* but he followed his orders with an impersonal little smile to reduce the rudeness of his abrupt speech.

He came to regard me as impersonally as he did the wooden filing case behind my desk. But I found Monsieur Gaumont no harder to get along with than the dour Mère Emilie.

Mademoiselle Alice

I was much relieved that Monsieur Gaumont had a wife and three children, and gave me no sign of being the lecherous type I had run into at my previous place of employment.

Chapter 17

FELIX-MAX RICHARD loved to talk about the time he spent three days and three nights on Mont Blanc. He had made the climb with one of his customers, Joseph Vallot, who became his good friend and who would later become a partner in the business of the Comptoir.

I met Monsieur Vallot when he came in to buy photographic supplies. He wore heavy clothes and had the rough, bearded look associated with that character we call the mountain man.

"Monsieur Vallot," Felix-Max said, by way of introduction, "was so enthusiastic about his expedition to live at high altitude for three days, I volunteered to go with him. It had never been done before."

"Was it terribly cold?" I asked the two of them.

"It was very cold," Monsieur Vallot said, "but that wasn't the worst part. The altitude made us sick. I hope you will pardon my vulgarity, Mademoiselle Alice, but the first thing we did when we got to the top of the mountain was to throw up."

"Then there was that terrific blizzard," Felix-Max said, "and an electrical storm."

"I stepped out of the tent for a few moments," said Monsieur Vallot, "only to find my body was swimming in electricity."

After this, I never saw Monsieur Vallot without envisioning little sparkles of electricity snapping all about him.

"We made up our tent and a bed," said Monsieur Vallot. "We had two guides with us and slept like sardines in a can to keep warm. When we woke up, the top of the tent sagged down as if something heavy had been piled on top."

"I struck the top of the tent with my hand," said Felix-Max, "and there followed something like a landslide. We looked out and everything was covered in snow."

Their faces glowed with satisfaction at the memory of their shared experience.

"The sunrise was a marvelous sight," Monsieur Vallot said, turning poetic. "Rosy clouds enveloped the snow-clad tops of the surrounding mountains. The rocky peaks emerged from the shadows clothed in pink and gold."

"I know what you are talking about," I said. "I have seen the Alps at sunrise from my Grandmère's in Geneva."

"You should hike up the mountain with us sometime," said Monsieur Vallot.

"When we came down the mountain," said Felix-Max, still reminiscing, "the people of Chamonix gave us a hero's welcome. They were hanging out of their windows, waving flags, and throwing flowers at us. It was wonderful. Since then, I have done a good deal of tramping in the mountains."

In this, my first year at the Comptoir, I came to appreciate that all around me was the excitement of scientific discovery.

One day, Felix-Max introduced me to his younger brother, Georges, who manufactured bicycles.

"Do you ride?" he asked me.

"I have not yet," I said "since, of course, I do not have a bicycle."

"Would you like to learn?"

"Most assuredly," I said. Bicycle riding was the latest sensation for the New Woman. In proper bloomers, she could go wherever she pleased without an escort.

"Sunday I can teach you," said Georges.

"Where?" I asked.

"The Bois du Boulogne," he said. "That is where everyone rides."

I promised to be there at 11:00 a.m., Sunday, for my lesson. My mother made over an old skirt of hers into bloomers for me. They were certainly not very flattering, but I was glad I wore them, for I disgraced myself repeatedly on that bicycle.

༄༅༅

I have introduced Felix-Max and Georges Richard, but this is a tale of three brothers, for Felix-Max and Georges had an older brother named Jules. It is an important part of my story since some of the events came before I got my position at the Comptoir and some came after.

The three brothers had inherited a precision instrument business from their father. In those days, precision instruments were made by hand, each one finely crafted by an artisan. Richard Frères was famous for its barometers which had found their way to a place of honor on ships in the French Navy.

Mademoiselle Alice

Jules was the oldest of the three brothers. He was eight years older than Felix-Max who was seven years older than Georges. Jules naturally expected to be in charge of everything related to Richard Frères.

Imagine Jules' annoyance when Felix-Max approached Monsieur Eiffel about installing barometers on top of the Eiffel Tower. Monsieur Eiffel liked the idea very much, and put Felix-Max in touch with his good friend, Elie Mascart, a physicist who was then head of the weather bureau.

Together, Felix-Max and his brother Georges, with the advice of Monsieur Mascart, installed a complete meteorology station on the Eiffel Tower, and earned a Grand Prix at the 1889 *Exposition Universelle*.

"Georges and I both received awards from the Legion of Honor as well," Felix-Max told me, "but Jules imagined that we had made representations to prevent him from also being decorated. That's when he conceived a mortal hatred, so to speak, against his two brothers."

"I cannot tell you," he continued, "how difficult Jules became. After two years of bitter conflict, Georges and I sold our interests in Richard Frères to Jules."

"I took the money Jules paid me for my interest in the partnership, and bought the *Comptoir Général de Photographie*. Georges used his payoff in the partnership to start a business manufacturing bicycles. Then Jules sued me."

"What for?" I asked. I knew I was being bold to ask him about a sensitive subject, but I was mature for my age and my sympathetic interest did not offend him.

"Jules required me to sign an agreement prohibiting me from selling or manufacturing any similar device."

"Did he manufacture cameras?" I asked.

"No, he sold barometers and other precision instruments."

Mademoiselle Alice

Felix-Max darkened visibly and mumbled something to change the subject. I had to find out the rest of the story later in bits and pieces, as time went by.

From what I could see, Jules Richard was a jealous and greedy man. He designed a camera called the Verascope which he patented in 1893, two years after Felix-Max bought the Comptoir. Jules Richard used the Verascope to take stereoscopic pictures of nude women. He then designed a handy stereoscopic viewer, the better to see the nude women in 3-D. This was an old technology in optics and, as you can imagine, very profitable for him.

Even though Richard Frères had never constructed or sold cameras before 1893, Jules Richard sued Felix-Max Richard alleging that he was in breach of their agreement by selling cameras. There was a trial, and the Paris court agreed with Jules Richard, enforcing the noncompetition agreement signed by the brothers.

Felix-Max filed an appeal which put off enforcement of the court's judgment for some months.

Felix-Max told me he needed to make arrangements just in case the Court of Appeal upheld the judgment against him. This is why he asked his good friend, Joseph Vallot, who was wealthy and had an avid interest in photography, if he might be willing to buy the camera and supply business. Then they both talked to Monsieur Eiffel.

"It was because of the conduct of my brother Jules and unworthiness of the trial that Monsieur Eiffel and Monsieur Vallot resolved to help me if necessary."

This happened a few months after Monsieur Eiffel found himself at loose ends because he had had to withdraw from his own engineering company.

Mademoiselle Alice

Monsieur Eiffel had been taking pictures for decades and was intrigued by the idea of owning a business that would occupy his questioning mind. He told Felix-Max Richard that, in anticipation of selling his business, he should hire a man to replace himself, someone qualified to manage the business day to day, so that if Monsieur Eiffel took it over, it would continue to function without his being there all the time. Within a few months, Felix-Max Richard hired Monsieur Gaumont.

It was but a few days after this that Monsieur Eiffel spoke to Felix-Max Richard on the telephone, and asked if he could use a stenographer. If so, Monsieur Eiffel said he would like to secure such a position for someone whom he could recommend.

Felix-Max Richard, wanting to accommodate the man who might be his salvation, replied that he most likely could use a stenographer to take his personal dictation. I started my job as stenographer-typist shortly thereafter.

℘ℭ

I was at the Comptoir when a pleasant young man named Georges Demenÿ brought in his photographic device, a whimsical camera that featured a glass disk with twelve pictures around the perimeter. When the disk turned, the viewer could see sequential pictures of Monsieur Demenÿ's face in motion, speaking and smiling.

Monsieur Demenÿ was looking for a manufacturer to help him market his camera.

"How happy people would be," he said, "if they could see again the living characteristics of a departed person."

Monsieur Demenÿ showed me his device several times, and then he showed it to Monsieur Gaumont. When Felix-Max

Mademoiselle Alice

Richard came in, he played the disk again several times for him. Felix-Max was very interested, but he was not able to invest in Monsieur Demenÿ's invention because he was still waiting to hear from the Court of Appeal. The court's decision would soon determine whether he would be able to continue in his business or be forced to sell it.

❧☙

My dear mother was one of those extremely proficient housekeepers and self-sacrificing wives left over from the Victorian age whose only ambition was to make her husband and children perfectly comfortable.

Because I was working downtown, she insisted that I do no work about the apartment. Anyway, it was easier for her to do things than to teach me to do them. Like many mothers, she let the accomplishment of home-keeping bring her the pleasure of waiting on someone she loved.

"If you were a boy, Alice," Mother said, "you would not feel called upon to do any housework. I am happy to have a daughter who is a business woman."

"If you wish," she continued, "you may give me fifteen francs a week for your room and board. That is exactly what I would ask a son to do."

"As a matter of principle, Mother?" I said.

"Yes," she replied earnestly, "because a son must be taught responsibility."

I started at the Comptoir at 150 francs per month, that was about thirty-seven francs a week. Fifteen I paid to my mother. Through a great deal of sacrifice, for I was fond of pretty clothes, I saved my first 150 francs over the course of a year.

Mademoiselle Alice

My second year's salary was forty francs a week, and I saved 200 francs that year.

My salary rose as I took on new responsibilities, but I liked to wear smarter clothes as time went by, and my savings each year did not enlarge proportionally with my salary. But I am getting ahead of myself again. To return to my story.

Chapter 18

I KEPT MY EYES OPEN and did my best to make a good impression on my employers. I racked my brains for bright ideas which might lead to their forming a favorable opinion of me.

I often remained at the office after hours. When someone else was unable to do his or her work I did it for them. I helped everyone and learned something of the duties of each. I learned so much about the business that I found it very easy to undo snarls, and I succeeded so well that I was often called on to undo all manner of snarls. Pretty soon it was generally understood that when Monsieur Gaumont stepped out, I would step into his place

My father had been a great advertiser in his day and had told me that, if I ever wanted to sell anything, to let that fact be known through the press. I noticed that the advertisements the Comptoir was running repeatedly in the newspaper were quite dull.

I suggested to Monsieur Gaumont that we might increase sales with some creative advertising. I offered to write a new advertisement for the newspaper. He merely said: "As you wish. Take care of it."

I sat down to think of a new way to showcase our cameras. I knew that women were accustomed to thinking of photography as something that appealed mostly to men, and that they were not as likely to take pictures with a heavy camera. My idea was to create an advertisement that emphasized a feature that would appeal to women. I settled on the small size and portability of the Photo-Jumelle, and its usefulness to a woman on vacation.

My first advertisement appeared in *Le Figaro* and I was well pleased with it: *Delightful travel souvenirs without embarrassment or trouble.*

A few days later, I wrote a longer ad, more specific and descriptive:

> *The Easter holidays are coming and promenaders are getting ready to take a tour—to the countryside, to the sea baths--to study the places where they might spend the summer. The essential baggage for the trip is a photography device. The Comptoir Général de Photographie provides Le Matin readers with the device of their dreams. Make sure you see the famous Photo-Jumelle, a wonder of convenience and lightness.*

Felix-Max, after seeing my ads, laughed heartily, and said they were most clever. Monsieur Gaumont noticed at once an increase in sales, and complimented me on my ingenuity.

ಸಃಧ

Mademoiselle Alice

Monsieur Eiffel was at the age when the pleasures of social life began to lose their appeal. When he was thirty, he no doubt fancied that he was courted because of his attractiveness. After he became financially successful, he came to understand that he was courted principally for what his income represented. This didn't interest me at all. What I wanted was that which would satisfy the cravings of my heart.

A match between Monsieur Eiffel and I would not have been a misalliance so far as our natural refinements were concerned, but from years of habit he shrank from marrying anyone, and our ages made us appear to be incompatible.

Nevertheless, his strong attraction to me prevented him from staying away, and he allowed himself to fall into the position of acting like a suitor without really being one. He used to call at Quai Malaquais on those summer evenings, and take me for a ride in his buggy. Many a happy hour we thus spent together enjoying the beautiful parks of Paris of which we were both very fond.

I was approaching the age of twenty-one and also had sufficient feminine instincts to discern that Monsieur Eiffel had a decided fancy for me, but the main reason my father had made him my guardian and trustee, and one of the reasons why I wanted to be close to him, was his integrity, and that stood in the way of my having him. It was evident to me that he considered me something along the lines of a fiduciary trust. He was so sensitive to his honor that he thought it some sort of breach of his duty to become involved with me in a romantic way.

What was I to do? I couldn't very well offer myself to him. Possibly if I had been nearer his age I might have found a way without sacrificing too much of my maidenly modesty. It might have been easier had I been absolutely sure that he wanted me, but how could I know unless he asked me?

I kept in mind something I had heard from Sister Martha: "I will tell you" she had said "why the ancients represented love by a little boy: the female is not supposed to be the aggressor in love. It is the male who makes the advances and is rightly represented by the boy who shoots the arrow."

My experience of falling in love was just the opposite. I was the aggressor and I was not willing to risk letting convention get in the way. If I was not the aggressor, I was sure, he might as well live on another continent because he was so eminently proper and reserved, he would never make the first move if I left it up to him.

I spent a long while thinking out a plan by which to overcome Monsieur Eiffel's scruples. Well, the day arrived when I was twenty-one, and Monsieur Eiffel invited me to his rue Prony apartment to explain his handling of my father's estate, and to turn over my property to me, but of course there wasn't any property unless you include worthless stock.

It had become evident to me that if I wished to break down his scruples, I must throw argument to the winds and use feminine methods.

When I arrived at rue Prony, he led me into his little study where he had spread some papers on a table. We sat down side by side that he might instruct me.

"My dear Alice," he began, "as your guardian and trustee, it is my duty to give you advice. Since you are now twenty-one, my trusteeship terminates. Your father no doubt expected that, by this time in your life, I would be turning over your business affairs to your husband."

"But I don't have a husband," I said flatly.

"Well, naturally, if you did he would be the one to look after your business matters, and he would find everything in order."

"I am sure he would."

Monsieur Eiffel cleared his throat. I was not making it easy for him.

"Your father purchased fifteen hundred shares of the Panama Canal Company stock. These are yours." He indicated that a stack of papers on the table were said stock. "There is a new Panama Canal Company, reconstituted from the old, but it has not yet found funding to proceed."

I was not thinking of the papers or of his instructions; I was thinking of something far nearer my heart.

"It is hoped," he continued, "that one day the Americans might purchase the project."

"The Americans?"

"They are taking their own sweet time about it, but someday, maybe..."

The more he explained the more I pretended to not understand. I hitched my chair closer to his until we could be no closer. He showed me figures, but I pretended that the figures were so minute I had difficulty in seeing them. I leaned sidewise until my shoulder touched his. In this way I crowded him to the outer edge of his chair, and he could not move any further away.

"The Americans are pretending not to be interested," he said, "so I don't know when that might be."

He went on explaining, but I could see his mind was no more on the papers than was mine. My hair was done in a tumultuous fashion, and loose strands grazed his cheek.

At last he broke down and put his arms around me.

Mademoiselle Alice

"I have loved you for years," he said, "and might have told you sooner had not your father made me your guardian. It has not seemed honorable to me."

"Yes, I know all that," I interrupted, impatient at having to draw him out. "You have been very stupid. You should be ashamed of yourself."

"Oh, I am, I am," he said kissing my forehead and then my lips, "I really am ashamed. You have no idea—"

I put my arms around his neck. He drew me close to him, clumsily, desperately, and years of loneliness for both of us dropped away.

൦൯

I was young, and visions of all sorts of pleasures danced in my head. There were feminine hearts, I was told, who had loved and lost where Monsieur Eiffel was concerned. But I smiled and went on to my fate—for I loved this man of gentleness and charm.

Monsieur Eiffel and I were both of an artistic temperament, and there is nothing more pleasing than the companionship of one with congenial tastes. One of my favorite afternoon recreations was the picture gallery in the Louvre, open gratuitously on Sundays, and overflowing with eager students and connoisseurs. We wandered through it, admiring the works of art together, with the luxury of a lunch at the café, and I formed my taste for art among the paintings there collected.

We were both fond also of music and literature. His appreciation for music was of the keenest. We visited what galleries there were, and then went where we could listen to music and read together from the works of our favorite poets.

After he built the Eiffel Tower, he had become very well off and it seemed to him that he could afford to allow a woman into his heart, at least, if not into his house. He was at the age when a man takes leave of his youth, but not willingly. Men of his age at that time were not likely to court a woman near their own age, but frequently found themselves attracted to a much younger woman whom they might have married had they been twenty years younger.

He would come by the office after Monsieur Gaumont had left, just as the sun went down, with a request that I allow him to drive me over to the Bois du Boulogne for a picnic supper with a moonlight sail on the lake to follow.

"I will be your gondolier," he said.

He often brought bread, cheese, and wine.

"Bread and cheese and kisses," he called it. This was a joke about a bachelor's attempt to make dinner for a lady.

The trees made a cathedral on the banks of the lake where his little boat was harbored, hidden under branches and shrubbery.

He took the oars, dipped them under the water lilies, then pulled away from the shore, gliding into deep water. Moonlight shimmered everywhere, transforming bush and shrub into a fairyland tapestry

Sometimes we would row, sometimes we would drift aimlessly through rushes. There's nothing like some rushes, some calm water, and a few overhanging boughs with a man and a woman in a boat to make the picture of romance.

All the delicious little nooks which bordered the lake we visited again and again. We pulled into a little cove with a tiny beach overhung with wildwood, and I remarked what a charming spot it was. As the moon turned the waters to gleaming silver, he tenderly leaned toward me and I nestled my head on his shoulder. And then we wandered off into a beautiful nonsense land where only lovers dwell.

I did not think very much about anything except that I loved him and wanted to be with him always, where I could feel his arms about me and answer his caressing words in kind.

My affection had begun as schoolgirl hero worship, grew steadily into genuine regard, and blossomed into love. In my eyes, he possessed all the imaginary virtues of the heroes I had met in books.

❧☙

In August, I went to Geneva to see Grandmère. I came up through the old garden, fragrant with memories. Grandmère's cottage was as dearly familiar as the apple tree next to it where I had sat in the old grapevine swing, swaying idly to and fro.

Always, I told Grandmère all my secrets, and she never bossed or irritated me like my mother did.

I had the feeling that, of all her grandchildren, I was her favorite. What caused her feeling for me is hard to specify. It was not that I was a strong character, for I was not. I was not only heedless, but blind to the result of my heedlessness. But in her eyes, I was lovable. She seemed to love me for my faults rather than my good qualities.

I used to tell Grandmère more about what was going on with me than anyone else. Why I did this I don't know, unless it was because she realized and therefore sympathized with the conditions under which I lived. She candidly admitted that I possessed traits which had shown themselves in her when she was my age, and it is more than probable that I inherited those traits from her.

Mademoiselle Alice

"Always remember," she advised, "that anything you desire in life will come to you so long as it is a good desire. You must never want that which belongs to anyone else, and you must never want anything wicked or harmful to anyone."

I frequently considered this advice, and it was thus that I had learned to trust the power of my imagination to bring forth good things from the heart of the world, and as I grew up, I developed a rather trusting nature.

While Grandmère endeavored to guide me out of the effects of my indiscretions, she never lectured me for having been indiscreet. She realized that indiscretion was a trait born in me and was not likely to be eradicated until I had grown beyond the age when it would lead me into trouble.

I had often gone to her in a light-hearted way with my perplexities, but this time I gave evidence that what I had to tell her was of a serious nature.

"You look pale my dear," she said, "and your eyes are tired."

"Grandmére," I said "I have done it now and no mistake."

"What is it, child?" she asked.

"I have fallen in love with Monsieur Eiffel."

"Not," she said, feigning shock, "a clandestine affair?"

"Mother knows him."

"Oh, you dear child!" she said, chuckling, and, "Oh, you delightful girl!"

She listened earnestly, delighted to be made my confidant in a love affair.

Grandmère read romantic novels continuously and never tired of talking about love and matchmaking.

"He has the kindliest eyes" I said, "and he is so sorrowfully romantic, but he is the jolliest companion."

Mademoiselle Alice

"We all have these fancies my dear. It's just like something I was reading the other day," she said, "a charming book. I'll lend it to you."

"It is sort of like a fairy tale," I said.

"He's in love with you, I know it."

"Always I find you here, among your flowers, always understanding my rebellious, childish moods."

"A choice made by one in love," she counseled, "is a love choice, and not the result of good judgment. You have, I dare say, chosen through love. Even if I knew Monsieur Eiffel well enough to make a choice for you out of good judgment, it would avail you nothing, for you would not think of abiding by it."

"You remember the old fairy tales," I said, "and your gift for making different stories of each to satisfy my demand for just one more?"

"Look into your heart, my dear, and let that alone decide you."

I longed to rest my wayward head upon her dear shoulder as she wove for me a new fairy tale of a prince and princess, or of a king and a beggar-maid, but always, always, with a happy ending.

ಬಂಡ

One day, Monsieur Eiffel asked me: "Have you been to the top of the tower?"

"No," I said. "I have been only to the first level."

Monsieur Eiffel had an apartment at the top of the tower and only the privileged few got to go inside it.

"Would you like to ride the elevator up to the top?"

"I would, very much," I said.

Mademoiselle Alice

On the second level, he stopped to place an order at the *pâtisserie* so we could have tea brought up to his apartment.

We rode up silently. He affected an air of nonchalance, but I could tell he was bursting with pride in his signature achievement, although he restrained himself from waxing fatuous. When we reached the third level, a thousand feet above Paris, the gleaming balcony seemed as remote and as distant from the crowded streets below as the clouds above.

I removed my hat and let the cool breeze fan my forehead.

When I laughed, I could hear my laughter ring like musical bells up and down the tower. We walked around the promenade and came upon a curving ladder stair.

"A ladder stair!" I said. "Where does this go?"

"There's a flag pole up there," he said, "and some weather equipment."

"Shall we go up?"

"Go ahead," he said, "I'll follow you."

It was another fourteen steps to the very top.

"This is scary!" I laughed. "Let's go back down!"

Then he showed me his apartment, furnished in masculine style, all dark wood and crimson velvet.

We had tea and *petit fours*. He played some cylinders of recorded music for me on a phonograph like the one given to him by Thomas Edison. His passion for music was even greater than my own, and his phonographs were among his most cherished possessions.

༄༅༅

That first Christmas Eve after I had started working at the Comptoir, my mother and I were invited to Monsieur Eiffel's mansion for dinner. He greeted us at the door.

Mademoiselle Alice

"Come on in," he said joyously. "The dinner is waiting and the champagne is icy cold."

The dinner table was loaded with a haunch of venison at one end and a wild turkey at the other, the interval being filled with other delectable viands. The sparkle of cut glass and polished silver made the table most inviting.

Monsieur Eiffel sat at the head of the table, while Claire's husband, Adolphe Salles, sat at the other end. Children and other members of the family crowded the table to its capacity.

A large bottle of champagne was in an ice bucket beside Monsieur Eiffel's chair, and as soon as we were seated, it was uncorked and our glasses were filled.

Monsieur Eiffel raised his glass.

"To the folly of youth," he said. Since he was clearly referring to himself and he was the oldest one in the room, everyone laughed.

"Always start a party with champagne," he advised everyone. "Remember what Napoleon said."

"What did Napoleon say?" returned Monsieur Salles, the perfect straight man.

"In victory you deserve champagne—in defeat you need it."

After dinner, Monsieur Eiffel got out the latest in lantern slide projectors, and showed us his slides, all of which he had taken himself.

Chapter 19

A YEAR'S HARD WORK at the *Comptoir Général de Photographie* hadn't worn off the enthusiasm I felt for photography and all its myriad possibilities. That was when Louis Lumière and his brother, Auguste, came into the office to invite Monsieur Gaumont to a little surprise party. I was sitting right there and so it happened that they invited me too.

"What is it?" asked Monsieur Gaumont.

"You will see," said one of the brothers. "It's a surprise."

We were more than surprised. We were astonished when we went to the meeting of the *Société d'Encouragement l'Industrie* at 4, Place St. Germain, and saw moving pictures projected onto a sheet. The short film showed the Lumière brothers' factory at closing time when its employees poured forth from a wide door. Larger-than-life men, women, dogs, and horse-drawn carriages moved across the wall.

We went back to the Comptoir in stunned silence. Georges Demenÿ's glass disk with twelve pictures on it seemed suddenly quaint and old-fashioned. Its novelty had been eclipsed by this new development.

Mademoiselle Alice

It was only two months after the Lumières rolled out their moving picture, when the Court of Appeal finally decided that Felix-Max Richard should give up his business in accordance with the contract he made with his brother some years before.

Felix-Max Richard sold the Comptoir to his dear friend, Joseph Vallot, and to Monsieur Eiffel. A third partner, Alfred Besnier, a shipping magnate, was brought in by Monsieur Eiffel.

Monsieur Gaumont was anxious about being left out, and wanted to become one of the partners in the company. He had to put up a sizable sum of money which he borrowed.

At last, the partnership agreement was executed, and the company was named *Gaumont et Cie* after its youngest partner. Monsieur Eiffel was president, but he did not want his name on the company since he was still suffering from the undeserved contempt of the public.

Monsieur Gaumont had not been to college and was not yet an engineer. Monsieur Eiffel, the master builder and engineer became Monsieur Gaumont's patron and friend.

Monsieur Eiffel was a kind master to Monsieur Gaumont. They worked together on improving the photographic development processes and the cameras, for these were still quite imperfect affairs.

Monsieur Gaumont would demonstrate each camera for Monsieur Eiffel, explaining its clumsy motions, occasionally looking up, calling attention to some defect that needed improvement, and then to another that, after much thought and experiment, had been corrected.

Monsieur Eiffel looked down critically on his apprentice, and at the many contrivances required in the advancement of photography, at all times exhibiting that zeal necessary to the breaking down of obstacles which stood in the way of accomplishing great results.

With the excitement attendant upon developments in photography and moving pictures, these endeavors were absorbing to both of them.

೩෨ೡ

Meanwhile, Monsieur Eiffel and I played a merry game of hide and kiss when he came into the Comptoir.

"I will have to keep you waiting," he would tell a customer, "while I discuss a business matter with Mademoiselle Alice. I will not detain you long," he added in a low tone, as I followed him into my private sanctum. Then when the curtains had been carefully adjusted, he caught me up in a masterful embrace, and at the same time put a little note into my hand asking me to have luncheon with him.

He called for me at my apartment building every Thursday night and took me out to dinner and to the theater at least once a week. Occasionally, we whirled off to the opera. Had we been living in a country town, everybody would have said we were keeping company.

Monsieur Eiffel would telephone me at the office "just to listen to that melodious voice of yours." Naturally, I was pleased at his many compliments, and before the telephone call was finished, we had made another engagement. Then came boxes of flowers and candy and other indications of a lover's affection.

As we lived in Paris, and were both reticent as to our personal affairs, nobody knew anything about us except for my mother. My mother, on occasion, accompanied us to the theater and opera, but since she found Monsieur Eiffel the

Mademoiselle Alice

model of good manners, she quickly persuaded herself that he was a perfect gentleman and no chaperoning was necessary.

Our courtship frequently meant roof garden lunches on the top of palatial department stores, and nice little dinners in the many beautiful nooks of that great city where romance and banter abide.

But in the office, to each other, we were always Mademoiselle Alice and Monsieur Eiffel.

I admit I usually thought a wee bit about Monsieur Eiffel as I put on my very best blouse in the morning. It may sound rather trite, but those early years in the inner office, as secretary to Monsieur Gaumont, with the knowledge that Monsieur Eiffel might pop in at any time, ready to take me to luncheon or supper, were the happiest I have ever known.

There were times when I could think of nothing else but Monsieur Eiffel, though you may be sure that I tried to banish the foolishness. But it would not be banished because it was love—love, the unexpected and the unreasonable.

ଚଓ

Through the humble doors of 57, rue Saint-Roch came often those known to fame. Monsieur Eiffel had many friends in high places, and since the hobby of photography was still too expensive for most people, this association with celebrities helped the business to flourish.

This was before every branch of the arts had become commercialized, before those who were intellectually inclined were divided into groups as they are now, with the scientists forming one group, the musicians another, and the literary people still another. At that time, refined persons took some interest in all branches of art and science. It seems to me that the commercial spirit of the present age has in great measure blunted our sensibilities.

I had seen enough of society to learn of its hollowness, and while I was working in the office, I rather dreaded seeing someone I used to know. Having been born in affluence and suddenly reduced to poverty, my economic condition and social position had changed drastically.

One day, a young society woman I recognized as a friend of one of my sisters, glanced carelessly at me behind the counter. I tried to look away but then her glance changed to one of recognition.

"Why, Alice," she exclaimed, "who would have expected to find you here?"

I looked back at her as dispassionately as I could, with a steady gaze.

"My friends of a more prosperous time," I replied, "have long ceased to expect anything from me."

"That is unfair of you dear. You yourself have been much to blame for the seeming neglect. After your father died, you disappeared completely."

I could feel my face flaming.

"Father's investments were unfortunate," I said, and immediately regretted it. Making excuses to someone who does not care is likely to do nothing more than illuminate their cold appraisal. And then I made it worse, continuing to blither on helplessly, making further unnecessary excuses for that which was neither my fault nor anyone else's.

"I was left penniless, and was obliged to seek work," I said. "You know there were no working girls in our circle."

After this former acquaintance left the office without exhibiting a scintilla of empathy, I felt absolutely wretched. Thereafter, I learned to keep my memories in reserve. Even the most favored were unable to learn anything of my past or present from my own lips.

Instead, I became known for rounding up notables and wringing from them their secret thoughts, where others had failed in their approach. I was frequently left to entertain interesting customers.

"Mademoiselle Alice," Monsieur Gaumont would say, "Monsieur So-and-So is coming in a little later. I have to leave but I will be back shortly. Would you kindly keep him entertained until my return?"

"Of course."

"My trust lies in you."

In the evening, my mother liked to hear about the society people that came into the Comptoir. We would sit at evening exchanging confidences.

"I saw the Duchess d'Uzes today," I would say. The Duchess was the richest woman in France and Mother had met her while working with society ladies at *Mutualité Maternelle*.

Mother would lean forward expectantly, awaiting the glowing descriptions sure to follow.

"Did she wear a plumed hat or one of velvet?"

"She wore a small, shaped hat," I said. "Very tasteful."

I met real princesses and deposed queens, but it was even more fun to meet adventurers such as Jean Charcot who built a sailing ship to go to the arctic, and Salomon Andrée who tried to do the same thing in a balloon.

Although I was not rolling in money, I was no longer on the edge of starvation, and gratefully acknowledged my own luck and good fortune. Positions such as the one I had did not grow between the curbstones.

Monsieur Gaumont, on the other hand, prided himself on becoming comfortable by his own hard work and good judgment. It seemed that for every thousand francs he made, he hardened his heart. His boast was that he owed his success to strict personal attention to detail. His failure to acknowledge the assistance he had received disturbed me, so I asked him:

"Didn't help from your friends, fate, or luck having anything to do with it?"

"Not a bit," he said. "Never had any luck in my life. What I've got, I've made in spite of luck."

༄༅

Those were the days when automobiles were just being invented. The first automobile inventors came from the ranks of bicycle manufacturers who cobbled two bicycles together with a motor between them, and tried to resolve the resulting problems from there.

When Felix-Max Richard had to discontinue manufacturing cameras, he joined his brother Georges in the manufacture of bicycles and then automobiles. Georges Richard became famous for his bicycles, and we sold them at 57, rue Saint-Roch with a camera case attached for those interested in touring and taking photographs along the way.

Still, automobiles had not yet come into vogue for conveyances, but were merely a rich man's toy. A person of means who could afford an automobile would be likely to take it out to the park on a Sunday, and drive it around for the novelty of showing off his machine, or for the amusement of being carried along without the effort of walking or pushing pedals.

One of the first automobile races was held only two months after the Lumière brothers demonstrated their moving picture camera. The contestants drove from Paris to Bordeaux, some 360 miles, and back at the breakneck speed of thirteen miles per hour to cheering crowds. The winner, driving a Peugeot, arrived back in Paris after forty-eight hours and had to wake up the judges who had retired for the night. The driver in last place limped into Paris two days later.

Monsieur Eiffel, naturally interested in new inventions, was also fond of automobiles, eventually having several in his garage, and he kept them all in order himself. He acquired all the tools he could need, and whenever anything in one of his cars broke or became disarranged, he would don his overalls and fix it.

One memorable Sunday, I happily spent the afternoon handing him wrenches and bolts, watching while he worked under one of his cars long enough to become begrimed. Having repaired the damage, he decided to try out his automobile with a view to seeing if what he had fixed would hold.

"Want to go for a ride?" he asked.

He did not change his overalls or wash the smudges off his face. We started down the road and he looked for all the world like a greasy mechanic. And since society in Paris was used to seeing him in a suit constructed by a fashionable tailor and a colorful silk cravat, no one recognized him.

༺༻

My sister Rose and I were both girls of a keen sensibility. We were inseparable as children, and often when together Rose would mention something that I was thinking or I would say something she was thinking. At the time we thought it was just a coincidence, but at last we came to wonder if it were not because we had both been babes in arms when Grandmère took over for our mother when I was born and Rose was only two years old.

Mademoiselle Alice

It was when Christmas was coming that year, the year of the moving picture camera and the first automobile races, when both Rose and I had the sense that we should visit Grandmère, now in the sunset of her life.

We all, my sisters and mother, gathered in her kitchen the day before Christmas, helping her make her delicious old-fashioned candies, as we had done when we were little girls, tying them in dainty, gift packages for her favored friends.

We were still with Grandmère the day after Christmas. While she was out in her garden, she was suddenly stricken. We rushed to her assistance, but she passed peacefully away in our arms.

I had developed a numb little place in my heart where the old memories were kept. Rose and I went up to the loft to sort through Grandmère's treasures in an enchanted old chest.

When we opened it to look over its contents, a tumult of emotion swept over me. After the trunk tray was placed on the floor, we took out dainty clothes, slippers, parasols, and hats.

Folded away with my childish dreams of fairies and my fairy godmother, was Grandmère's lavender party dress.

It had a quaint bodice tied with violet ribbons. The full skirt of the dress was covered with violets scattered quaintly over its lavender surface. Under the folded party dress were Grandmère's tiny slippers laced with ribbon.

The dress brought clear, bright pictures to my mind of being cuddled in Grandmère's arms, my sisters seated nearby, listening to some fairytale. I saw a candy pull on a stormy night, the old kitchen echoing with laughter. The longing to go back to the days when I was a tiny girl brought tears to my eyes.

"It is foolish to bring back the old dreams," I said to Rose, "for there are no fairies, no fairy godmother, anymore."

Rose was always wiser than I was, and protective of my feelings.

"Do you remember," she asked gently, "what Grandmère said?"

"About what?'

"About losing five of her eight children?"

"I never asked her about it. I cannot imagine any horror such as that."

"She told me 'we must not forever grieve.' She said we must laugh and be happy, for life, after all, is before us, and life is good."

"Just like her kitchen plaque—every cloud has a silver lining," I said, bitter tears springing forward, wishing I could believe it.

Chapter 20

THERE WERE HOURS when my time was practically my own, and affairs proceeded at the office without my constant supervision.

"It sounds childish," I complained to my mother, "and I have been childish for too long, but I would like my future to be occupied with bigger things than working in an office. One has only to realize the importance of Loie Fuller's life in order to learn the insignificance of one's own."

Loie Fuller had taken Paris by storm. She was an American girl, not pretty in any sense, but she had fashioned miles of silk into a costume she could manipulate with wands she held in her hands. Over her head she swirled her fabric while spotlights of various colors made her performance magical.

"Mademoiselle Fuller has a talent all her own," my mother admitted.

"Another one is Yvette Guilbert," I said. "She doesn't even have a good voice. She takes off her dress—well, I don't want to do that!" I said.

"Convent girl takes off dress!" my mother said reproachfully. "I should think not!"

Mademoiselle Alice

"There are other things that can be done on stage," I said.

"The stage is for poor girls who cannot do anything else," my mother said emphatically. "They are forced to go on stage." My mother still had the old-fashioned idea that the girls on stage were the same as girls on the street.

"I don't know," I said. "Some of them have talent."

※

The Lumière brothers had made ten films and they were shown all day, every day, from two locations, on boulevard des Italiens and boulevard Capucines. I saw people lined up to get in, and they each paid a franc to see the ten films, each barely a minute long.

There was one film of a couple feeding a baby that was charming. There was one of a man watering his garden, and the one of the workers leaving the factory which I had already seen. Most of the films were nonsensical and lost their appeal as soon as you had seen them once.

The magic was in seeing larger-than-life characters on a screen. People looked behind the screen, unconvinced that something wasn't happening behind it.

Coincidentally in Germany, Professor Wilhelm Roentgen had discovered the X-ray. He came to Paris and gave lectures on the discovery at the Hotel Scribe, the same hotel where the Lumières' moving pictures were shown in the basement.

Messieurs Eiffel and Gaumont collaborated with each other in duplicating Roentgen's ray. I packed off Crookes tubes, induction coils, fine wire, and a six-cell battery to Monsieur Eiffel's vacation house in Beaulieu-sur-Mer so that he could mount experiments reproducing the X-rays described in the science magazine, *La Nature*.

Mademoiselle Alice

After these experiments were successful, we X-rayed everything. Monsieur Gaumont sold tickets to show my foot inside my shoe and my bones inside my hand. Needless to say, the X-ray was very popular as an amusement before we knew it was a dangerous thing to play with.

Meanwhile, the Gaumont company was quickly developing its own motion picture camera and projector. One of Monsieur Gaumont's good friends, René Decaux, was hired to modify the camera Demenÿ had shown us so that it could be used to project films. Monsieur Decaux became Monsieur Gaumont's right-hand man, and there developed hostility and competition between me and Monsieur Decaux.

I was sent over to Dr. Marey's *Station Physiologique* to try out the new camera. Dr. Marey had developed a camera based on Monsieur Janssen's photographic revolver with which he could take sequential pictures in the laboratory.

This was thought to be the best use of the motion picture camera. The moving pictures of birds flying, horses galloping, and people running were a great advance for science because they allowed scientists, for the first time, to examine fast-moving phenomena in slow motion.

I mentioned to Monsieur Gaumont that we could probably make something fanciful that would appeal to those among us who were not scientists.

"With the addition of costumes, scenery and actors," I said, "we could put a vignette on film."

"You're not serious?" he replied. "That sounds like a silly, girlish thing." For him, my idea was frivolous, like the table decorations at a baby shower.

"It could be some kind of story," I said, "short and sweet."

Mademoiselle Alice

"You think you can write a story that fits on one minute of film?" Monsieur Gaumont asked doubtfully, always in a hurry, as if I were wasting his time.

"I think I can," I said, although my ideas on what constitutes a story were still unformed in my mind.

"Well then, take care of it," he said, brushing me off impatiently. "After you finish the mail, you can go."

In France we spend a couple of hours at luncheon, and this gave me a little time when I could put together something interesting and amusing. Monsieur Gaumont let me use his backyard to set my scene.

I chose as my subject the birth of infants. On the way to Montmartre one day, I saw an exposition of a new invention: the incubator for human babies. I paid fifty cents to enter a large room full of tiny babies in incubators. They broke my heart. Where were their mothers and grandmothers? Why were they in those cold, glass and metal boxes? The incubator was not yet accepted as a benefit to babies born small. We did not even call them premature. We called them weaklings and, prior to the incubator, it was believed that their survival had to be left to Fate.

I preferred the story of my own mysterious birth, the story Grandmère told me. She said she found me in the garden under a cabbage leaf and that she had loved me ever since that day. It was certainly more picturesque than being housed in those awful boxes.

Memories of scenes in Grandmère's tangled garden when I was a tiny girl came back to me as if borne on a drifting breeze. In a spirit of sudden longing, I realized that in all the days of my girlhood, my grandmother's home was the only real home I had known. I have never forgotten the magic of those times.

Mademoiselle Alice

There was a poster advertising the exposition of baby incubators which showed in its artwork tiny babies surrounded by vine leaves, the blossoms on the vines being little sleepy heads. This is where I found inspiration for my first film.

I had the cabbage leaves cut from stacks of card in the workshop where Gaumont cameras were being constructed, and then I spent hours painting them bright green and fashioning them into oversize cabbages. My father had told me about huge cabbages he saw when he was in California during the gold rush. The land around San Francisco had never been cultivated before, and the cabbages grew to be enormous—big enough for a small child to hide behind.

This was just what I wanted. I rounded up all the small children I knew and got them dressed in little green smocks and leafy hats.

The story was a simple one, but required the art of pantomime. I envisioned a pair of newlyweds on their honeymoon, walking in the country. They come upon a field of cabbages tended by a farmer. Two friends of mine played the couple, and Anatole Thiberville, the young fellow whose task it was to turn the film, stepped from behind the camera long enough to play the farmer.

In this single scene, the husband whispers into the ear of his bride and asks her if she would like a baby. Of course, she says yes, and the young man then asks the farmer if they might look behind the cabbages. The farmer shows his annoyance, but he allows the couple to search his field.

First, the husband discovers a baby, but, alas, it is made of card printed with a baby's face. The newlyweds show by their facial expressions great disappointment. Then the wife puts one hand behind her ear—she hears something. It's a baby softly cooing behind a distant cabbage. She runs toward the sound and discovers a beautiful baby. She brings it in triumph to her husband. After paying the farmer for their *petit chou*, the young couple leaves with their new baby.

When I saw my little film projected, I was dismayed at my mistakes. Since film in those days did not pick up multiple variations of gray, my cabbages, painted bright green, were too dark. My backdrop also gave me a pang because it had not been securely fastened to the wall behind it. Every time the wind blew, it ruffled prettily, reminding the viewer that it was not a real scene, or even a perfect fantasy, but a painted backdrop.

The newspaper described it as a "chaste fiction of children born under the cabbages in a wonderfully framed chromo landscape," and no one had ever seen anything like it.

We used this romantic story film to sell a moving picture camera-projector to the Comédie-Française. *La Fée aux Choux*, *The Fairy of the Cabbages*, or *The Birth of Infants*, as it was called at that time, was put to good use as an afterpiece for the classic play, *L'Ami Fritz*. It was shown almost every day from April through December, and was worn out from being fed through the projector time and again.

Thus, my career in art started in this curious way and was to carry me to the very heights.

While I was busy creating this delightful fantasy, I escaped sadness with respect to losing my grandmother by thinking joyfully about Rose, who was great with child, as that condition is described in Scripture, and the new little life that would be coming to us very soon—before May, as it turned out.

ಲ⊙ಣ

Mademoiselle Alice

Monsieur Gaumont used my film to show our customers what our new motion picture camera could do. There quickly arose demand for more films of an entertaining nature. Since my first film delighted those who saw it, I was allowed to make another and another.

I was so absorbed working on my picture plays, that at 2 o'clock, I would remember with dismay that Monsieur Gaumont always hustled back to the office after lunch, and I had quite forgotten my promise to type his correspondence that must get off in the outgoing mail. With my usual impetuous rush, I would run wildly after a vanishing cab, finally landing on the footboard, in close proximity to the astonished driver, whose little black moustache curled up higher than ever when he discovered a flushed, young woman suddenly flung his way.

The office soon came in sight and I had to rush to finish all my work.

We did not yet have a studio or the advancements in lighting that would allow us to take natural-looking films indoors. Monsieur Eiffel preferred that we take all of our films *en plein air*, out of doors, for the advantage of natural light. Monsieur Gaumont was always conscious of costs, so it was often more economical to find a scene than to build the scenery. This is why the dozens of films we made in those early days are charming street scenes of Paris.

All my scenarios had to be approved by Monsieur Gaumont, who viewed every story with all the skepticism that the hard-headed man of business brings to bear upon the fanciful dreams of a fiction writer. If it was a comedy or had burglars on the roof, he often gave his approval without much thought or consideration. But what I aspired to write was love stories.

Mademoiselle Alice

"For heaven's sake, Mademoiselle Alice," he said, "drop lovers and stick to crooks," as he handed me back a story dealing with the tender passions. And I did stick to crooks, though I was determined that someday I would write love stories that would make viewers sit up and take notice.

But a storyteller needs a rich and broad experience in life, and must not be strictly conventional or too bound by the laws of society. One must enlarge one's scope for story writing, so I developed a knack for writing stories about the underworld which made my scenarios acceptable to Monsieur Gaumont.

In my study of human nature, I acquired a taste for what was considered low company, the crooks and chorus girls of Montmartre. I began to frequent places where I could meet crooks, and I tried to absorb the authenticity I felt was needed for picture plays concerning the underworld. I made the acquaintance of some disreputable characters who knew I would never squeal on them. Crooks don't mind seeing films about themselves at all, they rather like it provided nothing about their identity is revealed.

One day, during my quest for a roguish type of character for a story I was writing, I looked into the dingy window of a café that seemed coated with just the exact kind of villainy I wanted to picturize. I entered this dreadful little den and glanced about the room, scanning the quaint assortment of faces. Here I found good-humored conversation, and dropped into a chair opposite a scruffy-looking man. He was so flattered by my attention, by my quiet listening, that he told me a few vivid tales, and my mind was set alight with powerful plots.

The cabarets also furnished a look behind the scenes, a look at the lives of chorus girls. The dancers were creatures of hot lights, starry-eyed and beautiful until the curtain rang down, when suddenly they became weary and bedraggled.

But I could only do this spelunking during the day, since a woman could not then go out unaccompanied at night without being taken for a prostitute.

The dances of many countries seemed to me to be a particularly good subject for film, a story without words, needing only the addition of music that could be played on a phonograph alongside the film.

I became infatuated with the tango, that romantic *pas de deux* from South America enjoying a revival in Paris. Hoodlums of the day, calling themselves Apaches, gathered at the *Caveau des Innocents*, an imposing set of old cellars transformed into a late-night restaurant, where they danced their own version of the tango.

"You cannot go there by yourself," Monsieur Eiffel said, "but if you like the tango, you have to see the Apaches dance." He took me late one Saturday.

The furnishings were simple—wooden tables and straw-seated stools. The fare offered, onion soup and beer, was neither cheap nor good, but in spite of that the place was packed and the amount of beer consumed gargantuan.

The men who called themselves Apaches were stylishly dressed in boots, flared trousers, horizontal-striped shirts, and red neck scarves. Their partners in the dance wore tight dresses and high-heels. They danced to the strains of a piano. The excitement came from their violent style of tango which included mock slaps, punches, and falls. Not surprisingly, some of the girls were injured in the dance. I resolved to one day create Apache dancing on film.

Mademoiselle Alice

One day Monsieur Gaumont said to me: "We need some kind of trademark." He showed me the Pathé Frères emblem, a rooster with a stylized morning sun with radiating spikes in the background. I set out to draw something with the Gaumont name on it. I doodled drawings with the name in the middle and came up with a daisy, like the one in Faust. Each petal was shaped like a heart. He loves me, he loves me not. We used this trademark for several years.

Because I was liked, I managed to keep in harness a dry humor with which I caused my own and other persons' mishaps and shortcomings to appear amusing. If taken to task for a blunder, I learned to soften it by a joke so apt that it assured my being forgiven. Then, too, I had a keen appreciation for the foibles of human nature. I realized that most people like to see the shortcomings of others, especially, shown up in an amusing way.

One day one of my fellow workers said to me, "Why don't you put some of these funny things in your films?"

"I have never thought they were worth it," I replied, but it gave me an idea. For a month, I kept notes of what seemed to amuse others and put the best of them in proper form for a humorous film. We used these ideas, and from that time forward something funny appeared in our films every week, and after a while these bits of humor began to be copied by other filmmakers.

The reception of some of our films was slow at first, because there was a zest in them that required a little time to percolate through the thinking of those who saw them. It would require some time to educate the public, but these films appealed to certain persons who introduced them to others and they grew in favor.

❧❦

I found inspiration wherever there was beauty or strong emotion. I often used lines from poems for the intertitles. Humor and pathos mingle to register a story that teems with human interest. A fine painting, a rhythmic poem with a beautiful thought, or an entrancing piece of music pleases and lingers long in the mind. I wondered for a long time how to put an opera on film.

I had continued my early morning walks and was fascinated by the gypsies who lived on the outskirts of Paris. I saw them tramping along the road, their shaggy old horses drawing their small carriage houses.

The wagons were gaudy with fresh paint, blue, red, and gold. Lace curtains tied back from tiny windows revealed intimate glimpses of drowsy children peeking shyly out.

Once they arrived at a spot suitable for camping, they would set up a picturesque little village crowded with horses, dogs, and dirty children clothed in rags. The men made baskets, chairs, and shoes to sell, while the women sold candy, crullers, and pancakes.

I was struck with a mixture of envy and pity for these families. They had almost nothing, sheltered only by the tent roofing on their wagons, yet they were united by love and necessity.

I was looking for anything with entertainment value, and gypsies are entertainers: jugglers, acrobats, tumblers, tightrope walkers, tossers of balls and knives, trainers of performing animals, such as bears, goats, dogs, and organ grinders with their monkeys.

I loved people who were struggling to put something of beauty into the world. Sometimes they didn't have a dime in their pockets, but that was of no moment to them. They were full to overflowing with good fellowship and always ready to share what they had.

Sometimes, when searching for a new story, I would get my hands on a newspaper and read the public notices. I could build a story around each one, complete with a setting, cast of characters, sequential events, and a climax, sad or glad, as my mood suggested.

I sketched costumes for the costumers, laid plans for the sets, and made the rounds looking for props and incidentals, the finishing touches that provide atmosphere and authenticity. One has only to watch the images unroll to see how the pitiless camera picks up every mistake. All parts of the production require an artistic vision.

But I was always on a strict budget. Monsieur Gaumont did not see some of my artistic choices as necessary, and was constantly after me to reduce my expenditures.

Once a week, Monsieur Gaumont made the staff sit in silence watching our last week's productions. He stood glowering over us, his hands in his pockets, a malignant expression on his face. We sank down in our chairs while he grumbled, growled and snarled, criticizing every detail, with special attention to the cost of each item, making all of us feel like we were dodging bullets in a shooting gallery.

Chapter 21

IT WAS NOT AT ALL PROPER FOR a single woman to travel overnight with a single man, but my mother's trust in Monsieur Eiffel was unflinching. Also, I think she thought it would not be the worst thing in the world if I married him.

One of the most romantic places in France is the coast of Brittany. It is wild and beautiful with picturesque, stone farmhouses. Artists go there to get subjects for their paintings, which they find not only in the countryside, but in the simple peasants who live there.

Monsieur Eiffel had a beautiful beach house in Trouville, a resort town surrounded by jagged rocks and cliffs, and he invited me for a trip through Brittany, to take three of his young grandchildren to the seashore, and to photograph the first drivers to finish the Paris-Trouville automobile race.

From the little railroad station in Trouville, we journeyed in a brightly painted coach drawn by two gray horses. We passed the rows of conveyances drawn up before the entrance of the *Hôtel des Roches Noires*, where the fashionable set liked to go to show off their new clothes. The Paris newspapers contained reviews accompanied by illustrations of what vacationers in Trouville were wearing. We were the only passengers to the beach house a short distance away, like a little sister of the grand hotel.

The coach went down a narrow lane shaded by cedars where the marsh grass grew sparsely in the sand. I took my hat off to the fresh breeze and gratefully inhaled the invigorating salt air.

The house proved to be a rather large structure placed just above the high-water mark. It was painted pink, topped with turrets and spires, its many windows and decorations making it look like a wedding cake. The front door swung open to a large, furnished room. We threw wide the shutters, raised the window sashes to the salt air, and got out the porch furniture.

Except for a layer of dust, the house was in perfect order. I decided to sleep in one of the turret rooms. There was little for me to do save to arrange my cot in the little room and unpack my things.

"Ah," said Monsieur Eiffel, "you found a turret room."

"I have always wanted to sleep in a turret," I said, remembering the castles of Switzerland, "just like a princess."

While the children played in the sand, we walked on the beach, caressed by a soft breeze, tasting the sensation of two hearts drawing together, delicious as a swallow of rare wine.

We took some pictures of the automobile race contestants as they came into town. I remember perfectly: Marcel Renault was the winner. After that, we avoided the crowd.

Monsieur Eiffel had arranged by letter for our meals to be sent from the hotel. At sunset, a boy brought a basket containing an excellent dinner which we enjoyed on the balcony overlooking the wide sweep of sand. The waves broke softly on the beach while the sky flamed with colors that faded into purple as the stars came out.

ଧଓର

After the children went to bed, Monsieur Eiffel and I sat with a table between us. We had been playing euchre when I suggested a game of hearts.

"Oh, no thank you," he said. "I am not so foolish as to play hearts with a coquette."

I was looking down at the cards, but presently raised my eyes to his. In his worn and comfortable clothes, he was handsome in a cuddly and wholesome way.

"Shall I tell your fortune then?" I asked.

"Please do."

I shuffled and distributed the cards on the table in four piles. Whenever I turned up a card, I paused and studied it.

"I would like to know," he said, "what process you are using to determine my fortune?"

"It is one I learned from a fortune teller."

"Oh, I see. Was she a scientific fortune teller?"

"She most assuredly was. She had a crystal globe and a stuffed owl."

"As the spider waits for a fly," he said, "she cannot be expected to tell the truth."

"This fortune teller spent a lot of time with me, explaining everything."

I put down four cards, then another four, one of them being the knave of spades.

"That's you," I said.

"You're calling me a knave?" he said with mock indignation.

"Yes, but you're awfully smart. You scintillate my mind with your bright sayings."

"Have you utterly no regard for a poor bachelor's heart?"

I laughed. There was warm admiration in his gaze.

Presently the ten of diamonds turned up.

"That's a wealthy woman who is angling for you," I said.

"What's her name?"

"The cards reveal not."

"Because the fortune teller doesn't know?"

"Exactly."

Next fell the two of spades.

"Ah! A black deuce!" I said. "That indicates that she is crafty. Look out for her. She will cause you a lot of trouble."

The next card I turned up was the ten of hearts.

"That's the girl who really loves you," I said, knowingly. "She is true of heart, and if you return her love she will make you very happy."

"Why are the ten spots always female?" he asked with a puzzled expression, "and how do you infer these things based on where the cards fall? I don't understand the system you use to make these pronouncements."

"Of course, you don't," I said. "What kind of fortune teller would I be if I told you?"

"Just like the fortune teller who taught you."

I put all the cards together again, shuffled them, and began again, this time laying them in six piles, so that all were exposed. The third card was the ten of diamonds and the fourth card was the jack of clubs.

"Unfortunately," I said, "the unexpected has happened."

"As expected, we get the unexpected."

"That's right. Sometimes, when Fate shuffles the cards she stacks them unfairly. The rich woman has thrown you over for a man who is brutal."

"That is the strangest fortune telling system I have ever seen," he said.

The ten of hearts turned up again, and I let my hand rest on it. He quickly put his hand on it at the same time. We both laughed.

"Don't tell me," he said. "This is the girl who loves me."

"How did you know?" I asked.

"Isn't that what you were going to say?"

"I don't know. Do you believe in love?"

"Of course I do."

"Then you believe in magic," I said. "There is no difference."

I raised my lashes and looked into his eyes with something that might have been inviting, or it might have been reproachful. It was whatever he chose it to be.

We spent the rest of the evening on the couch. I could not resist his charm.

Chapter 22

THE 1900 EXPOSITION UNIVERSELLE was in full swing. Everywhere there was music and color, merriment and laughter. The crowd pushed through the entrance gate in a continuous stream. Inside the grounds, there were great numbers of visitors wandering from one exhibit to another, fashionably dressed people from many countries.

The Gaumont company had an exhibit of cameras and films. Also our competitors, the Lumières and Pathé, were well-represented, along with the American motion picture companies, Lubin and Edison.

My sisters had moved back to Paris and were star seamstresses in the great fashion houses. With them, I visited the *Palais du Costume*.

The same men who had founded *Mutualité Maternelle*, executives in the needle trades, built a rococo pavilion where there was displayed thirty-five splendid tableaux with period furnishings and life-like wax figures wearing fashions of times past from Cleopatra to the present. Each tableau was a scene worthy of the stage. The jewelry worn by the figures and other articles in the scenes were copied from museum specimens. One scene was of a snake charmer casting his spell on the raised head of a stuffed reptile.

"That snake is revolting," said Fanny.

"I think it's entrancing," I replied, "but it would be even better with a live snake."

"Oh my word!" said Fanny, while I wondered how I could ever film such a scene.

"Look at this," said Rose calling us over to the interior of a modiste's shop, reproduced in charming detail. A wax lady stood before a mirror trying on an elaborate bonnet while the modiste brought forward another hat from a glass case.

Above us, looking down from a balcony, were gentle wax ladies wearing that curiosity of fashion, the steeple headdress: a tall cone with a veil sprouting from its peak.

"I think those are my favorite kind of hats," Rose said.

"They're princess hats," I said. I decided then and there to use the steeple headdress in my next version of *La Fée aux Choux*. Why not? Medieval ladies, no doubt, had babies in medieval style.

Julia was much taken with a tableau of Catherine de' Medici consulting the Italian astrologer, Cosimo Ruggieri.

"She believed everything he told her," Julia said. "He told her she would have ten children and she did. Balzac wrote a story about it." Julia knew Balzac, backwards and forward.

The most lavish scene was that of Empress Josephine being fitted for Napoleon's coronation, her train embroidered with golden bees. Napoleon stood looking on with his elbow on the mantelpiece.

After a morning in the *Palais du Costume*, we visited *Old Paris*, an entire medieval city constructed along the Seine inspired by Victor Hugo's novels. It was an instructive and praiseworthy attempt to reestablish the city of our ancestors.

Hundreds of actors in authentic costumes gave life to the miniature city. Winding through it were narrow lanes marked by brightly colored street signs such as *The Sow that Runs, The Old Donkey*, and *The Four Sons*. The restaurants were true period pieces serving meat pies and small birds, popular in Marie Antoinette's time.

A girl playing *Esmeralda* with her pet goat danced like an elf on the brim of a fountain. I had read Victor Hugo's novels, of course, and was captivated by his description of Esmeralda with her flaming eyes, salamander body, and nightingale voice. She also had a pet goat as I did when I was little.

In the Grand Theater inside the *Old Paris* exhibit, we saw performed an abbreviated version of *Esmeralda* and also a scene from *Les Miserables* called *On the Barricade*. Both proved to me that one could adapt a very long novel to a very short film.

ஜௐ

Wandering around the Exposition, I once again stumbled upon the tent of the fortune teller, Madame Zanubia. She seemed to recognize me, at least, she said, "Wait, I have some news for you."

She held back the tent flap invitingly and, under the spell of some sudden impulse, I entered and sat down on a three-legged stool while she read two schoolgirls' fortunes who were ahead of me in line.

She took their palms in her own and read them glibly, promising fairy tale futures as all schoolgirls love. I remembered myself sitting there years before, drinking in her encouragement.

"I see much happiness for you," she told them.

Then it was my turn. I was perhaps just as willing to believe her as I was when I was sixteen. She reverently held my palm in hers. Even as an adult, to my ears, her words had the ring of truth.

"You have traveled along a pleasant road," she began. "The sun shone on you every day, but then came a time of storm and trouble, and the way led through a dark winter of death. Then there came music and the sound of many voices, and through it all a love song."

She paused and then said, "Now, the future."

"I see two men. You are indifferent to one of them, the other one loves you. The love-light shines in his eyes. I see a marriage and a journey to a warm land where the sun shines, and the birds sing all winter. Brush off the butterflies. Love and happiness cannot be bought with money."

She dropped my hand suddenly and said:

"I have spoken as it is written in your hand."

"What else?" I wanted to know.

"It is enough. The rest you must do yourself."

୨୦୧

One Sunday, Monsieur Eiffel took me to the *Parc de Vincennes*, near where I was born, to see numerous hot air balloons take off in a race. Then we watched fencers in competition. After that, we went to the *Petit Palais des Beaux-Arts*, where the book-binding exhibit was.

Books were displayed in glass cases. They were bound with leather, their covers tooled and stamped and colored in the most artistic way, each suited to the literary work inside.

Among the most expensive of these was James Tissot's New Testament. James Tissot had spent years in the Holy Land creating soft pastels and watercolors of scenes from Jesus' life and death. With the recent inventions in photogravure and chromolithography, his artworks were reproduced with great accuracy. A book binding for the limited edition of Tissot's New Testament was created by a wonderful artist, Antoinette Vallgren.

I cannot describe to you my feelings as I looked longingly at this cover. In the center panel, emerging from an olive wood, stood the Virgin Mother holding the baby Jesus in her arms. She stood between two trees, and above her there were angels holding two banners on which were engraved the title, *Vie de Notre-Seigneur Jesus-Christ*. The trunks of the trees were delicately traced with vines, and here and there, peeping out from the foliage, were the heads of babies. They were probably intended to be angels, but to me they were babies. Below were coiled two serpents amid olive leaves.

I fell in love with this New Testament, but I could not afford it. Neither could I afford the version with a plain stamped cover. I put 800 francs down on the plainly-bound version of Tissot's New Testament which was only about half its price. That was my rent for a year.

Monsieur Eiffel saw how much I loved the elaborate New Testament.

"I know the woman who did this art," he said. "She is a friend of my lawyer's wife."

He was able, without my knowledge, to transfer my 800 francs to the more expensive version, and he made up the difference. It remains to this day one of my most treasured possessions.

Chapter 23

*M*ONSIEUR EIFFEL LIKED unusual young persons of decided action. Alberto Santos-Dumont was one such person. He was heir to family fortunes both in Brazilian coffee and Parisian jewelry. He wore beautifully tailored suits and a soft Panama hat.

He was small, like a jockey, and he was obsessed with the future of flying machines. He was famous all over Paris for his dirigible which he liked to use as a conveyance to his favorite restaurant where he found ingenious ways to crash nearby.

Frenchmen had been flying in balloons for a century, but they could neither steer nor land by design. Alberto Santos-Dumont added an automobile engine and a propeller to his dirigible years before the Wright Brothers made their first flight.

The Aero Club, of which Monsieur Eiffel was a member, offered to pay a cash prize to anyone who flew his dirigible around the Eiffel Tower and back to Saint Cloud in thirty minutes or less. Alberto Santos-Dumont was the only person to attempt such a feat. He tried three times. The first time, the wind was against him. The second time, he crashed into the roof of the Trocadero Hotel.

The third time he made it, but his assistants on the ground were slow to catch his mooring ropes and, although his dirigible was back in Saint Cloud in thirty minutes, the board of the Aero Club denied him the prize.

The spectators were so disappointed in the decision of the Aero Club, the board told the crowd they would reconsider.

Monsieur Eiffel invited Alberto Santos-Dumont to luncheon at his apartment on top of the Eiffel Tower to await the board's decision. I was there to chat with Alberto since he was known to be very shy. I was his age exactly and, of course, I had been to South America where he was born.

To break the ice, I brought gingerbread cookies which were made in the shape of his dirigible. Alberto was the toast of all Paris, and enterprising bakers made cookies in his honor.

"This is almost like having lunch in my airship," he said to me as we looked out at the view. "Looking down on the clouds—no dining room can be as marvelous in its decoration."

"What did you have for lunch in your airship?" I asked trying to draw him out.

"Everything I wanted," he said, "hard-boiled eggs, roast beef, cheese, champagne, cake, coffee, and Chartreuse."

"Are we having cake and champagne?" I asked Monsieur Eiffel.

"Yes, we are."

"Tell me more about this lunch in your airship," I asked.

"Well, I had dined sumptuously, as you can imagine, and then I was finishing my little glass of Chartreuse when I entered a fog. Visibility was zero. It felt like I was hanging in a void."

"Was it just fog or was it something worse?" Monsieur Eiffel asked.

"The weather changed rather dramatically. I had to crash."

Whenever Albert said the word crash, I couldn't help but giggle. He gave me the feeling that he would have lived in his airship if he could have.

"What do you do when the weather is bad?" I asked.

"On those days when the wind or rain prevent me from taking my airship aloft, it sits in the hangar, and I am so glum."

"The glum aviator," I said.

"Yes. Very sad."

Since Monsieur Eiffel had been forced to wrestle with the problems of wind resistance while building his bridges and the tower, when it began to look like flying machines might be possible, he became very interested in aerodynamics.

"How many airships have you built now?" Monsieur Eiffel asked.

"This one is Number 6." Alberto said.

"And the one that crashed into the Trocadero?"

"That was Number 5. I improved the wind resistance by substituting the ropes with piano wire."

"Indeed?" Monsieur Eiffel was very interested in this. "And that's strong enough to hold everything together?"

"So far it is. It is only eight-tenths of a millimeter thick."

"I saw you!" I said. "The wires were invisible. Were you frightened?" I asked him.

"Not in the least!" Alberto said. "If I was a passenger in an airship, perhaps I might have been afraid, but you see I have to work all the time. Even when the airship is falling, I have no time to think. My only thought is, try something to stop the fall. Then if that doesn't work, try something else. I have to keep working to the last and have no time to be afraid. Besides, I am what you might call a fatalist. I believe that one can die only once, and when the time comes, well, it comes, that's all."

"You say you are a fatalist, but I see you are wearing a Saint Benedict medal." I pointed to a gold medal hanging from his bracelet.

"You have discovered my superstition. I had it on when I crashed into the Trocadero. My motor had stopped, the wind caught the ship on the broadside, and drove it against the hotel. My poor airship popped open like an eggshell. After hanging on the ledge of the roof for perhaps half an hour—it was fifty feet from the ground—someone threw me a rope. I tied it around my waist and was hoisted to the roof. Of course, I knew all the time that the people below—there were hundreds—were frightened. You see they had nothing else to think about. I am used to all that because I have fallen so many times."

Monsieur Eiffel looked concerned. He worried about Alberto's safety.

"Why don't we take your airship to Monaco Bay," he said, "and fly it out over the Mediterranean? The climate is genial and that way you won't be running into steeples and such."

We had a lovely lunch and when we were done, the Aero Club awarded Alberto Santos-Dumont the prize. He divided the money among the poor and his employees.

○₰◯

Monsieur Eiffel was well-acquainted with Prince Albert of Monaco, who had a long affair with the Spanish dancer, La Belle Otero, twenty years younger than he. Prince Albert took us on a tour of his oceanographic museum, a stone palace still under construction for the lodging of his collection of deep sea flora and fauna.

The Prince of Monaco was interested in Alberto's experiments in flying, and built for his dirigible the perfect balloon house: a long iron shed near the shore, looking out on one side at the promontory on which Monte Carlo is built, and on the other side, the rock peninsula of Monaco with its fortified walls. The little bay of Monaco is sheltered against wind and cold by the mountains behind it, and on both sides by the heights of these two promontories.

It was the ideal spot. The protected bay and open sea beyond afforded clear space for Alberto to operate his airship which could be stored, filled with hydrogen, in the balloon house. Alberto could dart out whenever he desired, and then back again at the approach of squalls.

On this sunny winter morning, Alberto was ready to fly his airship from the balloon house and we were there to take pictures and to hover helpfully in the water below just in case he crashed into it.

"Take my camera," I said to Alberto. "If you have time, take a picture." I put my camera on a strap over his head and showed him how to take a picture with it.

"How much does this thing weigh?" he joked. "Every ounce counts, you know. I had no breakfast."

"If you don't take my camera," I said, "you will have to take me!"

In Monsieur Eiffel's steam launch, we followed Alberto from below, while across the cloudless blue he rushed in his dirigible. He clung to the slender supports as his dirigible swooped, up, up, up above the bay and then glided evenly along, high above the water. Swiftly, he sped out to sea over the open Mediterranean.

People had flocked into the street filling verandas and doorways. From every possible vantage point, thousands of people were assembled on the terraces and along the boulevard up the hill leading to Monte Carlo.

"There he is!" they called to each other. "There he is!" We gazed up in awed silence and watched until the ship of the sky sailed far into the distance, its whirring and burring little engine sending back no sound

On he sped until his airship seemed no larger than a great bird. Then he turned around and came back. When inside the little bay, Alberto Santos-Dumont made a circle, approaching so near to us that he was able to wave and call acknowledgments. A pleasurable excitement stirred within me, tingling to the tips of my fingers. A thousand handkerchiefs were fluttering around the bay.

Then he was out to sea again making a mad caper around in another circle, an exhilarating show to the little boats gathered below, and to the sight-seeing crowd on the shore.

"I feel like I have slipped back to my childhood days," I said. "Surely, it's unusual for a grownup to go racing around, chasing a big balloon. I used to chase the fire truck when I was little."

"Let's keep up the game for a while," Monsieur Eiffel said. "We are not often privileged to return to the happy hours of childhood."

When the wind became gusty in the afternoon, the airship was put away in its balloon house, and most of the crowd dispersed. We were left with a select group of admirers on the shore chatting with Alberto Santos-Dumont and others.

Mademoiselle Alice

Alberto gave me back my camera and said he had taken a few pictures.

The former Empress Eugénie, who had fled France after Napoleon III's debacle with the Prussians in 1870, had been in exile for decades in England, but now she lived in a villa on Cap Martin, two miles east of Monte Carlo. She came out of seclusion to see Alberto Santos-Dumont fly. I met her in the balloon house.

A servant who accompanied the Empress presented everyone inside the balloon house with an invitation, a little note with a crest on it, for 5 o'clock English tea at Empress Eugénie's villa.

We presented ourselves at the appointed hour and found the former Empress in her sumptuous Italian renaissance chateau built on a promontory that looked out on three sides over the Mediterranean.

We were introduced to several princes, a duchess, and other magnates. They were all very civil to Monsieur Eiffel considering that he was a common Frenchman with no title. At first, I was both delighted and amused at mingling for the first time in my life with real aristocracy, but then it made me nervous, and I felt intimidated. I felt much out of place among the golden throng.

"Five o'clock tea," I whispered meaningfully to Monsieur Eiffel, trying to make a joke about remnants of the French monarchy migrating to England where the monarchy was still in place.

"I don't get it," he said.

"It's funny. After twenty years in England."

"What's funny about it?" He still looked puzzled.

"In Paris, we call it the green hour for the great quantities of absinthe consumed at that time of day."

"France has changed," he said, "and for the better."

"I don't know why I'm so nervous," I said.

"When you are around aristocrats," he explained, "or someone who thinks their superiority is established by their wealth or heritage, it's possible to be somewhat bowled over by it. I have learned that royal figures like being surrounded by artists and intelligentsia because there are so few intellectual lights in their own families."

I looked at him, doubtful as to my own social status.

"True hearts are more than coronets," he said.

"What does that mean?"

"There is but one kind of nobility," he said sympathetically, "the kind that springs from the heart."

As evening approached, Monsieur Eiffel said to me:

"I want to show you the casino. It was remodeled by the same architect who built the Paris opera house."

"But I hate gambling," I said, "I am afraid it ruined my father."

"But you love beauty," he said. "You must see it."

I knew Monsieur Eiffel never played games of chance, strictly adhering to games of strategy and skill. He was different from my father and Alberto Santos-Dumont in that he had not one reckless bone in his body.

We took an automobile cab back to Monte Carlo, riding along the winding, coastal roads called the serpentines.

I did not count the number of zig zags, but there must have been more than twenty. On the hill side of the road, new villas had been constructed here and there, with the idea that the Cote d'Azur might become the winter resort of the wealthy, independent of the gaming tables.

On the sea side of the road, the descent broke away, sheer and awful. Along this narrow shelf, between the cut hillside and the outer darkness, our automobile sped. It was with a sense of exhilaration amid the cool fragrance of the southern night we were brought up sharply to the open doors of the casino, surrounded by brilliantly lighted gardens.

On entering the palatial gambling pavilion, I tripped on a low step, and one of my shoes came off. I looked around, but everyone at the tables was far too engrossed in play to notice my embarrassment. The croupier was giving his monotonous call:

"Make your bets, ladies and gentlemen, make your bets. Red or black."

A crowd was gathered around a spinning roulette wheel, while an orchestra, hedged about by ferns and palms, played classical music.

I looked around at the faces of those at play to observe the stylish gamblers of the higher class. On this, my first and only visit to the famous casino, I expected to see wild turmoil and high drama with women fainting over their losses and men throwing money in the air. I was disappointed.

If this crowd had been sitting around a low dive playing Old Maid, they could not have exuded less excitement. They were all making a quiet business of it, caught in the maelstrom of Monte Carlo.

Chapter 24

ONLY TWO WEEKS AFTER I got back from Monte Carlo, we lost Rose—she had consumption. Mother took care of her until she died. I have found that words fail, except in poetry. Music also is often too eruptive to listen to.

But there was a song, *Le Secret de Bébé*, popular that year, about a little boy whose older sister had consumption. He heard the doctor say that his sister would die by the time the leaves fell off the trees. The little boy desperately wanted his sister to live, so he tied the fallen leaves back on the trees with bits of string.

If I could have saved my sweet Rose by tying all the leaves that fell from the trees back on, I would have.

It seemed unfair though, almost cruel, sometime later, to have the privilege of visiting Rouen, whereas Rose was denied this pleasure. Rose and I were always staunch admirers of Jeanne d'Arc since our first history days. We had both wanted to visit the scenes of Jeanne d'Arc's triumphs and misfortunes.

Monsieur Eiffel was invited to Rouen by one of the Gaumont company's customers, a family of circus performers and operators of a big tent. Since there were still very few motion picture theaters, many of our customers came from the ranks of traveling shows.

One of my films was part of the entertainment, and it was enlightening for me to watch the audience, but the real treat was the three-ring circus. I had never been to one, and I gave myself up to the delights of the biggest show on earth.

The spectacle began with a procession around the center ring with a blare of trumpets and a band. Then there was a glittering pageant of pretty girls and animals from many countries, all in costumes right out of *Arabian Nights*. The music seemed calculated to lure the genii of Aladdin right into the big tent.

Then the romp in the rings began. Our heads were turning left and right, trying to see everything at once. Bears rode bicycles, elephants played ball, and ponies pranced in high-step while equestrians did stunts on their backs. The audience was stunned into suspenseful silence watching the acrobats tempt fate by swinging from the heights.

Then came the clowns, a dozen of them, with their ridiculous baby buggies, jitneys, and patrol wagons.

The next day, Monsieur Eiffel and I explored the glorious old gothic cathedral, from the crypt to the belfry tower, a wonderful specimen of architecture. We made several sketches of the nave as well as the exterior.

The countryside surrounding Rouen is very pretty and, after sketching, we took a long walk. The fields of grain and vegetables were bordered by flowers blooming in riotous profusion. Buttercups, bluets and wild poppies grew to fill a pitcher on a kitchen table or to garland a girl's hat.

Feeling rather tired and hungry after walking for six miles, we stopped at a farm for lunch. The farmer's wife, a typical belle of Normandy, was most kind to us. She spread out a feast in a vine-clad summer house in her lovely garden.

She put a square of white linen on a yellow painted table. On top of that she put a yellow pottery jar filled with a bunch of yellow poppies.

The colors of that lunch brought pleasure to my eyes. On thick plates of yellow pottery we were served large baked potatoes, a puffy omelet, and a fresh tomato salad. Finishing the meal was a blackberry tart, served with a pitcher of thick cream and cups of delicious coffee.

"How did you evolve this magic?" I asked the hostess, as I marveled at the *mise-en-scène*.

"You are the kind of person," Monsieur Eiffel told me, "who sees beauty in her environment—you look up at that blue sky, you smell the blossom-scented air, and hear the faint buzzing of the bees. There is so much beauty all around."

In the distance we could see the tower where Jeanne d'Arc had been imprisoned.

Monsieur Eiffel chatted amiably with our hostess who told us a few stories concerning Jeanne d'Arc's life which history has failed to record. She showed us her most cherished possession, a rosary she kept in a little tin box that she said was used by Jeanne d'Arc. She insisted that it had the power of consolation, however great the sorrow may be, and I believed her.

৩০০৪

If I had not made pictures on film, I would have made pictures on canvas. Monsieur Eiffel, as well, had spent his life making art out of iron. But few people know he was quite a good painter. He perceived in me those artistic inclinations he had in himself, and he insisted that I should see Italy and that he would take me.

"Italy and Spain," he said, "are the choicest depositories of art. Italy is regarded as the world's center of art, but there are some very famous pictures in the galleries of Spain, such as the paintings of the great Murillo, famous for his Madonnas."

I remember how excited I was the day before we left on our trip to Italy. Everyone in Paris vacations in August. Even Monsieur Gaumont went to the vacation home of the Lumière brothers. It was the last day in July, when the thermometer was at 95 degrees, my desk was stacked head-high with papers to be disposed of that day, the two telephones were ringing fiendishly, and everything went wrong. I worked hard in order to get ahead with my office duties. After Monsieur Gaumont left, I locked the door and left the frenzy behind.

A couple traveling for pleasure have nothing to do but enjoy each other's society, and the novelties they see together add to their enthrallment.

Monsieur Eiffel owned a splendid yacht, the *Aida*, big enough to sail anywhere in any waters by its competent crew.

"Let me show you to the galley," he said as he led me below decks."

"Here it is, every convenience. The best range made, china from the finest manufacturers, and all the necessary cooking utensils."

Also below decks was a dining room—for those occasions when we might not want to dine on deck—a round mahogany table and a sideboard to match.

"You have a library on board!" I said. It was a beautiful library, too, with elegant bindings on the books.

Our voyage to Italy consumed eight days, during which the weather was delightful, the sea smooth, and the nights moonlit from start to finish. We left from Beaulieu-sur-Mer, near Cannes, where Monsieur Eiffel kept his yacht.

At the time of this journey, the foliage on the multitude of hills surrounding us was of many colors. We would sit on the guards during the day looking out upon the ever-changing panorama, passing under some high bluffs and then sailing by some verdure-clad hills. In the evening, we would stay up on the deck to watch the lights on the shore go by.

Monsieur Eiffel was not a globe trotter, and he had no interest in traveling for the sake of saying he had traveled. He had intellectual tastes, and liked to visit the principal points of interest. He took two hotel rooms in Florence for us and was familiar with the city and all its art treasures.

We took breakfast together on the hotel piazza, and then roamed the wonderful countryside in a carriage. He found pleasure, as I did, in the relaxation of country hills.

In the afternoon, he introduced me to the rich art collection that is housed there. The former palaces, Pitti and Uffizi, are now picture galleries separated by the Arno River, connected by an ancient bridge, the Ponti Vecchio, still crowded with merchants.

We sauntered through the galleries of that ancient city and admired the works of art together. In the Uffizi, Monsieur Eiffel paused before one of Botticelli's Madonnas.

"This so reminds me of you," he said.

We went behind the Pitti Gallery to the Boboli gardens where the medieval method of cultivating flowers is still employed. The perfume alone is conducive to romance.

The next day, we rested from our sight-seeing. Seeing the artworks made him want to paint me, and I was a very good model. I could hold a pose for an astonishing length of time.

Mademoiselle Alice

I arrayed myself in spotless white, clinging drapery that showed my figure off to the best advantage. My coiffure was of the simplest.

"Paint me as I am," I said to him. "Don't flatter me. If you make a Madonna out of me, I will not like it."'

"I was going to paint you as the Saint of the Lilies," he said.

"You better not!"

"You'll make a very good saint," he teased.

After peering into each other's faces for hours, we quite naturally became quite enthralled with each other. I was as much absorbed in the artist as the artist was absorbed in his painting.

When the picture was finished, I did not think it looked like me at all, but it was a beautiful picture. He later placed it in a conspicuous place in his home, and it was much admired, but nobody recognized it as my portrait.

We visited what galleries there were, went where we could listen to music, and when we were tired of walking, we sat on the hotel piazza reading together from the works of our favorite poets.

In the evening, we walked along the Arno embankment. When the lamps are lighted there, it is as near a fairyland as any scene that can be produced.

We went to the opera at the *Teatro della Pergola*. *Faust* was given and given beautifully. Monsieur Eiffel sat entranced by the music, and he seemed also under the spell of that legend which contains the story of humanity in condensed form.

After the opera, we rode back to the hotel. We went to the lounge where he ordered a cognac.

"I feel," he said, "that I am Faust and that Mephistopheles is dragging me to hell."

"And by the same passion he secured Faust's soul?"

"Yes."

"And who," I asked, as if I did not know, "is Marguerite?"

I spoke the words so low as only to be heard by one who is intent on hearing them. His hand was near mine and he took it in his.

"You are my Marguerite," he said in a whisper, "you little humbug!"

I laughed, knowing that he meant that he was besotted with me, and not that I was destroying him. Monsieur Eiffel spoke about his love for me, such love as pertains to the emotions without any reference to marriage.

"So, goodnight, my beloved," he said as he tenderly kissed me.

ഔരു

Next, we travelled to Bellagio. The hotel where we stayed was on the very edge of Lake Como, the water splashing against its marble porch. On the evening of our arrival we dined at one of the tables there.

The lake was surrounded by mountain peaks, which stood out in bold silhouette against the twilight. On the opposite shore, village lights glimmered on the line between the base of the mountain and the lake. We drank champagne and chatted merrily.

The next morning, Monsieur Eiffel hired one of those delightful little boats abounding on Lake Como, furnished with cushions and a canopy, to say nothing of a boatman to do all the work. The boatman jogged along over the water which splashed softly against the boat. The reflection of the mountains trembled in the lake.

And then there was Rome, the Eternal City. Monsieur Eiffel had been there before, and was well versed in its history. He took me to the top of the Pincian Hill to show me the panorama of the city. Then he took me to the Forum, the Coliseum, the baths of Caracalla, and all the while he made these structures live again with the people of earlier times.

He told me stories, pointing out different objects of interest within view, and naturally I listened to it all with rapture.

We reached Sorrento on one of those afternoons when the Mediterranean reflected a perfect blue sky. This famous resort town is built on a cliff several hundred feet high. The hotel was surrounded by orange groves, a bounty of fragrant fruit on every tree.

On a road winding up the cliff, a short distance from our hotel, was a square cupola overlooking the bay and surrounding mountains. We sat on that balustrade together under the queen of the night. As she caused the tides to ebb and flow, she also drew our hearts together.

Below was the water, to the north the isle of Capri, and to the west the cone of Vesuvius, a faint trail of smoke hanging over its summit.

Monsieur Eiffel described that scene nearly twenty centuries before when, in the lurid light of the fires emitted by Vesuvius, the fleeing Pompeiians struggled in darkness under a cloud of ash. Monsieur Eiffel spoke of the artifacts that had recently been discovered of that horrible night when parents, children, and lovers lost one another in the darkness.

"Neither success nor riches bring happiness," he concluded. "Just two things count for much in this world: kindly deeds and love."

Sometimes, something very big will fail to move me, and sometimes a very little thing will give me the emotion of my life.

I could well feel the losses of those people of Pompeii, the unluckiest of all people, centuries before, but I did not want to. I was in love, and the man I loved was with me. In that moment, that was all I needed to be happy.

Chapter 25

WHENEVER THE GAUMONT company needed to expand its facilities, a meeting of the partners was called and a request for investment by all of them was made. In the end, though, it was usually Monsieur Eiffel who came up with most of the needed capital to build a studio, and the one that they built near the Buttes Chaumont park was like a glass cathedral.

I thought it was a wonderful idea to put opera on film, however, it was not my idea to build a stage similar to that of the opera house, with its flying bridges, trap doors, inclined floors, and assorted gadgets dear to the heart of an engineer.

The floor to the Paris opera stage is inclined five percent to enable the audience to better see the performance, but since the motion picture camera can be placed higher than the eyes of an audience, this was unnecessary and somewhat hazardous for the players.

Monsieur Eiffel loved the opera. He had engaged opera singers to sing at his daughters' weddings and at his birthday celebrations. His yachts were named after his favorite operas, *La Valkyrie* and *Aida*.

It was only natural for him to invite opera singers to come to the studio to be filmed. This is where we produced many scenes from operas. The arias were recorded, and then the films of the performers were made separately, synchronized with the music.

It was not yet possible to film the entire opera in one piece, but I liked to assemble a number of these musical films to create a condensed version of an entire opera—for example, *Mignon*, the story of a little girl who is separated from her parents when she is stolen by gypsies. Her mother dies of grief and her father almost loses his reason. He joins traveling minstrels and looks for his abducted daughter. Mignon grows into a young woman and is made to dance by a cruel man who beats her with a stick. When Mignon is a young woman, her father finally finds her again, identifying her when he hears her recite a prayer that she learned when she was small.

ଥଠ

Monsieur Eiffel was very versatile. He was the best whist player, the best billiard player, the best horseback rider, the best swimmer, and the best fencer. The days of dueling had long passed in America, but it lingered in France and Germany.

From a child born at a time when the military was the only profession for a country boy, Monsieur Eiffel had learned the art of fencing. His father had been a military man in Napoleon's army, and had sent his son to the University at Heidelberg for a short time. There he had joined the dueling corps and had shown a special facility for handling the sword. He had worsted one antagonist after another and, shortly before leaving the university, had been declared the champion of the corps. The members of this dueling corps proudly exhibited a distinctive scar on their cheek called a *schmitte,* or bragging scar.

Monsieur Eiffel's hand-eye coordination, his steady nerves, and his skill had rendered him remarkable in fencing. Physical strength had little to do with his success. It was all art. Often of an afternoon he would challenge one of the numerous sportsmen of Paris to a friendly contest with foils and he would usually come out the victor.

Because Monsieur Eiffel had gone on to a civil engineering career, he had no wish to look like a gangster. This was the reason he always wore an artistic Van Dyck beard: it concealed a great scar that lay across his cheek.

One memorable afternoon, Monsieur Eiffel led me to a fancy restaurant, the *Ambassadeurs,* for luncheon. A gentleman at the neighboring table turned to look at Monsieur Eiffel with wondering eyes, and exclaimed loud enough for all to hear, in a deprecating voice, with a foreign accent:

"*La tour Eiffel!*"

Now Monsieur Eiffel was a dapper gentleman, always fastidiously groomed, and sensitive on one subject and one subject only: his height. He was five feet five inches tall and it was clear to all observers that the man at the next table had insulted him.

Monsieur Eiffel whipped out a card with his name on it and flung it down on the neighboring table.

"What have you done?" the man's companion exclaimed. "Don't you know who that gentleman is? He is Monsieur Eiffel, the best swordsman in France!"

The man thought over his position.

"If you do not apologize," his friend told him, "according to the code, you must fight."

"What code is that?" the man asked, mystified. The *code duello* is well known to every Frenchman.

"He challenged you," his friend informed him. "Therefore you have the choice of weapons—pistols, foils, any weapon you like. You also have to choose the time and the place of combat."

"I choose feather dusters," the man said, and then he apologized. Needless to say, the duel did not take place.

Monsieur Eiffel could be stubborn and pugnacious when there was something to be stubborn and pugnacious about, but usually he was easy going and gentle. I have never known a nature like his, strong and dominating, yet with such personal charm of manner that it never occurred to me to dispute his word, or perhaps I had no wish to do so. His masterfulness swept away all my objections.

If it was chilly and I was wearing a gossamer wisp of a dress, he would not hear of my leaving behind my coat. He held it open for me and buttoned it up to the chin. Then he tucked me most comfortably into his car.

"How's that?' he asked, "comfy?"

Invariably, when he took me to lunch or dinner, he did all the ordering.

"You look a little thin," he would reply to my protestations. "You need more than lettuce and anchovies to keep yourself healthy."

Then he would order me a huge steak, some fine vegetables, and a good pudding for dessert.

"You eat that," he commanded, "all of it."

"Aren't you the dictatorial one," I said.

"I have found it is the best policy when I know I am right. You can tell me if I'm wrong."

But I didn't because I knew he was right.

Mademoiselle Alice

ଊଓ

Travel films were exceedingly popular, supplementing the adventure fiction that had sparked the imagination of armchair travelers ever since the railroads and steamships made travel possible for almost everyone. It was Monsieur Gaumont's idea to obtain travel films in Spain, and so I was sent there along with Anatole Thiberville, a cameraman who had been operating the motion picture camera from the start of the Gaumont company.

It was my idea to use this trip to obtain the scenes necessary to create a film version of the story of *Carmen*, Bizet's splendid opera.

The very mention of Spanish place names conveys magic and romance: the storied Alhambra, the stately Alcazar of Grenada, the magnificent cathedral of Seville, the famed Giralda, the royal palace of Madrid, the monastery on Montserrat—all are artistic treasures and symbols of a rich history.

The breeze in Seville is laden with the perfume of a thousand orange gardens. I shed tears of rapture when I beheld the Golden Tower, an ancient and enormous watchtower standing on the shore of the Guadalquivir. When the sun sets, it appears to be made of pure gold.

I needed some Flamenco gypsy dancers, and I wanted to look for a girl who looked like the ideal Carmen. I thought I could find one among the girls working at the famous cigarette factory in Seville.

There were thousands of Carmens, or cigarette girls like Carmen, who were employed in that tobacco factory. Attired in colorful dresses and mantillas, they tucked flowers under their ears and laced them in their hair, just like the heroine of the opera. Adjoining the factory was the artillery barracks, and it was not hard to imagine an impressionable Don José fascinated by a real-life Carmen.

What attracted my attention was the number of cradles and baskets with babies. Many of the young women had a baby to take care of while they worked. Sadly, I did not find a girl that looked like my ideal Carmen. Sometimes it is possible to make movies from real life, but sometimes it is not.

❧☙

On my return to Paris, I had to contend with the foreman of the workshops, Monsieur Decaux, who was a close friend of Monsieur Gaumont's since they had worked together long before we all came to the Comptoir.

Monsieur Decaux was always in a frame of mind to undermine me. He attempted to dislodge me on numerous occasions, but was never so effective as when I was doing the work preparatory to making a series of films about Jesus' life and death.

My treasured first edition of James Tissot's New Testament, which brought to life the many scenes engraved on my imagination from my religious training, was my inspiration for this series of films. The story I read most frequently was that of Mary Magdalene, where after Jesus raises her brother, Lazarus from the dead, she expresses her gratitude and devotion by washing Jesus' feet and drying them with her hair.

We used the forest of Fontainebleau, full of romantic beauty and rocky scenery, for the scenes of Jesus in the garden, Judas' betrayal, and the resurrection.

The costumes were very expensive. They required little sewing, but many yards of fabric, lavishly draped and gathered on numerous cast members. This expense was more than I originally estimated.

But it was the scenery that threatened to put me over budget and out of favor with Monsieur Gaumont. More than twenty sets were painted based on the wonderful scenes in my New Testament. We were very proud of these sets.

What was my horror to find that, after one cold night, Monsieur Decaux had cut up the decorations, both the paintings and the frames, and used them to wrap around the pipes in the workshop that were in danger of freezing. He could have used some older scenery that had been used for earlier films, but he destroyed the scenes that had not yet served their purpose.

This was a disaster for me. Each one of the sets had to be reproduced, a full ten days of work for several employees.

When Monsieur Gaumont discovered how much I was over budget, his face was like a thunderstorm. He was not interested in the details, only in the bottom line. He frequently ridiculed art as frivolous, and told me that it was silly to apply artistic standards to picture plays.

He told me my work was useless, my aims purposeless, and my ambition not worthy of me. Finally, in a fine frenzy of rage, he fumed about the Roman arches.

"The public doesn't know the difference between one Roman arch and another Roman arch. There are Roman arches all over Paris. Why would you need to paint so many Roman arches?"

This from a man who went to church only every other Sunday.

"It is your own fault," Monsieur Gaumont told me, "for spending so much money on the sets. It was a waste of time and money."

He glowered and fumed about me to Monsieur Eiffel who, fortunately, came into the office that day. Monsieur Gaumont told him he was thinking about giving my job to someone who could stay within a strict budget.

Monsieur Eiffel was a man of wide understanding of human nature, and of extreme tact in handling the disgruntled. He was also president of the company, its largest investor, and had the power to put the brakes on Monsieur Gaumont's temper.

Behind closed doors, he spoke to Monsieur Gaumont with reason and persuasiveness to put Monsieur Decaux's malicious acts in perspective. He later told me about their discussion.

"Certainly," Monsieur Eiffel told Monsieur Gaumont, "you do not believe it is Mademoiselle Alice's fault that Monsieur Decaux destroyed her scenery?"

"It is always and only Mademoiselle Alice's fault that her films are over budget!"

"But she had to replace the scenery that Monsieur Decaux destroyed."

"She had too many sets and they were too expensive to start with, and now they are doubly so."

"I trust the quality of the scenes will make up for the loss. When the films are finished, that is when you will be able to make a final judgment."

Monsieur Gaumont went into this conference with a severe case of peeves and complaints against me, but he came out with an apology.

Chapter 26

I AM NOT ASHAMED to admit that I was a born flirt. However, I never regarded it as a serious endeavor, with object and intent. When I reached the age of twenty or so, my mother insisted that I stop flirting and get married. I promised to think about it, but before I had finished thinking about it I was twenty-five, and by the time I was thirty, I was much harder to please.

I was a little troubled by the fact that when I looked in the mirror, I saw unmistakable signs of age on my face. I was comely, but I had passed beyond what was considered the best age for a woman to marry. Had it not been for my being in love with Monsieur Eiffel, I might have been married long before.

Coincidentally, because of the cool demeanor I acquired over the years, none of the young men of my acquaintance aspired to my hand. All the men seemed to have grown backward, and were nothing but boys. I rather prided myself on my aloof attitude toward young men—I was simply indifferent to every one of them.

Then one morning, I awoke to the realization that I was drifting into spinsterhood. This prospect did not please me. In my childhood, I had been long deprived of that affection which exists in families, and I was averse to passing the latter half of my life without a husband and children.

Also, the fifteen years that had passed since I had begun to emerge from childhood had brought changes in my surroundings. I was far more alone than I had been. Social life had lost its charm. Those of my friends who had married had replaced me with their children. Although they were always glad to see me, their little ones had taken my place in their hearts. Needless to say, I envied my friends their children.

I was approaching the age of thirty-three and still unmarried, whereat people wondered, and sometimes asked the obvious but unwelcome question:

"Why are you not married?"

I was in this frame of mind when I met my husband.

❧☙

"A new man came into the office today," I told my mother one evening. "I haven't seen him yet as I have been at the studio most of the time, but all the girls seem mad about him."

"I hope you will make yourself as agreeable as possible," Mother said, knowing there was little chance of my following her instructions.

As I entered Monsieur Gaumont's office the next day, I saw for the first time this fine-looking young fellow sitting in a chair in front of the desk. He was British, of that I was certain. The shaggy brown tweed of his coat and his peculiar air of detachment were my first clues. From the manner in which his legs projected beyond the chair he was sitting in, I judged him to be rather tall.

He exhibited an ease that could only come from being city-born and city-bred. His smooth hair was shiny like black lacquer, and his tiny mustache gave him a frivolous air.

I dared not stare at him, but my eyes traveled up his legs as far as they might go without an embarrassment of curiosity. He looked up at me with a captivating smile.

I did not wonder why silly girls were disposed to make fools of themselves in front of him. When he looked at me out of his warm brown eyes, and smiled his confiding smile, I was seized with an irresistible desire to obtain his approval. I liked him. I liked the nice steady look in his eyes and his square chin.

"It is positively wicked," I thought, "to be so good-looking."

"This is Herbert Blaché," Monsieur Gaumont said, "just over from London. He wants to learn more about our cameras, and I have asked him to accompany you to Provence."

My usual cameraman, Anatole, was sick, so it was to be my job to train Herbert, and he was happy to learn.

As I left Monsieur Gaumont's office, Herbert followed me with his melancholy eyes, full of a longing I could have understood had I been the girl who was currently tormenting him, but I was not.

He was the kind of man who always holds in his mind a competition for the prettiest girl. He was the sole judge and the contestants were girls he chanced to see anywhere. It was a game that made every day an adventure for him.

Thus, the day he met me, he regarded me as so gracefully proportioned, so fresh of face, so sweet of smile and soft of hair, that I won the contest. At that moment, he probably thought I was the prettiest girl he had ever seen. He was no doubt drawn to me on account of the feminine mold in which I was cast rather than by my mind or aspirations.

The railway trip to Provence took the better part of a day. After some leafy towns came valleys white with cherry blossoms. When I wasn't looking out the window or reading my book, I could not help glancing at Herbert occasionally, and I had to admit that he had a casual, devil-may-care attitude and modesty uncharacteristic for someone so good to look upon.

Whether or not he was encouraged by my occasional glances, or because he admired me, too, he gazed at me continually as we made the journey to Provence.

"I beg to offer an apology," he confessed, smiling at me whimsically, "for looking so intently upon you. You excited my admiration the moment I saw you."

"No apology is necessary," I said, and went back to reading my book. He seemed a little piqued that I paid so little attention to him. I was always polite to him, of course, but there was a reserved air about me which I am sure nettled him. I treated him with a sweet friendliness that was maddening to him as well as disheartening.

I knew we were in an ancient part of France when I saw an increasing number of limestone temples and aqueducts, a medley of Roman ruins. The train slowed as we neared the station.

I had never before been to Provence, and its scenery was unlike any other I had previously regarded as beautiful. It was not the beauty of the mountains and forest, but of the desert, with its austere lines, its low, red hills in the distance, tufted by olive trees and vineyards.

Stepping off the train, the warm fragrance of the sunflowers and lavender, together with their glorious colors, gave me the sensation of stepping from a cool and mechanical world into one of warmth and abundance.

The landscape and the heat tempt one into idleness, but the mistral, a gusty wind from the north, drives the residents out of Eden into homes with thick walls and tiny windows. The mistral passes by leaving implausibly blue skies and diamond-bright light.

Having arrived in Nîmes, Louis Feuillade, Herbert, and I took a carriage from the train to a hotel with a large patio. Englishmen are great walkers, and while Louis napped, Herbert and I spent a pleasant excursion visiting various points of interest in the vicinity. Herbert had been educated in nearby Montpellier, and acted as my tour guide. That was the beginning of our acquaintance.

Herbert propounded some leading questions, the replies to which convinced him that I would be glad to see as much of him as he liked during our stay. Herbert touched my heart by declaring that he was in a lonely condition. At the time, I failed to remember that, in his case, this condition was easily remedied. Still, in a way, I remained far removed from him in attitude and confidence. Like a dream maiden, I walked at his side, my thoughts elsewhere.

The next morning, we were to film the spectacle of the bullfight, and before this there was the ritual running of the bulls down the streets of Nîmes. It was during this event that fate stepped in once again to play one of her tricks. Events followed in such quick succession, I can scarcely separate them.

The bulls were shepherded by guardians holding pitchforks at the ready, riding milk-white steeds. We trudged alongside the bulls, the fiery face of the sun beating down on our bare heads. Herbert and I, walking together absorbed in our conversation, failed to notice that we had found ourselves along the inside of a fence.

I had just opened my collar and raised my sleeves in deference to Old Sol, and I was looking up at the sky over which white clouds were sailing lazily. The next moment, a death-dealing force was driving at us from behind. A deep shadow, accompanied by the sound of horse's hoofs, caught Herbert's attention. Glancing behind him, he saw a furious bull running toward us. Seizing me roughly by the arms—I was slight and he was strong—Herbert fairly tossed me up over the fence, then got over himself without a moment to spare.

The bull bellowed angrily as he covered the ground between us with amazing speed in so clumsy a beast. We had barely made it to the other side of the fence when the great black bull charged it with all his strength. The bellowing animal rushed the fence like a whirlwind, thankfully, to no avail. In all my life, I have never felt such sudden, life-threatening fright as I did at that moment.

One of the guardians, who had also seen the errant bull, galloped toward us. He could not change an angry bull into a lamb with a blue ribbon, but he had that pitchfork. The bull lifted his ugly black head and rolled his bulbous eyes toward the pitchfork, feigning indifference.

The bull stopped charging the fence, his angry bellow diminishing to a low mutter. He looked at us through the fence as though he was merely curious as to why we had invaded his domain. He pawed the ground a few times, evidently satisfied with being left supreme, and walked away.

I looked at Herbert and swayed slightly toward him with the power of the emotion that held me. Herbert, seeing that I was about to faint, sprang swiftly forward. I slipped straight into his arms and found myself caught firmly by a hold that promised to last forever.

I am sure I passed out for a few moments.

The next thing I knew, I was looking up into Herbert's anxious eyes. His hands were clasped under my shoulders, his face not far distant from mine. It was then that I realized I was holding him in a frantic embrace.

"Are you hurt, *mon cherie*?" he asked.

"No," I said, "but what a harrowing experience!"

"Thank goodness I was on the spot," he said fervently.

Perhaps it was propinquity, my liquid eyes, my pink lips so near his own, or perhaps it was the realization that words are a poor medium for expression. For whatever reason, he drew me nearer to him and kissed me. Then there was a little cluster of kisses after which we proceeded to the bullfight.

I admit I failed to fully recover my equanimity. I was half sobbing, silly with gratitude to Herbert because he had saved my life

Six bulls were killed that day, the spectacle of which unleashed a torrent of emotion in me. I was crying and hiding my face from the horror. Some people were laughing at me, but Herbert was solicitous. I could not help but remember the admonitions of Grandmère, so simple and true: be kind to the dumb animals. At the same time, I could imagine those animals taking their vengeance on my own body.

Later that evening, our crew gathered at the hotel patio restaurant for *soupe pistou* served family-style with toasted bread and tumblers of rosy wine.

The twilight cast a golden glow on our party. Herbert presented the picture of serene relaxation in an immaculate white flannel suit, his mandolin in his lap, singing pleasant songs in a melting baritone.

We watched the evening sky fill with stars while Louis Feuillade recited some verses from the Nobel prize-winning poem, *Mireille*, which we were to begin filming the next day.

In epic fashion, it begins with the words: *I sing of a maiden of Provence and of her girlhood's love.* It is a pathetic tale, and glows with images of the strange and lovely landscape of Saintes-Maries-de-la-Mer.

ೞଔ

Through fields of gray-green artichokes, we traveled further south to where the Rhone separates and forms a large delta called the *Ile de la Camargue*, a vast and sandy desert broken by lagoons, sparsely clothed in coarse grasses.

We went all the way, seemingly to the edge of the world, to the seaside village of Saintes-Maries-de-la-Mer, a toy town of white-walled and red-roofed houses, where the fierce sun and fiercer wind forces the sprinkling of trees into odd shapes. The endless sweep of land and sea, arched over by an opalescent dome of sky, gave me a curious sense of grandeur and desolation.

Our host was the colorful Marquis Baroncelli-Javon who greeted me with a lordly bow and swoop of his hat. He had a large ranch house, called *Mas de l'Amarée*, on the edge of the village. Ten slender-limbed white horses, for which the Camargue is known, were stabled next to the house.

The Marquis, a scholar of the language, traditions and history of Provence, was both a poet and a cowboy.

"These horses were born," he said "from the foam of the sea which deposited Aphrodite on the beach."

"There's so much marshland," I said, "where do they run?"

Mademoiselle Alice

"They tread the salt water marshes with ease—they are believed to have descended from the watery steeds who powered Neptune's chariot."

The Marquis was so very gallant and gracious to us perhaps because he was a close friend of Frederic Mistral, the author of the poem I had come to picturize.

"Would you be so kind," I asked him, "as to allow us to film a few scenes on your property?"

"My home is yours," he said. "I would like to compliment you on your noble choice of subject. There is only one place, where this story can be brought to life, and that is right here. This landscape is the stage on which tragedies written by God himself are played."

The ground floor of his ranch house consisted of a large dining room filled with the rustic furniture associated with Provence. Adjoining it was a kitchen. Halfway up the stairs leading to the bedrooms, was a window which presented a magnificent panorama of the sea and the Camargue.

It was indeed a wonderland. The light changed magically, in ever-varying pastel colors. Rising in the not-too-distant blue of sea and sky, was the church of Les Saintes Maries with its Roman belfry and buttresses. As if drawn by a magnet, Herbert and I walked down a sandy path to that lonely, tenth-century church.

We crossed a white bridge that stretched across the salt marsh. As a matter of fact, it had never been painted, that bridge, but after years of exposure to wind and weather, the wood had taken on a soft gray tint that blended with the silver tide ebbing and flowing under it.

Flights of wild flamingos soared above us in glorious clouds of pink, dazzling to view. It seemed to me that Herbert and I were drawn nearer together by the vast expanse of land, sky, and water all around us.

From olden times, gypsies have come from all parts of Europe to this village by the sea to pay their devotion to the two Marys—mothers of the apostles, John and James—also to Saint Sarah, their devoted servant.

The legend is that the three women were sent away from Egypt during a tempest, cruelly, in a boat with no oars and no sails. It is said that the waters were suddenly calmed, and an azure path opened before them. Sarah held up her apron as a sail, and a divine wind gently guided them to Saintes-Maries-de-la-Mer.

When the gypsies make their pilgrimage each year, figures of the saints standing in a little boat are held aloft and brought down to the water to bless the sea.

The story of *Mireille* is just as beautiful, but ends tragically. It was made into a wonderful opera by Charles Gounod which Monsieur Eiffel and I saw performed at the Opéra-Comique.

Mireille is fifteen. Her parents introduce her to three wealthy suitors, but she loves poor Vincent, the son of a basket weaver. The difference in wealth is too great, and her parents violently oppose their union. One day, the maiden, in despair, rushes away from home across the island of Camargue to the Church of Saintes-Maries-de-la-Mer to meet her lover and to pray that her parents will change their minds. Distraught and in haste, Mireille has forgotten to wear a hat. Under the Provençal desert sun, she suffers from sunstroke and dies in Vincent's arms.

ಬಂಧ

Mademoiselle Alice

Our last night in Provence was calm and beautiful with a pale moon rising out of the east like a bride behind a cloudy veil. We sat outside, drinking rosé in the changing light. The surrounding lagoons danced constantly with the fevered breath of mirages, not unlike the *ignis fatuus* of my childhood. Stone walls appeared to rise out of the marshy plain giving the impression of a sunken city springing from the water.

The next day, we finished our work and took the train back to Paris. Herbert immediately went on to Berlin where the Gaumont company had opened a new office where he was to be assistant manager.

I did not think I would ever see Herbert Blaché again, but I knew then, and nothing has altered my view since, that we are only toys in the hands of destiny.

Chapter 27

A FEW WEEKS LATER, pursuant to Monsieur Gaumont's orders, I traveled from Paris to Berlin in a second-class coach. Strangers on the train were talking very earnestly in German, a language I did not understand.

Arriving in Berlin, it was the same story. The streets were crowded with soldiers as though it were a garrison town. I was hedged about by men who wore brass-buttoned jackets with insignia on their collars. I could not help but notice the ritual fencing scars on their faces and felt like the alien being that I was in that country.

Herbert Blaché fetched me to help him explain how to work the Gaumont Chronophone to our new German clients. Herbert translated my French into German for their nodding approval.

Then Herbert took me sight-seeing, and as I have said before, two people with nothing to do but sight-see are in a fair way likely to fall under each other's influence. There is something unifying in being thrown together in a foreign country. We visited coquettish little towns along the Rhine, full of half-timbered houses and vineyards, transporting me to

Mademoiselle Alice

the pages of a story book. The good villagers in their embroidered costumes pursued humble crafts such as wood carving and pottery.

In this romantic ambience, I shared with Herbert the many problems I had working under the thumb of Monsieur Gaumont. When I told Herbert about the incident with the Tissot-inspired scenery that Monsieur Decaux destroyed, and about Monsieur Gaumont's desire to blame me for the cost of it, he said:

"Monsieur Gaumont dislikes anything that is frivolous, whatever, in his view, does not strengthen the mind."

We were the only two people from the Gaumont company in Berlin for a week. I was concerned at the equivocal position in which I had been placed, being a single woman alone with a single man. Everyone back in Paris knew how handsome and charming Herbert Blaché was, and I was afraid they would gossip.

I told Herbert that the circumstances in which we were thrown together would not preserve us from scandal.

"They should preserve us," he agreed, "but they will not."

"There are always some people," I said, "who will take advantage of such a situation and cast a slur."

"What do you propose to do about it?" he asked.

"I have no idea," I said.

"There is but one recourse for us," he said conspiratorially.

"What?"

"To be engaged."

"Engaged in what?"

"Engaged to be married."

"To be married?" I replied. "Don't be silly. That would just make it worse. Aren't you the rash and romantic one," I added half-joking, "to propose marriage to a woman of whom you know nothing!"

"We met an entire month ago!" Herbert said emphatically, and I laughed. "Marriage," he said, "often unites two people who scarcely know each other."

"Don't you care to learn about my antecedents?" I asked.

"No, I do not wish to marry your antecedents. I know you have character and refined tastes, and I am willing to risk the rest. Anyway, I expect to be a much better man under your influence."

I admired his frankness, but it seemed to me that he was a trifle selfish.

We continued sight-seeing without further talk of marriage. I assumed it was only in jest that Herbert proposed, but in later discussions he proved to be more serious.

"I do not approve," he said over dinner, "of the ancestral custom of parents choosing mates for their children." This assertion won my respect.

"Nor do I," I said. "I am a believer in love, and that marriages should be made for love."

"On the other hand," he argued, "I do not believe that, however long a man is acquainted with a woman or vice versa, that they can learn the other's good and bad qualities. To discover each other's good and bad qualities, they must be married for some time."

I realized then that Herbert was proposing again, that he was actually making an argument for marrying me.

"It is only natural," he continued, "that I should take pains to conceal my faults, and wish to appear to you in as favorable a light as possible. Therefore, you have gained only a superficial knowledge of my character."

"That is certainly true of me as well," I said.

"I propose a trial engagement of six months," he said. "I will agree to show myself to you just as I am, if you pledge yourself to do the same."

"Did you not just say that we can never really know each other without having lived together as man and wife?"

"I did," he said laughing.

"In that case," I said, also laughing, "I see no hope for marriage in our case."

"My disappointment is very great."

"I know you are a gentleman and I think you must be a good man."

"You are not certain?"

"I am deeply touched," I said, "by the compliment you pay me. I am not surprised that you look upon marriage as a leap in the dark. I have always considered it so, and perhaps that is the reason why I am not yet married."

I did not wish to say that I was not in love with him and could not make any promises.

Herbert continued to argue amicably weighing bachelor life against married life and, to his credit, he found the advantages and disadvantages of equal weight. On one side, there was someone to tie to. On the other side, there was the threat of loneliness that increases with age. He granted that if a marriage turned out happily, the advantages outweighed the disadvantages, but if the marriage failed, it was unbearable.

"But, you see," I said rather definitively, "I may not marry."

Herbert did not ask me to explain why. No, he was a wise young man and accepted my decision cheerfully.

"A beautiful woman such as yourself may or may not, as she chooses."

Mademoiselle Alice

ଛଓ

On my way back to Paris, I considered my situation. Herbert had offered me his troth and I had neither declined nor accepted him. I had not declined him decisively because I was not sure that I wouldn't regret having done so if I did, and I had not accepted him because I did not feel as I expected to feel had I been stricken by Cupid.

I loved the idea of marriage, but I also loved my work. My writing and film-making, my dear friends with whom I collaborated and worked in the studio, were a big part of my life. I was neither a clinging vine nor the independent type.

Now, how is a girl to be sure of her heart? She might say yes one day and be filled with regret the next.

Back in Paris, the picture postcards came thick and fast after that—letters, photographs, and bulging little packages—all addressed in Herbert's bold hand.

I became rather cross and fretful, which condition was not ameliorated by my mother, who liberally showered reproaches upon me when she learned that I had not accepted Herbert's suit.

"You are wasting your opportunities," she said. "You won't always be young. One by one these young men who wish to marry you will begin to drop off until they are all gone. And then what will you do?"

"I'll make sure the last one doesn't get away."

I was flippant with my mother, but her astute observations made more of an impression on me than I cared to acknowledge.

"This idea of marrying," she said, "without giving due consideration to practical realities pertains to the young and foolish, where romance is more important than common sense."

"I am not in love with Herbert, Mother."

"I promise you, these light romantic visions of yours will vanish in the reality of sensible devotion."

I remembered an earlier occasion when my mother spoke to me about the unlikelihood of my marrying Monsieur Eiffel, telling me that when a gentleman becomes devoted to a girl beneath him in station, only trouble results. I resented this because what she meant by station was yearly income or an inherited fortune. What woman has yearly income to match a man's? I turned a deaf ear to what she said, so infatuated was I with the man who was charming me.

"You have always had the cart before the horse," Mother insisted. "The courtship begins after the engagement."

As it did in your case, I thought, but I did not say it. My mother's suggestions were rather too businesslike for someone like me who had such romantic dreams of the man I should love and marry.

But as the summer months went by, her tone became unusually strident.

"How much money did your father leave you? Nothing. How much do you suppose you will have when I die? Again, nothing."

When the first crisp days of autumn came, Herbert returned to Paris to work in the Paris office, and to renew his impressions on me. He courted me with British determination.

I had merely intended to drift into a mutually helpful companionship. I knew that I had several years beyond him, not only by actual count, but in experience, yet Herbert charmed and refreshed me. I looked up into his face and drank in his frank regard for me.

"I want a wife now," he said in a persuasive voice, "one who in the future will realize that she was the inspiration for all my success. I don't want to look back when I get older and remember a lonely struggle. I want my wife to share all of the building with me. Life must be a thing of partnership if it is to be a happy one."

His lips were smiling but his eyes reflected unwavering purpose. I smiled at him, still uncertain.

"I love you, *mon cherie*," he said, "but if you will not marry me now, I will not ask you again."

I believe I unwittingly nodded a yes.

"You are mine and I am yours forever, *mon cherie*," he said, adopting a masterful tone and kissing my hand.

My ill-advised flirtations, not my favorite subject, had never led to marriage before, or even an engagement.

"So, it is written that we shall marry," he concluded happily. After he left, I said:

"I know I ought to love him, Mother, but I just can't make up my mind."

"It is difficult," she said, "but, after all, Herbert is a thoroughly good man, and I promise you within a year or two you will be living contentedly."

"Yes," I sighed. "I suppose after a few years together, it is all the same, so long as one marries a considerate type of man."

My mind was taken over by a mysterious melancholy, illuminated by occasional flashes of high spirits. It did seem absurd to decline Herbert's offer. He was a pleasant and gentlemanly fellow with delightful manners. There was nothing against him.

I guess I'm engaged. I thought. *How delightful!*

And then I was plunged into an emotional dungeon. Why this curious complexity of emotions? And the answer flashed across my mind as a meteor flashes across the sky: I was in love with Monsieur Eiffel and I was engaged to Herbert Blaché.

I groaned deeply on this. For the briefest moment, I had gloated over the hopeless agony that Monsieur Eiffel would suffer when he learned of my engagement. Then I began to be sorry for him and by the time I turned off the light and got into bed I was crying and saying to myself: "What am I doing? What am I doing?"

I resolved to speak to him as soon as possible.

ಬಂಡ

After several nights of tossing and turning, I came to the conclusion that I must marry in order to have a home and children. My mother had convinced me that, plainly, Monsieur Eiffel's comfortable unmarried state was well-established. Between us was a romance, but what had it led to? I needed a man who would go to business in the morning and return in the evening to play with our children. So what if I wasn't head-over-heels in love? I could lavish my excess affection on my children. But this was not altogether satisfactory to me. What if I could marry Monsieur Eiffel and have children with him? That was what I really wanted.

Monsieur Eiffel never mentioned to anyone his age unless he was required to legally, and then he did so with a sense of irritation. He looked many years younger than he was and he often heard his well-meaning friends remark: "It's a wonder you never remarried."

The fact remained that as young as Monsieur Eiffel looked, I was still much younger than he was. Putting all that aside, Monsieur Eiffel, on a good day, could put through a complicated business deal, walk six miles in the country, eat rich food at a banquet, and listen to speeches until midnight. Then he would go home and sleep like a baby, after which he would wake up next morning feeling just fine.

At my next tête-a-tête with Monsieur Eiffel, I worked up my courage to broach the subject of marriage.

"Why can't we marry?" I asked him. "We can never be sure of anything."

"We can be sure that people die when they get older," he said.

"But you always say that good health is the greatest blessing in the world."

"Yes, but here I am priding myself on keeping young, and at the same time breaking out all over with the symptoms of age."

I began crying hysterically like the child that I always was with him. He put his arms around me.

"Don't cry little one."

"Nobody takes you for a day over sixty," I told him, laughing, in spite of my tears.

"I am an old fool," he said, "old enough to be your father."

"But you are not my father," I said pointedly.

Then I came out with the whole story about how I had met Herbert, and that Herbert wanted to marry me and that I might not be in love with him. I meant not in love with Herbert, but I think looking back on it Monsieur Eiffel took it to mean I was no longer in love with his older self.

I had no sooner spoken the words than I regretted them, first because I knew they would cause him immense pain, and second because I was sure that my heart did not gush for

Herbert the same as it had gushed for Monsieur Eiffel since I was a girl.

I knew that while the older man is not aggressive, he is still vulnerable.

With infinite melancholy Monsieur Eiffel told me that he would freely give me up to the man of my choice, and that he loved me so well that he could not stand in the way of my happiness.

"I cannot be sorry for my foolishness," he said, "because this foolishness brought me to you, and I cannot be at all sorry for your tears. Tears prove the existence of a heart."

"How can I help but love you, my dearest?" I said to him.

"I am old, child," he said sadly, "old in years with an unruly heart still young enough to love."

Monsieur Eiffel made himself scarce after that. All the while I went about wishing to tell him that I loved him, only him, had not meant what I had said, but I didn't think he would believe me, and it would not make any difference anyway. No one can be expected to believe two sides of a story coming from the same person.

⁂

I tried to make myself think that happiness with Herbert might be possible after all. I have always believed in marriage, domestic life, children, and all that. Like the heroines of the novels I had read, I naturally clung to something stronger than myself.

I let Mother do all the wedding planning.

"Madame Marier is coming tomorrow," she said, "to do the white sewing. We should finish up here and go downtown to pick out the embroidery for your petticoat."

"I can't bear the thought of fussing over a silk dress and serge suit," I said. "I don't like the conventional path for brides, the new china and silver. I want Grandmère's blue-rimmed teacups and nothing else."

Mother, who had been looking forward to these festivities with childlike anticipation, seemed disappointed. She tried to talk some sense into me.

"It's just nerves, Alice," she said. She explained that I had made a mistake in not marrying when younger, and that I should rectify that error before it was too late. Any time was time enough for marrying for companionship, but it would soon be too late to marry for children. Love after marriage, she said, was, after all, but an intensified companionship.

"Young persons haven't any sense about marriage," she said. "Girls are caught by trifles. Until they are older they don't usually realize the difference between what they call love and what they call romance."

I looked at her dolefully.

"Trust me," she said. "Herbert is a good man who will love you, and you will learn to love him. You will have a home and in time will be the mother of a happy family."

"A marriage based on common sense," she continued, "is worth a dozen based on infatuation."

I repeated my mother's advice over and over in my head, and then I made the mistake of talking sensibly to Herbert as my mother had to me. I admitted my mistake in not marrying when younger. Any time was time enough for a home but it would soon be too late for children.

Finally, Herbert said to me:

"You have convinced me. A marriage based on common sense is worth more than one based on infatuation."

The comfort of having him agree with me lasted but a moment.

"I have been considering another woman," he said. I looked at him, trying to discern his meaning.

"She is not as smart as you, but she is an excellent cook."

At last I found my voice.

"Your words are positively brutal!" I said. He burst out laughing and took me in his arms.

"Am I any more brutal than you?" he asked.

※

After the Christmas holidays, I did not relish telling Monsieur Gaumont that I was to be married, and to one of his employees, no less. Being a natural wet blanket, he tried to cast doubts on my value as a wife.

"My dear young woman," he said, "I am sure that you can understand how sometimes a man will hamper his chances by taking on the responsibilities of a wife and family."

"I will not hamper his chances," I said indignantly, not knowing what on earth he was talking about.

"Oh, pardon me. I was under the impression that you have been working in an office ever since you left school."

There was an awkward silence while I pondered why he failed to note all the work I had done creating films for his camera business.

"How long have you been working here?" he asked.

"Thirteen years."

"Do you think you are perfectly proficient in your line of work?"

"Moderately so."

"Then you have nothing more to learn?" he asked.

"On the contrary. I learn something every day."

Monsieur Gaumont, without further comment, went back to his work, and I was left feeling strangely perturbed.

Within weeks, Herbert and I were treated to a big surprise. Monsieur Gaumont was sending Herbert to the United States. Herbert had met a German orchestra conductor in London by the name of Max Faetkenheuer who expressed interest in buying a number of Gaumont Chronophones with a view to installing them in multiple theaters in the city of Cleveland.

This was more than I had bargained for, and I never felt so beside the point in my life. I could go with Herbert or stay, and Monsieur Gaumont did not seem to care one way or the other.

The truth was I could no longer endure working side by side with Monsieur Gaumont. I had stood it for almost thirteen years, and I was quite sure that much of the success of the company was due to my own discrimination in selecting subjects for our films, but he only criticized me and took all the credit himself.

In bed that night, I lay awake for a long time wondering whether it was Monsieur Gaumont's idea or Monsieur Eiffel's idea to send Herbert to Cleveland. Perhaps it was Monsieur Eiffel's intention to both get Herbert out of the way, and to tempt me into staying home. Clever man!

Like my mother before me, if I married Herbert, I would also have to leave my family, my friends, and the country of my birth.

ഈരു

Herbert was surprisingly romantic about this new adventure. He assured me it was only for a year.

"Dry your eyes, Alice," he crowed, "and just to spite Monsieur Gaumont, you go down to the office tomorrow and tell him to take his old job and give it to anyone he pleases."

In this context, the subject of my continuing to work after being married had suddenly been moved to a column entitled "optional," and Herbert revealed his preference for a home girl to one who earned her own living.

"You cannot be married," he said, "and continue in your position—at least, I would not have you do so."

I knew from bitter experience that the care of a family without adequate income is misery for all concerned.

"What assurance do I have that you will continue to earn a living?"

"If I have to pinch and struggle," Herbert said, "for comfort or even necessities, I will."

"I am afraid that when poverty comes in the door, love flies out of the window."

"Well, my answer to that is true love begets energy to provide for its enjoyment."

I wasn't used to being the practical one, but I was reassured that he was at least a romantic. There was a silence between us, which was broken by Herbert.

"I would have no respect for myself," he said, "if I loved a woman whom I could not take proper care of."

The next evening Herbert said to me: "Monsieur Gaumont is all right, after all. He called me in today and said he would give me two weeks' vacation when we are married, and five hundred francs as a wedding present."

"Isn't that splendid!" I exclaimed, my resentment toward Monsieur Gaumont abating not in the slightest.

I began preparations for my future which seemed to be taking a new turn. I indulged in a few new dresses while my mother updated all my old ones. She hemmed towels, stitched monograms on bed linen, and embroidered tablecloths and napkins for me. I would go to Herbert a well-dowered bride.

Chapter 28

I SAT IN MY BEDROOM and cried over a letter. "Dearest, I cannot bear this silence—this separation. In pity let me see you once more." The scrawl ended abruptly, and the sheet was torn off as though in haste.

It was nine in the evening. On the morrow I was to become the bride of Herbert Blaché who was a very estimable young man, and obviously in love with me.

The days had gone by so fast since my engagement that I had had little time to regret. I scarcely believed it. Me, marry? It was not until Monsieur Eiffel's letter came that the floodtide of memory came sweeping back on me: the little boat rides, lunches and suppers where we had had such intimate conversations. It had been a glimpse into a wonderful world for me. Now it was to be closed down abruptly.

I had barely seen Monsieur Eiffel since Christmas. He had little reason to visit the Comptoir or the studio. The Gaumont company had gone public in January, and the presidency of the company had been turned over to a bank.

Herbert's father had come to Paris to seal the bargain with my mother. Although I did not care to be handed over like a package, it had all been very decorous, and—well, I was to marry Herbert on the morrow.

I read Monsieur Eiffel's letter again through blinding tears. It was only a little congratulatory note saying that he was dining alone that night at the little table at Brébant's which we used to occupy, and that he would be remembering me.

The apartment was very quiet. My mother had gone to bed early in anticipation of the next day's momentous occasion. How easy it would be to escape for an hour or two, to fly to Monsieur Eiffel, to spend one last evening with him before the life ahead of me began.

With those memories of the past, I could resist no longer. I slipped on an evening dress and coat, and softly made my way to the door. The traveling bags packed for my departure, and the heavy fragrance of the white roses that had already arrived from the florist, threatened to derail my purpose, but I hurried past them until the door opened and closed behind me, and I was out.

I left my home that evening hastily and in an unenviable frame of mind. In a new wave of rebellion, it seemed to me that Mother and Herbert were too insistent in their demands for an early marriage, while I was not sure that I wanted to be married at all.

Half an hour later I entered Brébant's, and my heart leaped when I saw the well-remembered figure, my bachelor angel, solitary at the far table in the midst of a well-dressed crowd. The years I had passed in the company of this man were a dream come true for me.

He did not even start when I approached him, threw back my cloak, and sat down facing him.

"Alice, I dared to hope that you would come to me tonight," he said. "I willed it with all my heart."

"I had to come," I answered, "I could not start on my new life after I got your letter without letting you know." My voice broke indicating I was still his.

"Know what?" he asked gently.

"That I love you still," I answered. "I should not be saying this, but my marriage is not of love, on my side, at least."

"But you will still go through with it?"

"Yes," I answered, "unless you want to marry me?"

He looked at me with the concerned frown of love.

"You never were a quitter, Alice," he said.

We dined together. It was almost as merry as in the old days, for we resolved to banish all thoughts and cares of the present evil from our hearts. After the meal, we sat close together, heedless of the passage of time.

"I am glad to have seen you again, Alice," he said at length. "We had a wonderful time together. This will refresh my memory. I will carry it with me the rest of my days."

"I feel trapped somehow, with printed invitations sent out and all. There really doesn't seem to be one sensible reason why I should object to getting married."

"The only future you could have with me is taking care of me as I get older. You want to have children, Alice. You have always wanted children. I knew that when I saw your film of the couple finding a baby among the cabbages. It's all right, my dear."

The incredible thought going through my mind was that if I could stay in Paris, if I could just stay with Monsieur Eiffel, nothing could ever harm me. If I could have children with him, I would have stayed.

Then I glanced at the clock and was horrified to see that it was almost 1:00 a.m. I sprang to my feet in alarm. Trained in the ways of politeness, I could not bring myself to oppose the arrangements that had been made for me, for my future, and for my benefit.

"I must go," I said, "whether I want to or not."

He conducted me gravely from the restaurant. We were the last to leave. The yawning waiters watched us reproachfully as we went out. The street was brilliant with lights. There came the sound of music from the cabarets, and the voices of the late-night pleasure-seekers.

"That was lovely, thank you," I said wistfully.

"Yes," he said, "I shall get you a cab."

He took my hands in his and at the very last he lost his self-control.

"Stay with me, Alice," he whispered. "Stay."

The temptation was terrible. I fought it down silently before I could answer.

"It wouldn't be honorable, that's all. And I want to have children, as you said."

A mixture of misery and love was on his face.

"Of course," he said, "I want you to marry Herbert if he can make you happy, but he can't possibly love you more than I do."

"A year is not so long," I said. "It is only twelve months between now and the time I return."

"The Atlantic Ocean will be between us," he said. "I shall scratch off every day on the calendar as it passes until I see you again."

I bade him goodbye with streaming eyes and went home while he stood looking after me. When I reached a point where he would pass from my view, I looked out the window, threw him a kiss which he returned, and then he passed out of my sight.

Mademoiselle Alice

The guests numbered only a dozen, but my mother ordered a large cake, the white surface of which was covered with delicately wrought flowers and cupids of sugar. The wedding was set for noon Tuesday at the imperious looking *La Madeleine* where my parents wed.

We hear a great deal about the beatific bride and the gun-shy groom, happy nuptials, and all that. My wedding was more like going to a funeral. Dressed in white from top to toe, I clung to my mother and needed all her encouragement to induce me to marry even after all the arrangements had been made.

It was no one's fault save my own that I was in such a predicament. How different I would feel, I thought, as I fought back tears, if I was to stand at the altar with Monsieur Eiffel. But that was not to be.

I permitted my picture to be taken, hopelessness and despair there recorded.

Then I turned hot and cold, possessed of a wild desire to escape, and a still wilder one to be dragged to my fate.

"I am making a fool of myself," I thought, "and I can't stand it."

People were moving into the pews and an organ was playing softly. I could picture how dainty my mother must have looked in her bridal dress, standing beside her handsome young husband there at the lovely altar.

Then I became aware of another fly in the ointment. Where was the groom? This was the worst suspense of all, I decided, but I wouldn't cry, for I had to look nice and fresh for the ceremony.

Mademoiselle Alice

When Herbert arrived three minutes late, chords from the organ rose and rose in the almost empty church. I had no father to walk me down the aisle, and since no one could ever take his place, I disregarded all conventions and walked alone. I held a small bunch of fragrant white roses tied together with a white ribbon. Lilies of the valley fell in a lovely shower down the white satin of my dress.

A little smile ran around the faces of the guests, reminiscent perhaps of other wedding days.

Herbert took my hand and gently pulled me to his side. I stood beside him, and a man in canonicals began to read from a prayer book.

A sonorous *I do* from the groom, an inaudible *yes* from the bride, and it was all over. I still have a picture of us coming out of the church, a trail of pink bridesmaids behind us.

A slightly misty morning gave way to a beautiful day. Then there was an informal wedding breakfast, after which a party of our friends accompanied us to the railway station. They waved happy farewells with affectionate parting words, and threw rice at the windows of our coach. No tears shed, that was a blessing. It would have been a lot harder to leave home if my mother and sisters were there to make a fuss.

Having been duly married, we left on our wedding journey, a business trip to the United States. I was sailing with my husband for a distant country, which was as remote and uncertain to me as it had been to Christopher Columbus four centuries before.

Part Two

AMERICA

Chapter 29

I HAD TAKEN A MATRIMONIAL leap in the dark and Herbert suddenly seemed like a stranger to me. There was the usual bustle upon the sailing of a steamer. I stood, in deep mourning, on the deck of *La Touraine* looking out upon the landscape in which I had dreamed of so much happiness, grieving over the wreck of my hopes.

I watched the midshipmen draw in the gangplank. The time to ask myself questions was clearly over, but my mind was still turning over the same thoughts. There arose in my heart a great outcry against fate.

Was I to cross the Atlantic Ocean and leave my cat and my loved ones in the pursuit of a future, not of love, not of art, but of business? For the first time in my life, I envied my sisters because they were staying in France, spared the path of adventure so they could acquire a little furniture and a perennial garden.

It was indeed a great honor to be numbered among the Gaumont company's first business representatives in the American cities toward which we were traveling, but it was an exile from all I had known. I tried to think of it as an adventure, but the blank gray sea seemed to mirror my gloom.

As soon as we were out on the ocean, I began to feel ill. Herbert asked me if there was anything he could do, and I asked him in a coarse voice if he had any liquor. I did not normally drink hard liquor, but it seemed appropriate to the occasion. He found me some very fine brandy which he poured into a glass for me.

For the next nine days my *mal de mer* was a good cover for what really ailed me. I was disconsolate at having parted with Monsieur Eiffel—the waves, the wind, and the seagulls all kept whispering his name.

I felt wretched, and whenever Herbert left our little cabin, my eyes became misty. I kept to our cabin during the first day of the voyage, staying in my wrapper, and only later in the day went up on deck for fresh air. Getting out from the ship's smells helped me recover slightly from my *mal de mer*.

Every day was a repetition of every other: meals sitting on deck, promenades around the perimeter, and early to bed.

To take my mind off my queasiness, I tried to learn some English. I wrote a story in French about my father's experience when he was a little boy in the Swiss Alps. He had told me the gripping tale of how he was buried in the snow during a blizzard and was rescued by a noble pair of St. Bernards.

My father would have died and I would never have been born had not his parents lived practically next door to an abbey where dogs were trained for rescue work in the Alps. Fate is the strangest thing, otherwise—well, happenings would undoubtedly have been different.

Herbert helped me translate my French into English. This activity required the use of a French and English dictionary and was mercifully time-consuming.

"This would make a very good story for film," I said to Herbert.

"You would need snow," was his practical response.

"It's March. There may be snow in New York when we get there."

"Do they have St. Bernards in New York?"

"That I don't know," I admitted. "I don't think you could do it without St. Bernards. That's the whole point." I was already thinking about how I could get this story enacted when we arrived at our destination.

We fell to talking about my having given up my profession.

Herbert said to me: "You have a great deal of talent for art, but not genius, which is very rare. I know you would be disappointed in the end. It will lead you like an *ignis fatuus* to do something which will always be just beyond your reach."

"Herbert," I said, "there is one matter for us to consider, a matter to which my heart is set, upon which you seem to be indifferent, but which is liable to make trouble unless there is a distinct understanding between us."

"There is nothing to settle between us," Herbert said with his characteristic charm, "because I propose to give way to you in everything."

"That's very sweet of you," I said, "but you don't seem to realize as I do that there is a good deal that is practical in married life, and is dependent on a husband and a wife having the same views."

"That's not true in our case," Herbert said, "because, as I have told you, your views shall be my views."

There was rather too much of the brush-off in this to suit me, but since I could not find fault with it, I proceeded to explain my concerns.

"I am very much interested in the struggle for the emancipation of women that has been going on for many centuries."

"Many centuries?" he said, laughing, and making me laugh, too. "What do past centuries have to do with us? We are modern people in modern times. I have no opinion concerning it. You can have whatever opinion you like."

I ignored this as it seemed to ignore my concerns and continued to try to get to the heart of the matter.

"My mother was left penniless after many years of marriage. What is a woman to do who is left alone like that?"

Now it was his turn to ignore the harsh realities of life.

"Man," he said, "when left to himself, without a woman's influence, becomes a brute. Ergo, he can only be tamed by a woman."

"Well, then," I said, "keeping her husband tame requires a lot of time, and then there is the household to look after, and the children, and a lot of other things," I trailed off confusedly.

"I thought you were going to argue in favor of the emancipation of women? Now you are saying that a wife is too busy looking after her domestic affairs to do anything else. Following that principle, the husband makes a living and the wife takes care of the house and children." Herbert could be persuasive.

"I believe in a division of labor," I said weakly, "or if you like, another way of putting it, certain things are attended to by the wife and certain other things are attended to by the husband." I felt my mind wandering down a dark path with no direction. But Herbert was given to diplomacy rather than open opposition.

"These days," he said, "a girl has the right to choose whether she wants to devote herself to domestic matters or follow some career that she is better suited for. But, there is no use," Herbert said, picking up my hand and kissing it, "in trying to cross a bridge before we get to it, so long as our differences are settled amicably from day to day."

I could think of no reply to this.

"There are but two arguments," he said, kissing my hand again, "which count for anything between a husband and wife. Her best argument is tears and his is kisses."

It was so very nice to have a man to comfort me in my trouble, that I yielded then and there and told Herbert that it made me happy to make him happy.

"You will find, *mon cherie*," he said "many disappointments in life. How can we meet them without sympathy? Whether or not you continue to pursue your profession, at least give me the right to love you and comfort you when you are distressed."

I yielded. It was a moment of feminine weakness. As soon as I yielded, I had placed more value on his happiness than I did on my own.

๛

We steamed down the coast, and entered the lower bay of New York, making our way north toward Ellis Island where emigrants must prove that they come within the laws governing their admission to the United States of America.

We were among those transferred from *La Touraine* to a smaller ship destined for Ellis Island. Surrounded as it is by water, it is not a disagreeable place to visit. I gazed out over the bay, wondering at the gigantic Statue of Liberty, rising in the mist, and at the skyscrapers of lower New York.

Monsieur Eiffel held the distinct honor of designing the structure holding up the colossal statue, and also of being the originator of the engineering calculations that made the skyscrapers possible. Again, tears rose from my heart and gathered in my eyes at the thought of being so far from him and everything else that was dear to me.

We passed with a motley throng into a large room where emigrants present their claims for admission. After a period of waiting, we were brought before an official for examination.

"What means have you?" he asked.

"More than fifty dollars," was Herbert's answer, and it was the correct answer for anyone wanting to enter the United States as a foreigner.

"How do you expect to live here in America?"

Herbert explained our business in America, bringing the Gaumont Chronophone to Cleveland.

After we passed our examinations, a little steamer took us from Ellis Island to New York City. The passengers on that steamer spoke many languages, but there was a current of language common to all people, felt not spoken, that bubbled up between us. The optimism and happiness of the other passengers was contagious.

People of very limited means from all nations were flocking to the United States where, it was said, there were great factories, plenty of rich land, and those who were skilled received wages that were unheard of in Europe.

"The people here have no king, no nobles," said an ecstatic Norwegian passenger. "No king! Think of it! All are on the same level so far as the law is concerned."

After we debarked, and while we waited for our luggage, I looked at some picture postcards for sale. I found one with a picture of the skyscrapers in New York City. Beneath the picture was printed: "This is a dull town because you are not here."

I repressed the impulse to send it to my beloved. I concluded then that as a girl, perhaps, I had been too emotional, and now that my big love affair had been smashed into the past, I should try to eradicate emotion from my nature.

Also, I was so glad to be off that ship, I resolved that, instead of thinking about my life in Paris, I would think about how my father came to America when he was young, and had a grand adventure in spite of his many misfortunes.

※

New York was a confusing whirl from the moment we arrived, but it was a great and noisy city. The noise emanated from over the streets and under the streets. A mass of human beings rolled up and down the avenues like an ebbing tide. And all night the whirl went on with people seeking pleasure under the glow of street lights. People of all sizes, shapes, and colors poured into the restaurants and theaters, and then they poured out again.

We strolled around Battery Park which inherits its name from an old fort. A century before our arrival, the houses bordering the park were occupied by New York's most aristocratic families. But by 1907, it was intersected by an elevated railroad, and those who loitered there were mostly immigrants or persons out of work.

The glorious odor of hot coffee wafted to me from a stall where it was served in chipped cups to the down-and-outers of that neighborhood.

Then we took a stroll along the East River where the outlines of the high curving bridges were framed by lights and reflected in the dark shining water.

We stayed at one of the best hotels in New York, the Lafayette. It had an elegant dining room that served French food. The prices were staggering—twenty-dollars a day for a room and forty-five cents for a cup of coffee. But I had decided not to let money worry me too much for a few days.

Dinner cost a day's wage, but it was a great comfort for me in getting acquainted with my new surroundings.

In the morning, there was a knock at the door and it was the bellboy. No one on the European continent takes anything but rolls and coffee for breakfast, and that's what he had brought us.

The first day we bought a few clothes. After that we devoted ourselves to pleasure.

It was snowing, and I talked Herbert into letting me take my new scenario about the St. Bernards over to the Edison studio on East 21st Street to see if they would be interested in producing it. Herbert said it would be an advantageous contact if nothing else.

The men working at the Edison studio were as idle as I had predicted they would be since there are so few snow stories. They liked the idea of the children lost in the snow, but where to get the St. Bernards? One of the men had recently seen a dog show, and a pair of St. Bernards had won first prize. While they went about obtaining the St. Bernards, I played the mother, hugging my fictional children goodbye and then welcoming them back when they were found in the snow by the St. Bernards. This little film won a prize.

Chapter 30

WITHIN A FEW WEEKS, we were on a train to Cleveland. When we rolled out of New York through the outskirts of the city, I saw miles and miles of houses, throngs of people, traffic of all types, and my heart sank within me.

I was a practical girl. I had met many young men who had gone to the city to make their fortunes, some of whom came back threadbare and hungry, and some of whom never came back, but I had never heard of anyone making a fortune. Many are those who struggle in a great city and are crushed under the juggernaut. But I repressed the feeling of despondency, gritted my teeth, and resolved that I would succeed, we would succeed.

I remembered the story of Dick Whittington who went to London a poor boy, became discouraged at the sight of the great city in the distance, and started to go back to his home. Dick heard the church bells ringing, and they seemed to say, "Turn again, Dick Whittington." He changed his mind, entered the city, and became enormously rich. This story, familiar to many school children, gave me a measure of courage. When we alighted from the train, I felt strong enough to meet the tide that seemed to be rising up to oppose me.

As for my marriage, the trouble began on our wedding journey. When I was the beneficiary of the prettiest girl contest, I was flattered. But as soon as we were married, it started to grate on my nerves. Whenever we went into a restaurant, Herbert cast his eyes about to find the girl who, in his opinion, was the prettiest. Then he would take a seat at a table that seemed to be in her zone. Everywhere we went, stores, offices, train stations, he could tell you which of the girls was the prettiest.

Herbert and I set up housekeeping in a little furnished apartment in Cleveland, and it was not long before I asked fate why I could not be a happily married woman. It seemed that my days were all for my husband.

When I awoke in the morning, my first duty was to see that he had what he liked for breakfast. I poured his coffee with my own hand. While Herbert was gone for the day, I saw to it that everything was in order for when he returned. In the evening, I asked him what he wanted to do. If he wanted to go out, I went with him. If he preferred to stay home, I stayed home. It seemed to me that I was working for Herbert.

And he? He worked hard all day, from his point of view, for me. Whether he met with difficulties or success, it was all for me.

It was also depressing for me to look around our bedroom and see my clothes flung on chairs. I realized for the first time that my mother had been picking up after me my whole life. To make matters worse, when I saw Herbert pouting over his burnt toast and watery coffee, I realized I had no cooking ability whatever.

For dinner, I depended on the delicatessen. Although at first it was sort of fun, like a picnic, we soon got tired of the German sausages and potato salad which was then the *pièce de resistance* of the deli shop.

Our money was fast disappearing, and I was lonely all those long, idle days for the companionship of my comrades and co-workers, the world outside our tiny flat.

When an active mind is deprived of that which has fed it, there comes a craving for something to take its place. I began to wonder what my new vocation would be.

One evening, I broached the subject of my going back to work, and Herbert, who was ordinarily quite mild of manner, was very much insulted, actually becoming quite angry.

"I think I can support my own wife!" he said, and he wanted to know if I had already stopped loving him. Of course, that settled it. I said no more just then, but I kept longing to put my years of experience in making movies to good use.

It should not be surprising to anyone that tensions arose between us, and they all seemed to come from my doing what was expected of me. I suppose I was what was then called a New Woman: not a good thing, by Victorian standards—how dare she? But vocations of all kinds were opening to the gentler sex, and I saw no reason why a woman should not have one.

I came to the conclusion that the differences between me and Herbert had arisen long before I met him. Herbert had never known hunger. He had gone to college and his parents were both still alive. On the other hand, I was not at all confident in the cradle of this world. What would happen to me if something happened to Herbert?

Naturally, our quarrels were nearly all from want of sufficient funds. I felt that if I could at least make some money, the troubles between us might be less likely to arise.

To accommodate Herbert's ego, my new vocation had to be something that I could do at home, something that did not take me out into the business world, but kept my mind occupied. I had always loved to write and I resolved to write scenarios for American film producers, and if they did not sell, turn them into short stories and see if I could, while improving my English, sell them to American publications.

One evening, about a month after we arrived in Cleveland, Gaumont's new client, Mr. Faetkenheuer, took us to dinner at a very smart new restaurant. It happened to be an evening when I was feeling very lonely, when it seemed to me that the only solution was to pack my trunk in the morning and go straight home. But I tried hard to enjoy myself.

Mr. Faetkenheuer was looking for an idea for the grand finale for the Hippodrome he was building in Cleveland. He was planning to install a massive water feature behind the stage.

My father had told me that, in the Swiss Alps, there were mountains where there had been valleys and valleys where there had been mountains. Whole sections of land had slid down into the sea and passed out of sight. This was partly the inspiration for the spectacular that was created for opening night at the Cleveland Hippodrome. One hundred and fifty players and 450,000 gallons of water were put to use before an audience of thirty-four hundred.

Here is the story I gave to Mr. Faetkenheuer. A wedding is in progress in the Swiss Alps when a storm suddenly comes in. The wedding is ended by a realistic cloudburst. The mountain streams swell, the mill dam bursts, and an entire village is swept away. The cattle stampede, people cling to floating roofs, and men on horses plunge into the raging torrent in an effort to rescue the drowning villagers. All ends in pandemonium, men, women, and beasts fighting for their lives.

For a first night opening, it was successful, but it was much too expensive to keep staging it.

I still wonder sometimes why audiences don't seem to like happy stories of happy people living well. I believe it is because pleasant pictures put one to sleep, whereas scary or unpleasant pictures arouse a variety of sensations.

※※

By the end of the year, it was clear that the franchisee had failed to incorporate the Gaumont Chronophone into his theaters. We were out of work and almost out of money.

Herbert sent a telegram to Monsieur Gaumont who, instead of bringing us back to France, asked Herbert to find an office for the Gaumont company in New York. Monsieur Gaumont promised to send someone over to discuss expanding Gaumont's business in the United States.

Herbert's new job would be to take over the distribution of Gaumont films and continue to install the Chronophone in theaters wherever possible.

We went back to New York City where we did not know a soul. The Gaumont films and cameras were then being distributed through the Biograph company, so we went there first. Cast two people adrift in a strange country and they will make friends.

Mademoiselle Alice

The Biograph studio was on the first floor of a formerly grand brownstone mansion between Fifth and Broadway. I still remember the address, 11 East Fourteenth Street. On the first floor, there was a spacious ballroom and concert hall. There the previous tenant had exhibited and sold grand pianos. Upstairs were cheap little studios full of artists, and we stayed there in a little room on the fifth floor for a time.

It was at the Biograph studio that D. W. Griffith and I met and became friends. He had seen almost all the films from France that I could name, and he was most interested in my work for Gaumont.

D. W. Griffith, who later became one of the best directors in the United States in the silent cinema, had not yet directed his first film. He had acted, however, on the stage and then in a few films, his famous one being *Stolen From an Eagle's Nest*.

For that performance, he had been required also to discharge the duties of carpentry and sweeping, for which he was paid a total of fifteen dollars a week. Those were the days when an actor in a moving picture might play a dramatic part one day and cheerfully paint scenery the next.

Actors came to the Biograph studio in the early morning and hung around hoping to get parts. I was willing to pitch in and lend my advice, but I did not feel free to lend my name as Herbert was still working for the Gaumont company, and Monsieur Gaumont was sensitive about loyalty and his competition in the United States.

I also became acquainted with Mary Pickford who had been a child actor in the theater. She was pretty and petite; her size was in her favor. D. W. Griffith hired her for a scenario in which the heroine was in the earlier parts a child and the last act a woman.

Mary Pickford made her film debut in *The Violin Maker of Cremona*. The original play was written by a famous French author, François Coppée, and I adapted it for the screen. Scenarios were much in demand during this period since there were so few writers of picture plays who understood the practical and technical requirements of film production.

My typewriter clicked incessantly with fine plots for the movies.

I adapted a heavy drama called *Resurrection*, Tolstoy in one reel. Later that year, the Biograph players produced my scenario, *The Crossroads of Life*, about a girl who is alienated from her father because she wants a career on the stage. In the end, the girl is reunited with her father.

I was there when D. W. Griffith directed his first film with his wife, Linda Arvidson, *The Adventures of Dollie*, another one of my scenarios, about malevolent gypsies who kidnap a small child and hide her in a barrel. The gypsies put the barrel in the back of their wagon and, as they speed away, it falls off just as they drive through a stream, down which it floats. In the end, again, the little girl is reunited with her father.

"It's kind of a lemon, isn't it?" D.W. Griffith asked.

"What's wrong with it?" I asked.

"The barrel. How do you control the barrel?"

And then I explained to him that the scenes with the barrel sailing, apparently uncontrolled, down the river could be achieved with the use of the strong, but invisible, piano wire, as Alberto Santos-Dumont had done with his dirigible, and as we had done in Paris in the comedy, *Histoire Roulante, A Story Well-Spun*.

Mademoiselle Alice

Although I was a city girl, fond of city life and music and all the arts, I loved to prowl about crooked lanes and ancient landmarks to find out, as far as possible, what kind of people inhabited those parts before my time. History furnished many themes for stories, and I was constantly on the lookout for plots and mysteries to solve, odd sketches of life, moments fraught with tragedy or joy—each a drama in itself.

These months at the Biograph studio were delightful for me because I was able to throw myself back into the work of the cinema. But it turned out to be a short season because I was expecting my first baby.

When I stepped outside the door of 11 East Fourteenth Street, I was in the heart of the theater district on Union Square. I liked to walk up Fifth Avenue, the feeling of life surging and hurrying around me.

Fifth Avenue was lined with shops, costly buildings, formerly the mansions of the very rich, ablaze with banners. Every day the sidewalks of that street were crowded with pedestrians, while the flags of many nations waved in profusion overhead.

While I was walking, I would make up little romances for those among the passing throngs whose faces caught my attention.

Whoever said New York is a town of strangers was right. It's the loneliest place in the world. I found myself frequently visiting the wonderful old churches, St. Patrick's or St. Thomas's, and finding in the silent walls a great amount of spiritual help.

And then my feet led me to the old Trinity Church, that church whose doors are never shut, day or night, to the worn and weary. I sat down inside and gazed at the wonderful windows, and my eyes rested on the one above the altar.

I stared at the Virgin Mother with her child in her arms, and my tears came unheeded. I remembered how Grandmère had petted and loved me when I was a baby, guarding me from all trouble and care. I prayed that my child would have a childhood similar to the early years I'd had with my grandmother, years of love, stability, and peace.

Chapter 31

THE FIRST BABY is the first chain to truly bind a married couple. In those days, husbands were made to wait in the waiting room while their child's birth was attended to by others.

After our baby was born, I saw the door of my hospital room slowly open. Then Herbert looked cautiously around the door with half his face, as if fearing to disturb me. The sight of me lying there with a little sleeper nestled up against me was too much for Herbert. With tears streaming down his face, he walked over to my bed and took me and our baby together in his arms.

I named our beautiful little girl Simone. Simone sounded so prettily romantic. I hoped that my little girl would know in childhood a real home and a united family, the human essentials I had been obliged to forego.

There is no magic of healing like that held in the hands of a child. Doting on our little girl, we naively had no fear of future disappointments. They would come, but the thought of our little one, we both believed, would ease their harshness.

We did not then count on the cold, gray dawn of the morning after.

The next six months were most difficult for me. I was not very strong, and the care of Simone, who was a lusty youngster, seemed to take all my time. We were harassed by bills, and had no money to spend for anything except the barest necessities.

I became more discouraged daily as I sat down with my moody husband to the unappetizing meals I had so little energy to prepare. I had to refuse almost all invitations because I had nothing to wear and no money to reciprocate.

I neglected my appearance and seldom left the apartment. I had no time to read and consequently little interest in what was going on in the world.

Herbert and I both looked forward to the first of the year when we hoped for a raise in his salary, but on the second of January he came home even more discouraged than before with the news that Monsieur Gaumont had given him an assistant instead of adding to his paycheck.

"Monsieur Gaumont wrote to me," Herbert said, "that I did not seem to be able to keep up with all the new work that was added to last year's business."

Herbert made new friends and often went out to dinner in the evening. The loneliness this caused me was terrible. At times I almost wished I had not had a baby, and yet when I felt her soft arms around my neck and her moist kisses on my cheek, I knew she was my greatest joy and only comfort.

I had kept a box of keepsakes—among them a withered rose, a crumpled dance card, the Faust opera tickets—of my years with Monsieur Eiffel, tied up properly with a blue ribbon in my top bureau drawer. I reserved to myself special occasions for looking at my keepsakes. After all, there had been many hours of enchantment and light-hearted irresponsibility to reflect upon. Sometimes it made me feel good to remember those precious moments, and sometimes it made me feel desperate. It was all I could do to keep from writing to Monsieur Eiffel and confessing that I was homesick and longed for him.

Nonetheless, if any attractive young woman came near my husband, I was seized with a terrible anxiety lest someone should take him away from me.

It was out of this loneliness I decided to go back to work. I was sure I still had a grasp of the tools and symbols of my vocation. I hoped I could earn enough money to pay for someone to look after my little girl, and keep her dressed in respectable clothes. I advertised for a woman with experience in housekeeping and child care.

"I know how to do only one thing," I told Herbert, "and do it well, and that is the work I was doing before we were married."

Herbert looked at me sadly, but he was tired of being short of money all the time.

I was writing in every spare minute. I brought out a chafing dish of my mother's and prepared savory meals in it. Then the typewriter clicked while the chicken stewed.

Late in the spring, Monsieur Gaumont visited New York on business as he did twice a year. He wished to be accepted into the Edison Trust, eight companies illegally combined for the purpose of dominating the film industry. The Trust imposed restrictions on theaters and film producers, and objected to the printing of Gaumont films in the United States. Monsieur Gaumont thought it best, for the time being, to cooperate with the Trust rather than make use of the studio he had built in Flushing, Long Island.

So there the studio sat, unused. I asked Monsieur Gaumont if I could rent the studio from him to make a few little films of my own.

"Oh, you don't have to pay me rent," he said sheepishly. "If you wouldn't mind, instead of rent, I would appreciate your writing me some scenarios I could use. No one else writes stories like you do."

"I would be happy to!" I said. I already had a few scenarios lying around I could spruce up for him.

※※

I called my company Solax and I drew the logo for it, a picture of the sun rising over the Alps, touching the tops of the peaks with pink and gold, as my sisters and I used to see from our little loft at Grandmère's.

I had always had a penchant for layering my meanings, whether they were clear to anyone else or not. The word *solax* means "grave oath" in gypsy legal disputes. If there were no way to determine the truth of an allegation, the matter could be decided on sworn testimony alone if the *solax* were administered. A witness was allowed to swear on the graves of his ancestors that what he said was true, for if one swore falsely upon an ancestor's grave, there was no doubt that great evil would fall upon the perjurer.

Gypsy lore also employed images of the sun and the moon which shine on everyone at the same time. It has always comforted me to know that while the sun is shining on me, the moon is guiding my loved ones on the other side of the world.

The first film I made for my own company was a family drama, somewhat autobiographical, *A Child's Sacrifice*. It was a story about a working man on strike, whose little daughter sells her doll to help her hungry family. The owner of the factory settles the strike, buys the doll back, and gives it to the little girl.

The Gaumont studio at Flushing was so small that most of the films we made there had to be filmed out of doors. This meant our production days were determined by the weather. I had to consult newspapers morning and evening, and sometimes call the weatherman himself, to guarantee that we would have good weather.

We took wagon loads of scenery and props out to a country place we called "the farm," two miles from the studio in Flushing. The advantage of the farm was that the landscape was formed in the shape of a bowl, a natural amphitheater. Almost all of my productions that were filmed in Flushing were staged at the farm because it lent itself to the building of deep sets, a most valuable element in achieving realism.

Somehow, the entire population for miles around heard that we were working out in the open, and came to see what it was all about. Children and dogs, women and farmers, all came to watch. They sat looking down on us from the rim of the bowl, and we had a hard time keeping them out of the picture.

Henri Menessier, an excellent scenic artist who had worked for the Gaumont company in Paris, turned up on my doorstep one day.

"Mademoiselle Alice," he still called me, and he asked for a job. I was delighted to see him and to have his contributions.

Henri wrote a story called *The Sewer* and its scenes were dug into the ground on the property where the Gaumont studio was located.

A large ditch was dug and filled with water and waste. Henri contrived an ingenious roof and wall for this representation of a sewer which shut out considerable light and yet allowed enough light for photographic purposes.

Long weeks of preparation, with the utmost care and attention to detail, were put into dives and dens, switches and pulleys, rats and traps.

It took a full week to train the rats which were to attack the hero. At first we used ordinary gray rats, but it was found that they were not amenable to reason. They would scamper away as soon as they were set loose. The white rats, however, were not convincing enough to play sewer rats. It was necessary to paint them red so they would appear to be a filthy, dark gray in the film.

We spent time filming in Fort Lee, New Jersey, where there were magnificent cliffs. In one scene dealing with the violent death of a bandit, the actors had to struggle two hundred feet above sea level on a narrow shelf of rock only two feet wide. We sent a dummy headlong over the precipice. It turned somersaults in the air on its way to the rocky edge of the waters below.

Working out of doors was adequate for westerns and adventures. But for love stories, one needed to film indoors. I longed for a real film studio. I began to think about how to expand the buildings on the Gaumont property, but I could not afford to make the improvements.

I formed a plan. Why not ask Monsieur Eiffel to arrange for an enlargement of the Gaumont studio in Flushing? That way the benefit of the expansion would remain in Gaumont company hands, and I could use it until Monsieur Gaumont resolved his problems with the Edison Trust.

Mademoiselle Alice

I did not dare risk this request by letter. The best way to ask for anything is in person, so I wrote to Monsieur Eiffel asking if we could visit him during the summer. He wrote back immediately inviting us to his lake house in Vevey, Switzerland. We set sail at the end of July for a six week trip.

Chapter 32

FROM GENEVA, WE TRAVELED north along a green-bordered road with Lake Léman, blue and sparkling, at its feet. Monsieur Eiffel's vacation house at Vevey, Switzerland, was a beauty, commanding fine views of the lake in front and the hills behind.

The house had been built by an architect who was also an artist. The grounds consisted of a dozen acres, beautifully laid out, extending to the bank of the lake. On a still morning, the hills are reflected in the lake, giving a perfect image of the original.

It was here that Monsieur Eiffel liked to entertain friends from the city.

On our arrival, I stood on the porch and Monsieur Eiffel came out and stood face to face with me, the girl who had left him four years before. We looked at each other for a moment without a word, then he put his arms around me and my head sank upon his shoulder. We wept in each other's arms.

I do not know what Herbert thought when he saw me do this, but I know it may have opened a window in his mind to a view he had not considered before.

The lake house was attractive as well as hospitable, and members of Monsieur Eiffel's family—daughters, sons-in-law, nieces and nephews—all remained there for many weeks during the summer, boating on the lake, climbing the mountains behind it, and visiting the sights in the neighborhood.

We enjoyed all of these activities for several days. Over dinner, Monsieur Eiffel explained how the Gaumont company had recently patented a way to make color film. Monsieur Eiffel was taking pictures and developing them in color while we were there.

On one of our group walks in the hills behind the house, I brought up the subject of building a larger studio on the Gaumont property in Flushing.

In response to this, Monsieur Eiffel said, "You should build your own studio."

Herbert took this as a refusal to expand the Gaumont property, and he wanted to leave as soon as possible at an appropriate time. But I wasn't ready to leave.

"Why should we stay?" he asked. "We are just imposing on Monsieur Eiffel, and lolling about, wasting our time."

"I need to ask Monsieur Eiffel something in private," I said.

"In private?" Herbert demanded. "You have something you want to say that I cannot hear?" Herbert's voice rose and I was afraid other guests might hear him.

"He knew my father," I whispered.

"Why did you not tell me this before?" Herbert was quite agitated at being left out of my intimate thoughts.

"I have not told anyone," I said. "I did not want Monsieur Gaumont to know that Monsieur Eiffel was a friend of my family's. It would have given me a personal advantage. You know how Monsieur Gaumont is."

After another day or two of recreation in which I looked happier than Herbert had ever seen me, he found himself unaccountably incensed by the whole indecipherable situation, and left me to find my way to the steamer and then home by myself. There was a decided chill between us.

Of course, I had left our daughter back in the United States with a friend of mine, and had not even thought of staying with Monsieur Eiffel or reviving our romantic relationship. It was all I could wish for just to see him again, to see the love light in his eyes. It was in those dangerously transparent moments that Herbert may have had an inkling of the secret I had kept from him.

೮೦೦೪

The morning after Herbert left, Monsieur Eiffel and I sat in wooden chairs on a point of land overlooking the lake, admiring the reflection of the mountains. The trees had been cut away leaving open a path down to the water.

"What happened to Herbert?" he asked, concerned. "Is he all right?"

"He had to go back to New York." I said. "I need to ask you something."

"Anything. Ask me."

"Tell me what was the trouble that came to my father when I was a young girl, and what was your connection with it?"

Monsieur Eiffel looked pensive.

"It is all so long ago," he said. "You don't really want to dig up those ghosts, do you? There is nothing to be done about them, now."

"It is something that I've always wished to know," I said. "What was the trouble that preyed on Father's mind? I am convinced it finally killed him."

Monsieur Eiffel regarded me for a few moments before he began, and I waited patiently.

"It was years ago," he said, "before you were born, when your father still lived in Chile. He came to Paris on business. I saw him on that trip, and one night he went into a saloon. At that time gambling was illegal in France, and the saloons that offered a place to gamble had a light in the window. The gambling den was always in the back, behind closed doors."

"Wait," I said, "why did you see him on that trip?"

"He traveled through Panama in order to find out for me where the Americans proposed to build the canal."

"Why?"

"Well, I figured that if the canal was ever to be built, the Americans would insist on being part of it. I wanted to make preliminary calculations, taking into account the interests of the United States. I wanted to bid on it, and I was not sure France would be able to build it alone."

"You were right about that," I said. "What about my father?"

"He spoke both Spanish or English. If anyone could find out where the Americans had gone surveying, he could."

"What happened later, when he came to Paris?"

"Well, he was very good at poker, as you know, and he was by himself. Your mother was back in Chile with the children while he was on business, and he was seeking a little entertainment. He went into the back room to gamble, and he was extremely lucky, and when he was lucky he was also amiable. His luck attracted attention. Strangers became friendly with him, and he knew how to play the crowd."

"I know that," I said, reminiscing.

"The trouble began when he won so much money that by the end of the night's playing, he was advised by the owner of the saloon that he should stay the night, that it would be hazardous for him to go out with so much cash on his person. So he agreed to remain overnight and was shown to a room."

Monsieur Eiffel seemed reluctant to tell me the rest. He tried to retreat, but I was determined to hang on until he told me what happened.

"I know all about the poker game," I said, "but not about what happened after."

"Are you sure you want to know this? It is not something your father would have wanted you to know."

"He died when I was seventeen," I said. "I am an adult now. Tell me."

"Well, during the night," he continued, "he perceived that there was someone in his room. He knew right away that he was trapped. He had to fight for his life. Somehow, he was able to get the knife away from his attacker."

"And then what?" I asked, holding my breath.

"Well, what do you think happened? He killed the other man."

There was a long moment of silence between us. I was not even breathing.

"It was in self-defense, of course," Monsieur Eiffel continued in a sympathetic voice, "but he did not see how he could explain it to the authorities. He got out of there as fast as he could and took the next ship back to Chile."

I was thinking in silent shock about my father on the run, blood on his hands.

"It was in all the newspapers," Monsieur Eiffel continued. "They reported your father had stolen seven thousand francs from the man he killed. That's what the owner of the den, who was clearly complicit in the attack on your father, told the police. Your father decided to remain in South America because there were those in France who would never believe in his innocence. In Chile, no one knew that he had fled from justice. Or rather, injustice. He came back to France only many years later."

Monsieur Eiffel told me the story, drawing it in as mild terms as he could so as to minimize the part he had taken in the matter, for he didn't want to boast about the time when, after my father came back to Paris, some men at the club recognized my father and wanted to lynch him.

I had noticed that my parents felt thankful to Monsieur Eiffel for something, but I didn't know what it was. Now he was saying that he had stood against a crowd that wanted to lynch my father. His defense of my father was a remarkably heroic act.

I stood up, very agitated, overwhelmed with the deep sense of loss my long separations from my father had caused during my childhood. Monsieur Eiffel stood up with me.

"Nothing more was done about the matter," he concluded, "but your father lived the rest of his life under a cloud."

I threw my arms around his neck, crying hard.

"I know, I know," I sobbed. "What you did was of the greatest importance to my father, but he never told me what it was."

"Also," he added, "I wanted to make amends for my innocent part in the events which lost your mother the money which might have educated her daughter and made her happy. I brought you into my home, and through the years I have been more than rewarded by your sweet presence which has seemed like a dream to me."

"The years have made you what you are," I said, "and that is why I love you."

He held my hands and kissed away my tears.

"I did my duty," he said softly, "to him and to you."

೫⃝ಌ

As I prepared to leave, Monsieur Eiffel promised to send me money to build my own studio.

"Few there are who make it in business," he said, "but if anyone can succeed, I believe you can."

He did not want the money he sent me to go into a bank account with my name on it or in one with the Solax name on it. As a founding director of the Gaumont company, he did not want it known that he was helping one of its competitors.

I was not one to look too far into the future, and did not see myself as a competitor at all, but just as a former employee who was trying to practice my craft and make a living.

He asked me to form a company with some other name and then open a bank account in that name. He instructed me to telegraph him with the information, and then he would deposit money in the company bank account. He didn't want anyone else to know the truth regarding my finances.

"If anyone asks you where you got the money, just tell them it was profit-sharing. You always earned more than your pay at Gaumont, and I feel I owe you something for the Panama Canal stock that you were never able to redeem."

I looked into his eyes for a long moment.

"Without this look into your eyes," I said, "without this touch of your hand, I could not go back to my life." He embraced me and said:

"I am always thinking of you. Never in my heart can there be room for other than you."

Chapter 33

MY SHIP LEFT LE HAVRE three days after Herbert left from Cherbourg. I arrived in New York four days after he did, and I was very anxious about what other people thought, if anyone had noticed that we had not come back together. Even more anxiously, I wondered what would happen between us when I got home.

How very strange it was! That may have been the first time I thought of New York as my home.

For all I knew, Herbert might have decided to divorce me, or perhaps he found comfort in the arms of another. There flashed through my mind visions of scantily clad, pink-robed damsels who might career over to the house offering solace to my husband.

Thoughts of my daughter tore at my heart. She had been learning to lisp baby words when I had left her six weeks before. I knew this little clinging thing needed me, and no one else could substitute.

Herbert and Simone were playing hide and seek when I came in the front door. The most important things are said without words. That is where silent film gets its poetry.

"Where were you, mama?"

"I was on a ship having an adventure," I said, "and I had to talk to an old friend and make arrangements."

"What arrangements?" Herbert asked. "I thought Monsieur Eiffel told you to go build your own studio."

"He said he would help me."

"Yes, but how much is he going to help you?"

"I don't know yet. We will see. Anyway, he said we have to be discreet about it. He doesn't want Monsieur Gaumont to know he is helping me."

❧☙

With Monsieur Eiffel's promise of assistance in mind, I began planning the building of a larger studio on the Gaumont property at Flushing. Even though Monsieur Eiffel had advised me to build my own studio, I could not imagine having enough money to undertake such an endeavor.

It was the biggest surprise of my life when I found much more money than I expected had been sent to the bank account Monsieur Eiffel asked me to open. I began at once to find a suitable lot for my own studio.

I had many times found picturesque backdrops in Fort Lee, New Jersey. There were forests and country roads, old homes and hotels, rose-covered cottages and the magnificent palisades that glorify the Hudson River.

One morning, I dusted my nose with powder, pulled on my sensible little hat, and put on my low-heeled walking shoes. I made sure my checkbook was in my bag and, with a little flutter of my heart, I started off to inspect a small chicken farm in Fort Lee which had been advertised in the morning paper. I hoped that the farm would prove to be the ideal spot.

Mademoiselle Alice

After catching the ferry across the Hudson, I found my way to the property where another prospective purchaser was looking at the chicken farm at the same time. He hoped to be producing chickens and eggs for a New York restaurant. Fortunately, he had only $3,500 in his bank account, and I had the requisite $5,000 to purchase the farm.

I had the time of my life that year. I went to bed every night planning that studio. I loved to imagine working in my own place, choosing my own picture plays, the scenes taking shape from my own imagination. After only a few hours of sleep, I woke up at dawn to contemplate floor plans, blueprints, and equipment.

Also, I was expecting another baby. My studio grew in size along with my belly. Two months after my little boy was born, the studio was finally completed.

My glass palace was four stories tall and allowed me to use natural light instead of glaring lamps. In addition, we had what were then the most modern devices. I felt very particular about the comfort of the actors, so I made sure the dressing rooms and makeup quarters were spacious and inviting.

We had a papier-mâché room for making scenery and props, as well as a large room where the actors, waiting for their scenes, often played pinochle.

A kitchen and dining area provided meals to my players every day without any deduction from their salary.

I also bought two conveyances which took the actors to the ferry when their day's work was done. I probably spent too much money on these things, but I was doing my best to make into reality that which had only been a dream for me: the ideal studio for making moving pictures.

CRSO

In my heart, I was still six years old. I had always loved stories which fed my fancy. The weaving of wonderful tales had become my chief delight, the game of make-believe a substitute for reality.

I wrote most of my own scenarios, but I was always on the lookout for good adventure stories submitted to me for consideration. I wanted soldiers of fortune fighting under foreign flags, or explorers shipwrecked and taken captive, or perhaps a big game hunter running away from angry elephants—something like that.

If nobody sent me an adventure story, I could look about and find human heart stories everywhere. I have always felt that, to make a story live and breathe, you have to hold your head close to the ground, close enough to hear the intense longings of Mother Earth, to feel her vast emotions, her love and heartbreak.

I have always been addicted to the personals column, because in some of them I think I see a romance, and I love to wonder what that romance might be. I like stories in which some parts are left to the imagination. What I know ceases to interest me. The part I imagine becomes a story in itself.

But these daydreams could not take all my time. After I became the manager of a moving picture studio, I was slightly overwhelmed with the fact that success or failure depended almost solely on me.

If one wants to see the workings of a studio photographing picture plays, let one visit a studio like mine while the work is going on. One would see actors and actresses lounging about, waiting their turn to appear before the camera. One girl waits to become a princess, another for her call to do a peasant dance. Some actors are dressed in somber suits arranged in a court scene. There might be a love scene or a murder at the same time, anything and everything pertaining to life on land or on water, portrayed on film for the wondering beholder.

How different this behind-the-scenes view is from the pictures moving smoothly before the eyes of the audience seated comfortably in a theater.

A story in a moving picture is different from most other stories in that the whole notion of the story is compressed. You might have a couple meet on a train, become acquainted during the first mile of the trip, fall in love during the second mile, and leave the coach a few minutes later to get married.

And then when the actors kiss for the camera, it is entirely different. I had to stand by telling the players just what to do. I would instruct the male actor to try to feel like a lover, talk like a lover, and act like a lover. Then I would tell the actress playing his sweetheart to draw continually nearer to him until her lips were very near his.

When their faces were only inches apart, I would tell them to stay there for a few moments for the sake of the viewers' pleasurable anticipation, but the male actor could often not stand so flagrant a temptation and would kiss the girl too soon. The result was that it had to be done all over again. The second and third time turned out no better than the first, and I would excuse them from another attempt, although the actors were usually quite willing to try again and again.

Westerns had come into vogue and I had my own ideas about them. I had loved to hear my father talk of the "halcyon days" as he called them, during the California gold rush. I could not get out of my mind his descriptions of that wild country, filled with wild men, dignified by the name of prospector. I could easily visualize my father going about in a flannel shirt, his trousers tucked into his boots, a pick and shovel on his shoulder, stopping here and there to dig holes for gold.

The Little Kiddie Mine was inspired by my father's stories about his years in the gold country. In that story, the baby daughter of a prospector captures both the gold and the desperado.

❦

While I was working at Gaumont, I had filmed many stories for children—Christmas stories, fairy tales, even my *Vie du Christ* had many children in it, playing angels as I had on the little stage at Ferney.

I very much wanted to film my favorite childhood picture book, *Dick Whittington and his Cat*, another story with rats. I spent weeks recreating the illustrations that had captivated me when I was a child: the kitchen in the house of an English merchant with its great old-style pots, antique bellows, and brass works, the large bells that rang out, "Turn again, Dick Whittington." Even the cat had to look like the one in my picture book.

We converted an old sailboat to look like an English caravel, the ship struck by lightning in the story, and then Herbert set off explosives so we could film it. This stunt proved to be disastrous as Herbert was badly burned about his face and much skin grafting was necessary.

We had barely finished *Whittington* when I went to a great deal of expense to film *Beasts of the Jungle*. It had all the wild animals I could want in a feature-length story about a little girl, not unlike myself, who adopted a cuddly, full-grown tiger for a pet and taught her tricks.

We took the tiger out to a film studio, a great, barn-like building on the top of a cliff in Shady Side, in the vicinity of

Fort Lee. A Sacred Heart church there was founded in 1873, the year I was born, making me feel like my place in Fort Lee was meant to be. The Sisters there had started a little school where I put my daughter while we filmed.

One day the tiger escaped briefly. We had to chase her down with pitchforks. I was rather worried that the children might be given a fright.

It was during this wonderfully creative year that I wrote the story of a little girl named Trixie, whose older sister contracts consumption. Trixie hears the doctor tell her mother that by the time the leaves fall from the trees, her sister will have passed away. Trixie takes this literally and, after she is put to bed, she finds a ball of string and goes out into the garden to tie falling leaves to the trees.

The story ends happily. A handsome, young doctor comes to the house with a new cure for consumption. He brings Trixie's older sister back to health and she falls in love with him.

I wrote a scenario called *A Terrible Lesson* about a gambler who is talked into staying overnight after a winning streak. He is startled during the night when his bed begins to be lowered into another room. I got this idea from a Wilkie Collins story. Unlike my father's experience, it ends happily, and no one is killed or falsely accused of murder.

Chapter 34

IN THE EARLY YEARS of moving pictures, the adaptation to the screen of a novel, play, or story had the status of a poor imitation, a cheap version of a legitimate work of art. Thus the public, although they enjoyed the movies in all genres, regarded them as somewhat vulgar.

If the form of the art is something the public is not used to, the art form suffers a period where it is not accepted as art. Plays in the theater had been accepted as art for centuries, and then we had moving pictures, more fun and cheaper than theater productions, but not accepted as legitimate art. I was sensitive to this withholding of approval, and tried to counter it with films as artistically rendered as I could make them.

I found that friends were far too kind to give a competent criticism, and professional critics, while they might be able to comment on what is a good story, when it came to predicting what the public would fancy, they were as much at sea as anyone else.

Some critics advised me that I was constantly firing over the heads of the people, the people being the great numbers of viewers with modest incomes, rather than wealthier people who could afford the theater and the opera and never darkened the door of a cinema.

Then I was told that the public wanted something on a subject which they were discussing, such as a current controversy. Again, I was disappointed in the public's lukewarm reaction.

"Why?" I asked Herbert.

"If you lean to one side of the question," Herbert said, "your work will offend everyone on the other side."

I was in despair. It seemed like all my work had come to naught.

Napoleon had been fond of going about incognito, dressed in ordinary civilian clothes among those he governed, surreptitiously hearing from them their views concerning him.

This seemed like a good idea to me, so I patronized the theaters that exhibited my films so that I could see the audience's reaction to them. I was surprised to find that the reaction was different from theater to theater.

Nevertheless, while I was making moving pictures, I took it personally when the critics did not like my work. Unfortunately, I still remember a critic who had referred to one of my pictures with the single word, execrable, a film which cost me months of work.

"Work?" Herbert said to me, when I bemoaned the critic's verdict. "In England we have a saying, 'all work and no play.' If you had been making a great picture it would have been the opposite, 'all play and no work.'"

"It's true," I said, "I struggled over that picture." But I did not accept that my work should be so easily dismissed.

"Genius," Herbert continued, "according to my interpretation of genius, doesn't struggle. What it does seems very easy."

"But there are geniuses," I argued, "whose work is recognized as something that is strongly appealing to present-day audiences."

"Unfortunately," he said, "the great bulk of films, as well as the literary arts, are occupied by the commonplace."

"True," I said, "but an artistic work may be a long while in gaining recognition. Unhappily, the risk seems to be in favor of its never attaining it."

"The public is the final judge in such matters."

"That is only because," I said, "the public buys the ticket. I would say that the public is slow to appreciate art in a new form."

"There you have it," Herbert agreed.

This was always the conundrum I faced. Should I produce moving pictures that the public could watch and forget, or expend a great deal of effort and money on a real work of art?

Also, I was torn because I adored my children, but I did not believe I could be happy if I was rooted in the purely domestic garden among the turnips and cabbages.

ଛଠଃ

In May 1913, an item in the newspaper set me back on my heels. An award for Monsieur Eiffel was given in Washington, D.C. Alas, he was not there! The French ambassador to the United States accepted the Langley Medal, a very high honor, on behalf of Monsieur Eiffel.

The ambassador apologized to the audience at the Smithsonian that Monsieur Eiffel could not be there, and told them that Monsieur Eiffel was one of the men of whom France was most proud. I could remember twenty years before when he had been the most maligned man in France.

The French ambassador spoke humorously of the way in which France and the United States had been competing with each other in aviation experiments as well as in many other fields of science.

The Eiffel Tower was, he said, "a thing of beauty," but it had finally been made useful with experiments in aviation and wireless telegraphy. These links, he said, helped bind France to the United States.

I had to smile because the article said that the Langley Medal was being awarded to Monsieur Eiffel for the exacting research work he had published between 1907 and 1911. He had been busy since I left.

ಬಂದ

Having had a strange fascination for horror ever since my convent days, I wanted to film *The Pit and the Pendulum*, and picturize my long wakeful nights. That the story takes place in a monastery is no coincidence.

We built a realistic set and employed a plague of rats to gnaw at the ropes that bound the luckless hero to his bed. The gruesome forcefulness of the tale was magnified by the quiet occupants in the dungeon: snakes, skulls, and—the sinister scourge of my childhood—skeletons.

While I was working on The Pit and the Pendulum, Herbert came home beside himself with hurt and anger.

"I quit," he said flatly.

"Quit? How could you quit?" I said, disbelieving.

"If I hadn't quit, Monsieur Gaumont would have fired me."

"How is that even possible? You are the president! And the vice-president! And the treasurer!"

"Monsieur Gaumont raged at me. He saw pictures of your studio and he accused me of stealing from him."

I knew at once as I should have known earlier what Monsieur Gaumont's reaction to my studio would be. He knew there was no money in my family. He knew I had been making films in the United States for little more than a year when I bought the property on which to build my studio. He also knew that the market in the United States was severely restricted by the Edison Trust, and that the possibility that I was making a fortune, much more than he was making, was very slim indeed.

"I don't understand," I said. "What is it he thinks you stole from him?"

"He showed me a Gaumont film that had a Solax trademark on it."

"That's ridiculous!" I said. "How did that happen?"

"The only thing I can figure out is that someone put it there to undermine me. Monsieur Gaumont sent someone to look over my shoulder last February, and perhaps, when he couldn't find anything, he manufactured something that would infuriate Monsieur Gaumont."

"So he thinks you sold Gaumont films as Solax films and made a fortune?"

"Exactly."

"Perhaps you can explain to him that I got the money through another source."

"I am not going to explain anything to him. I am mortally insulted. In addition to that, I have been dissatisfied. Maybe I can work here in our studio."

It was a terrible shock for Herbert and for me as well. Success had been within his grasp. He had climbed to the top of the Gaumont company by being the first from that company to come to the United States. Now he was out of a job and we had to do something immediately to save face. We could not let word get out that he quit for any reason other than that he had bigger plans to pursue.

My first press release regarding this was *trés gauche*, a little awkward. I wrote that Herbert was going to help me wherever he could, which made him sound like my lapdog. Eventually, we formed a new company called Blaché Features and under this name Herbert was able to borrow money, improve the studio, and make a few films.

My budget for lavish productions had been used up. It was a hard lesson for me.

※

I had been under the impression that the success of my productions was a matter of their superior artistic quality and fair competition with other artists. I believed, naively, that if the public liked my work, I would succeed and be able to remain in business.

This was not the case. We had a monopolist named Thomas Edison: many and myriad were the methods he employed to crush the competition, not just those of us who were making films, but anyone who had their hand in the movie business—theater owners, distributors, and manufacturers all suffered from the pressures brought to bear on them.

Thomas Edison was not by any means a pioneer in motion pictures, but he did everything he could to prevent other people from making money in the movie business. He shielded himself behind numerous patents, most of which he obtained by forcing competitors to go broke paying lawyers' fees, and then settling the case by giving up their patents.

He combined eight companies into the Edison Trust, also known as the Motion Picture Patents Company, whose sole aim was to destroy any good outside of themselves that might be created.

My studio was one of the largest in the business, and I could not be ignored by these fiends of unfair competition.

However, in the summer and fall of 1913, after Herbert lost his job, we were unable to pay the actors. We saw them leave one by one as they regretfully had to find paying work.

This slow trickle of stars leaving my employ was a red flag to anyone on the outside alert to a potential windfall. The sharks scouting for those in financial difficulty smelled blood in the water.

I was in my glass palace one day when I had a couple of visitors, a Mr. William Hershberg and another man who was bigger in size than he was on words. He silently stood by the door just to scare me.

"The object of our visit," Mr. Hershberg said, "is to tell you that this would be the very best time for you to sell your studio to the General Feature Film Company, as you are no doubt aware that we have almost all of the business now."

"I do not want to sell my studio," I said. "I am getting along just fine."

"It doesn't look like you are getting along just fine. You have lost a number of your employees."

"My employees can do what they want to do."

"Well, Madame Blaché, I am willing to give you my expert advice and then you can do as you think best. You know you have stayed in business a good long time. Almost everyone else is out, and you are still in, and if I were you, at this time, I would sell out and be done with it. Now if you don't sell your studio today, you might not get another chance. No one is going to talk to you any plainer than I am to you now. I would advise you to sell."

"And just how much money," I asked, "are you offering me for my studio and factory?"

"We are authorized to pay you $200,000 in stock in the General Feature Film Company."

"No money?" I asked, incredulous. "Nothing but stock? You expect me to hand over my studio for nothing? What guarantee do I have that the stock you give me won't be worthless in a few years?"

"Guarantee? What guarantee do you have that you will be successful in your business in a few years? This is the right time for you to sell. If it were not for that, I would not come here at all to make you this offer."

"I don't want to sell my studio," I said. "I intend to remain in business. I have helped build the motion picture business from its beginnings. I have worked hard, and I am wrapped up in the art of cinema and want to remain in it."

"Now, Madame Blaché, we are good businessmen, and we treat everybody fair and square. We are prepared to offer you and your husband a job with the General Feature Film Company."

"A job? What kind of job?"

"You can continue to work in the business of cinema at $1,600 per month for both of you. That is the going rate for directors in this business, and we can give you a contract for five years of work."

"I can probably do as well without your stock and without your contract!" I sat straight in my chair, and spoke slowly and evenly with all the icy indifference I could project.

"Now, Madame Blaché, there is no reason to get hysterical. I am the general manager of the General Feature Film Company, and we are a great big wheel, and you are just a small proprietor. You look like a smart lady, and I cannot believe you are going to be so foolish as to hold on when everyone else is selling out. The General Feature Film Company was created for the purpose of absorbing all of the feature film business in the United States, just as the General Film Company has absorbed all of the rental business. We were organized to control the business and to monopolize it, and that is what we are going to do. And you have got to get out of the way, one way or another."

I knew that the Motion Picture Patents Company was being sued by the U.S. Attorney General for anti-trust violations, and I was surprised at this man's blatant admission of breaking the law.

"I understand," I said evenly, "that the Attorney General may be taking a dim view of your efforts."

"Now, Madame Blaché, that is neither here nor there. We are in court all the time, we have the best lawyers, and we always win."

"We'll see about that, Mr. Hershberg," I said. "Thank you for your offer. My husband and I will consider it. Good day."

Of course, I never accepted their offer and I never regretted it.

Chapter 35

WHEN I ARRIVED AT THE FERRY one evening, I saw a man standing on the platform reading a newspaper. Big, black letters topped of the front page: *BELGIANS HOLD LIEGE.*

I asked the stranger what it meant, and he told me that all Europe had suddenly burst into flames. I bought a newspaper and read an announcement of the arrival of a ship in New York harbor bringing passengers from Europe, some of whom had left Germany on the last train that was allowed to leave.

That night, I had the most terrifying dream of my life. I dreamed that I was in Berlin. I was in the hotel situated on a square that I had stayed in when I had gone there to work with Herbert.

In my dream, I looked out through a window on the square below, thronged with people, all in a state of intense excitement. Some of them were throwing their caps up in the air and shouting, others were hurrying about, while carriages and automobiles were trying to get through the crowds without running people over.

Then, in my dream, without being conscious of a transition, I was on a train crowded with passengers. Every town we passed through was filled with soldiers, and everyone seemed to be hurrying. In the fields, women were gathering in the harvest, there being not one man left to help them.

Everybody and everything was moving in the same direction as the train I was on, while I was shouting in silence, "What is happening?"

Presently, we crossed a border into another country. This was followed by an audible sigh of relief by my fellow passengers. We passed through a valley over which loomed fortifications on both sides into which soldiers were hurrying. These two lines were so filled with soldiers dressed in dark uniforms that, as we passed them, they looked like swarms of insects.

Our train entered a city, and I was hurried onto another train with the other passengers. Soon we were again traveling across the country. Now, looking out the window, everyone, instead of hurrying in the direction I was going, hurried in the other direction. Soldiers marched in great multitudes, and presently I saw someone carrying a French flag.

I saw Rose's face on a train going in the opposite direction. She was looking at me with an expression filled with love and sadness for me, her baby sister, and a sorrowful longing to go back to the past.

"Rose!" I called. She heard me, of course, but passed by in an instant.

There seemed to be only one anxiety on the part of everyone on the train: to make it to the coast of Normandy so we could all catch a steamer to the United States.

During the next phase of the dream, I was on a steamer. It was rushing through the fog silently, and without lights.

Everyone was grouped below decks in terror. Stewards went from room to room stuffing pillows over the portholes to conceal every ray of light from within.

The next morning I awoke feeling utterly demolished, and then I remembered that I was in the United States already. This relief lasted but a moment when I remembered how many people I loved were still in Europe. My mother, Monsieur Eiffel, my sisters, Julia and Fanny.

I thought of Rose too, and was relieved, and then also saddened, that she was no longer there.

For months after the start of the war, fought almost entirely on French soil, I was in a daze. Every day I read every word of several newspapers. Finally, I was so upset, that Herbert took me to a rural part of North Carolina where the only newspaper was a weekly with almost no news in it at all except for what was of interest to the surrounding farmers.

I found some relief from my anxiety by making candles and soap, as my grandmother had done. But because I felt I must do something to hasten the end of the war, I rolled bandages for the Red Cross.

At last, my nightmare, my vision, or whatever it may be called, faded slightly, and I managed to go back to Fort Lee and to work. I continued to volunteer for the Red Cross, and my house became a gathering place for thrift teas, dances with proceeds for French orphans, and Mahjong parties with war savings stamps for prizes.

Since Herbert and I had too little capital to finance film productions ourselves, we allied ourselves with a company called Popular Plays and Players which had bought the rights to a number of literary works. As part of our agreement, we did most of the work in my studio. I cannot say it was the best deal we ever made, but it was necessary under the circumstances at that time.

One of the literary works I adapted for the screen was a twelve-line poem called *My Madonna*. By this time, I had written so many stories, I had a veritable grab-bag of story elements that steered my imagination into familiar corners. For this scenario, I wrote about an artist who paints a model as the Madonna. The model falls in love with the artist, but he leaves her for a wealthy woman. They meet again in church, in front of his painting of the Madonna.

The vice-president of Popular Plays and Players was named Aaron Hoffman, and he fancied himself to be quite a good writer as he had written a few vaudeville acts and some speeches. Under his orders, I wrote the scenarios and adaptations for a dozen films and he, being the vice-president, felt justified in putting his name on them. I was irritated by this but, as I said before, he was the vice-president. I noted later that after we parted ways, he did not manage to write a single scenario by himself.

∞○∞

Fast forward to 1918, or as we say in the movies, "An interval of several years is supposed to have elapsed."

The war was interminable and I could not go home until it was over. We managed to break away from Popular Plays and Players and made a few films of our own. One was *Her Great Adventure* starring Bessie Love, a lovely girl of nineteen. Herbert liked her very much.

I was jealous of Bessie Love and I hated myself for it. I knew I was only something comfortable to Herbert, like an old shoe, or a warm robe on a cold morning.

We attended a dance and Bessie was there, all curls and frivolity and fun. She had plenty of dance partners, and her laughter drew attention to her. Herbert danced dutifully with me, but he seemed scarcely aware of it. The absent look in Herbert's eyes and the turmoil of my own heart made the situation unbearable and, at last, I suggested that we go home.

Something took possession of me, and as soon as we were home, I accosted Herbert with my words.

"What do you think I am?" I shrieked. "I've stood your silly patter about that odious little minx as long as I can! I'll be no man's vicarious sweetheart!"

I left him with my head high and went to my writing room, where I threw myself on the couch in an agony of remorse. How could I have revealed my feelings in such a disgraceful and unladylike manner? My thoughts were unbearable.

It was hot and stifling in my room, so I changed my frock and went out to the garden in the moonlight. How soft and sweet nature is at this quiet hour. If only my soul were at peace. How long I paced back and forth in that garden I do not know. Somewhere a clock chimed, I don't know if it was two or three, and I decided to go back inside, but as I walked around the house, I saw someone sitting on the stone wall in the front yard. It was Herbert.

"What are you doing?" I asked.

"I had to think some place," said Herbert in a humble voice, "and this was just as good a place as any."

"Herbert, I am sorry I lost my temper. I never supposed that I could so forget myself. I don't want you to think—"

I paused, suddenly mute.

"Think what?" Herbert asked.

"Think that I care what you do with pretty actresses." I instantly regretted this as I knew I sounded brittle. Who did I think I was kidding?

"But I want you to care," he said.

I looked at him, exhausted, and he caught me to him in an embrace, whispering sweet nothings in my ear.

೫ଓ

After ten years of marriage, Herbert confessed that he set out to win me merely because he had heard that I was oblivious to all suitors. Someone in the office had remarked that there wasn't a man in Paris or anywhere else who had a ghost of a chance with me. Herbert had simply responded, "Oh, is that so?"

I resisted the temptation to also make a confession, to say that I had learned to love my husband only after his years of devotion to me and to our children. I did not see how making such a confession would do either of us any good.

I had faithfully tried to be a good wife to Herbert, and succeeded at least in keeping from him the knowledge of my own, what you might call, mistake. For as long as we had been together, in the depths of my miserable heart, was always a haunting realization of my love for another.

I said none of this aloud, however, and Herbert expected me to say something.

"Would you deprive me of knowing your feelings, Alice?" he asked. "Isn't there something you're hiding from me?"

I thought of Pandora and the box of troubles she opened.

"What have I to hide?" I said.

"Your true affection for me perhaps," he said.

I turned on him in a small fury.

"Is there nothing more important than your ego?"

"I believe that you do love me, Alice, while I have never ceased to love you."

"And if I love you or not," I said wearily, "what is it to you?"

He leaned forward intently and grabbed my hands in his.

"It is everything to me," he said. "Even if you can forget those old sweetheart days, I cannot."

But such intimate moments became harder to come by. While I preferred to read or to write as a diversion from the stresses of life, Herbert preferred amusements—dancing, theaters, racing cars, and to be eternally on the move. Also, as I have said, he was fond of starlets.

Many sighing maidens fell before his adoring, dark eyes—which had not been adoring after all, but faithless. As he had with me, he would first show devotion, rendering sympathy and helpful service. Then he would make himself necessary by his kindness, then abruptly absent himself to await the assurance of the young lady's anxious affection.

This was the source of the troubles between us. That which first attracted him, my falling into his arms and his conquest of a cool customer, eventually faded to an unsatisfactory experience that needed to be repeated.

My failing was that I could not accept the oxymoron of the business friendship. Herbert was absorbed in business, and after business hours he was absorbed in business associates. I could not bear the heartache of superficial attachments, the parade of gaiety for the benefit of people for whom I did not care. I was painfully aware also that in a room full of young people, I looked old-fashioned.

I was miserable enough to leave Herbert's guests to their own amusement. Herbert reproached me.

"Can you not read between the lines?" he asked. "I bring my friends home for you to entertain so they all might see your superiority. I'm proud of you, even though I know that they will never engage you intellectually."

One night, we had a terrible fight which ended when our dog bit his hand. Herbert went to Hollywood where the movie industry seemed to be migrating. I had to move to a small apartment in New York City, and enroll our protesting children in boarding school.

That was a dreadful year, and then I got sick with the influenza that swept the country. It was staggering how many people lost their lives to that flu. Theaters and factories were closed to help stop it from spreading. I knew several people, much younger than I, who died.

The flu put me out of my head so that I could not measure time. I must have been in that gloomy room, almost unconscious, for more than two weeks.

During long days and nights of pain and helplessness, I feverishly lingered on that terrible precipice that rears itself between life and death. I heard voices in consultation in the next room, the voices of a man and woman, pitched soft and low.

Consciousness was long in returning. My first waking glimpse was of the charming wife of one of my co-workers who had done a thousand and one comforting, soothing, and wonderful things at my bedside.

My progress was more rapid after that first glimpse, and I realized that the world was a good place to get back to. The war had finally ended, and although I had lost a great deal of weight, I was on the road to recovery.

But I was a pitiful sight. Herbert came back to New York and saw me looking weak and pathetic.

"Do I look old to you, Herbert, much older?"

"You always look just the same to me," he said gallantly, "the prettiest girl in the room."

I looked around and joked: "Well, I'm the only girl in this room."

He told me I should, when I was feeling better, come out to California. The sunshine, plentiful even in January, would do me good, and there might even be some movie work for me.

Chapter 36

I HAD ALWAYS HOPED that I would one day have the opportunity to go out to the western United States to satisfy my curiosity as to what life had been like out there for my father.

The train trip with my children through the plains and over the Rockies was spectacular. I savored the sight of every mountain spring, every waterfall, and every desert star.

Herbert met us at the train station in Los Angeles and took us to the Hotel Hollywood where he was living.

There were still vineyards and orange groves at the intersection of Hollywood and Vine. The streets were lined with graceful pepper trees, their lovely branches trailing softly in the warm evening breeze.

The recently-built library, looking like an oversize Swiss cottage with its high-peaked roof, seemed out of place between the only movie theaters, the Iris and the Hollywood.

There was no restaurant yet, but there was a general store with a counter where hearty American breakfasts were served. Many actors crowded the counter in the early morning to hastily consume waffles and flapjacks with maple syrup, orange juice, and coffee.

One moving picture studio had been set up in a large barn, another in an old saloon.

Actors in cowboy costumes gathered in front of Gower's Drugstore hoping for a part in a western. We called that corner Gower's Gulch.

At lunchtime, I walked down Prospect Boulevard, now Hollywood Boulevard, and met people I had known in Fort Lee. Actors and actresses in costumes and pancake makeup wandered happily among their comrades, giving the street the atmosphere of a carnival.

Almost all actors, directors, and producers made their home in the Hotel Hollywood which flattered its more famous residents with gold stars painted on the ceiling over their favorite tables in the dining room.

The hotel's veranda was lined with rocking chairs where one could watch the world go by or, more likely, where people in the moving picture business could meet to talk over their next project.

The chairs rocked excitedly. New stories for film were under constant discussion: who had written it, who would play the lead, who would direct. Nobody thought to have an agent. Invitations to meet with Mr. Zukor or Mr. Goldwyn were placed in the hotel's mail boxes.

Herbert was hired to direct several films that year and I assisted him on a couple of his directing jobs, but my vocation was being taken over by men, mostly because the making of a movie required large sums of money, and only men could borrow money from a bank.

My room was in the back of the Hotel Hollywood where there was a hill that had been turned into a Japanese garden with wonderful plants and exotic birds. I experienced once again the joy I had as a child awakening to the singing of those birds. There was a nest of wild parakeets in the tree beside my window, one red-breasted robin coming each morning to beg for his breakfast.

On Thursday nights, the hotel residents rolled up the Oriental carpet in the spacious lobby and danced until all hours of the night.

Herbert threw himself avidly into all the gaieties afforded by life at the Hotel Hollywood—yachting, dancing, swimming, and tennis parties—while I confined myself to the society of a few people I found sympathetic or intellectually stimulating. Herbert and I seemed to see each other only when our social circles collided inadvertently.

Leaving the role of belle to younger women, I frequently retreated to the billiard room. I'd had my share of social life in Paris, and Hollywood parties about power and money bored me. I had no appetite for free-flowing alcohol, feverish dancing, or musical bedrooms. I found that life in Hollywood came with a haunting emptiness.

"We dash past all the natural wonders," I told Herbert one evening after a party, "speeding by in our motorcar, intent on getting some place chic as fast as possible."

"We had a jolly time tonight, don't you think?" Herbert said. "The wine was good and the music merry, and you were there in your fragrance and beauty. What more does a man want?"

"A woman wants more," I said, "at least I do. I like to be as busy as possible. If I cannot express myself and use the abilities God gave me, then I am not living up to my own standards."

While Herbert's spare time was taken up by his social life, I had time to reflect and concluded that I wanted to be in a place where I was loved for the soul within me, where what counted was nobility of character. I was sick of being loved because my eyes were alluring or my clothes fantastic. After a month of living in the Hotel Hollywood, I moved into a little bungalow nearby.

The little box of memories was always with me, filled with treasured possessions, the closest links with my past. When I opened it to look over its contents, a tumult of emotions swept over me. The longing to go back to Monsieur Eiffel, long suppressed, brought tears to my eyes.

If I had not recently survived a brush with death, I might never have realized that some of the most important things in life were passing me by. When that piercing grief melted, I was left with a desire to live the rest of my life fully and worthily.

When the day came that prohibition was to go into effect on the morrow, we were invited to a last-night-to-legally-drink party for movie people in a private room at a restaurant that looked like a ship. It was called the Juan Cabrillo, and was docked on the side of the Venice Beach pier. At first I thought it was a genuine antique with its hull rotted out, but it was built as a replica, and a very good replica, of a Spanish galleon with a bar and hotel rooms.

The waiters were dressed as sixteenth-century naval officers. This was a feature of Hollywood in those days that I liked: the theatrical nature of the town extended to the restaurants, and it was not unusual for gregarious actors and actresses to be discovered while they were serving food to film producers.

But this was a night of debauchery with dancing and jazz. There were also many bewitching girls to gladden the masculine eye. We watched as vulgar singers, and even more vulgar dancers, attempted to arouse our jaded emotions. For me, it was a waste of time.

"I hate every vapid, meaningless hour," I said to Herbert "There is so much to do in the world besides thinking of one's own pleasure."

This struck a nerve with Herbert because it was not the first time I accused him of having frivolous friends.

"I think you might at least admit," Herbert said, "that the people with whom I associate are at least paying their way in the world."

I had not intended to flare up, but Herbert's words with their only slightly veiled contempt, roused me.

"I am afraid," I said, "I will lose my mind or my soul, if I don't steer away from this town."

ಐಜ

I had come upon a blank wall in the path of life. I was approaching a crisis and felt I must take decided and reasonable action. I wanted to go home to my own people and, after a rest, continue the profession in which I had had such wonderful experiences.

There was one old score I wanted to settle before I went back to France. I wanted very much to go to Mexico. My father had gone there to seek his fortune in silver mining after the California gold rush. He told me that he had left a tin box, half full of gold nuggets, buried under a rock formation near the little town of Gatlach, or Gerlack, something like that. I thought I could find it.

But we pay a price for everything. Perhaps I was deserving of another lesson.

I set off on my adventure with enthusiasm, but near the border my car was ambushed by bandits, and my daughter was injured. It could have been much worse if rescuers had not, by pure chance, showed up in the nick of time.

This forced me to confront the foolishness of my errand: I was pursuing a phantom, the *ignis fatuus* I had been warned about in childhood. I remembered words from a novel by Charles Dickens, the grotesque images of "forms and faces from the past, from the grave, from the deep, deep gulf where things that might have been, and never were, are always wandering."

The "always wandering" part scared me the most. I did not want to go on being a person without a home. The memory of Grandmère, who had lost so much and still retained her girlish delight, gently reproached me. We must not forever grieve, she had said. Life is for the living, but life reaching out for a link of sympathy by which we might regain our hold upon that chain of human affections which changes throughout our lives.

After this incident, I decided to go back to Paris right away. I had not been on my side of the Atlantic since before the war, and I wanted to reconnect with Monsieur Eiffel before I lost him for all time.

※

People were talking about the belle of the hotel who was a very young actress with lots of money and soulful eyes—an alluring combination, yes? Herbert had been seen now and then in her company.

I had to rationalize about our children. I told myself that if I stayed in Hollywood for the sake of the children, they would feel Herbert's rejection because he was close at hand, but if I took them to France, he would be on the other side of the world, like my father was when I was little, and that, I hoped, would take the sting out of his absence.

Herbert and I met on a secluded nook of the hotel veranda where we could hear the night birds calling now and then from the wooded hillside which rose behind the hotel.

"It's a beautiful night," said Herbert, always charming. The pleasantness in his voice had come to sound counterfeit to me.

"I want to go home." I said.

"To Fort Lee?"

"To Paris."

"Well, that's a long way from here. How will you make a living there? You know that movie-making in France has all but stopped."

"I have always felt," I said, "that the soaring aspirations of the soul should not be confined by the considerations of mere money, even though, by cruel necessity, they often are."

"I have to stay here," he said. "I barely get enough work as it is."

I often quoted lines from poetry. When Herbert first met me, he found this charming, but as the years went by I think it rankled him. Besides, I wanted to neutralize his enjoyment of pretty girls.

"I have another life I long to meet," I quoted Lord Byron, "without which life my life is incomplete.'"

"Have you already met this person?" he asked. He looked into my eyes and he may have seen the answer there. I looked away.

"The stars of our destinies," I said, "lead us in different paths."

"Quite right," Herbert said. "Good luck."

I was surprised to see an expression of relief on his face, as from a burden released. After he left, I shed a few tears of relief myself, and then I went home.

Chapter 37

MASTERS OF ROMANCE in song and story have always held that there should be just one love. Playwrights know instinctively that they should never bring a second love to the stage.

With all my soul, I longed for the vividly interesting evenings I used to have with Monsieur Eiffel. And my heart was achingly lonely for the sound of his laughter.

I betook myself to 1, rue Rabelais. I needed no invitation. He looked at me, recognition startled by reality. Like many survivors of the Spanish flu, my hair seemed to have turned white in a night, due no doubt to the unusually high fever.

The moment came when Monsieur Eiffel's puzzlement gave way to surprise, and then something else. Suddenly he flung his arms about me and drew me to him.

The separation of so many years was bridged instantly with his entwining arms. I wept copiously on his shoulder, and then I raised my head to look at him.

He was older and thinner, with eyes that questioned mine.

"You remained away so long," he said. "When did you come back?"

"Yesterday," I said.

"And your husband?"

"We are not together," I told him. "But I have two children."

"Where are they?"

"They are at my mother's."

"How is your mother? I always liked her. When I first met her in Chile, I liked her."

In his pretentious mansion, he was surrounded by costly furnishings and priceless tapestries. He could have been a very rich old man, but he was not. The Eiffel Tower had been closed for four years during the war, used by the military for surveillance and telegraphy. It had saved France. If he had any extra money, he had put it into the science of aviation. He had built an expensive wind tunnel which he let other researchers use for free.

"You look a little frail," I told him. "You are closeted too much in your tapestried room. You must spend more time out in your beautiful garden. You need fresh air and sunshine."

I caressed the curls, now white, on his forehead. He smiled with the deep-cut lines on both side of his mouth.

"When we have congratulated each other," he smiled, "upon our phenomenal successes, then it will be wiser to shake hands."

I put my arms around his neck and kissed him.

"It's all foolishness, isn't it?" he asked.

"It's the folly of youth, as you used to say," I said, "but I wouldn't trade it for anything."

"I have been waiting for you all these years," he said.

We sat down to untangle the skein that fate had wound around us.

The portrait he had painted of me was there, hanging over the fireplace in his library, and beneath it a vase of fresh violets. Claire managed to leave us alone together for quite a long time, and alone together our hearts spoke. He was an odd, gentle creature, this engineer, scientist and collector of tapestries.

"You have been successful, Alice?"

"I suppose so," I said, "at least I made some money. That spells success, does it not?"

"Sometimes it does, sometimes it doesn't," he said. "My life has been like that famous picture of Monet's. There have been blossoms along the way, of course, but the blossoms never lasted long."

"Well," I said, "things don't always turn out as expected."

"I remember you said that when you first came to my house!" He laughed, affectionately. "You said: 'The unexpected often happens where I am concerned,' just like Napoleon."

"Did Napoleon say that?"

"Not exactly. He said, 'I will control circumstances.' I have always felt that since Napoleon failed, we may be forgiven for going back on some of our resolutions."

"I followed the path I saw before me," I said. "It was not the path of a woman of business, but rather that of an artist. I realized I have a gift that neither the public nor the critics can take away—the gift to enjoy the beautiful and some power to portray it."

"I saw that in you," he said. "Artists are frequently misunderstood, particularly those artists who create a new path. Look at the Impressionists. They were completely rejected here in their home country for many years. The Americans were a step ahead and bought up most of their paintings."

I was not willing to let him fall into the comfortable role of mentor and friend.

"In all the world," I said, "I found that there was no success or fame or joy—apart from you."

"I have missed you, my dear," he said, "more than I can say. I found, Alice, that after you had gone, you had become such a large a part of my life."

"Well," I said, "we are two middle-aged people now. Fate seems to have decided our lots for us."

"Yes," said he, "fate has indeed decided."

Then, sitting in the house of memories, I answered all his gentle questioning, told him all that had been and, all at once, he was not an old man who sat there in the room with me but just my faithful Gustave, understanding and true. And I was not the little white-haired lady I had become, but still the girl he loved, Mademoiselle Alice, still sweet, young and fair.

He listened so kindly to me, this courteous old man to my confiding prattle, the same kind of prattle I had poured on him when I was a girl, and his keen eyes noted the mended places in my gloves, the wistfulness in my voice.

For a moment my hand thrilled in his clasp, for a moment his eyes grew tender before mine.

"You are just as I hoped to find you," I said. "It's like coming back home."

"I have discovered the meaning of that word home," he said. "Home is where the heart is. Oh! I sound like a sentimental old fool, don't I? You made your own home—you needed to do that—and now you are 'at home' with me."

He smiled wisely. And in my silent glance he read my thoughts.

"We're going to have to try to make up for the thirteen years we've lost," I said, and he looked at me with a look full of everything that is beautiful.

"I'm a little tired," he said. "Would you mind if I took a short nap?"

"Of course not," I said.

"You don't have to stay, you know."

"I want to stay, more than anything."

While he napped briefly, I sat at the desk in the sitting room adjoining his bedroom.

He had an *escritoire* there, much larger than the one I had been given for Christmas decades before, with many more drawers.

I am not ashamed to say that, while I have built a wall of reserve around myself, I am always nosily interested in other people's stories. That is my excuse, anyway, for pulling out every sandalwood drawer in that desk, wondering what secrets they would contain.

There were passbooks and promissory notes, but these did not interest me. At last I found the drawer holding the secrets. I found the photograph of myself with short hair that I had sent him when I was sixteen after I flirted with him, the misspelled letter that had accompanied that picture, the Faust opera tickets, and several articles of no more intrinsic value than these, but evidence of how dear they were to him.

I never believed I would fall in love with anyone else, and I never did. Even though I am now an old woman, it is the tenderest memory of my long life.

ABOUT THE AUTHOR

Janelle Dietrick received a B.A. in modern European History from the University of California at Berkeley. She is the author of two nonfiction books about Alice Guy Blaché: *Alice & Eiffel: A New History of Early Cinema and the Love Story Kept Secret for a Century* and *Illuminating Moments, The Films of Alice Guy Blaché*.